Return
to the Little
Coffee Shop of
Kabul

Also by Deborah Rodriguez

FICTION
The Little Coffee Shop of Kabul

NON-FICTION
The Kabul Beauty School
The House on Carnaval Street

DEBORAH
RODRIGUEZ

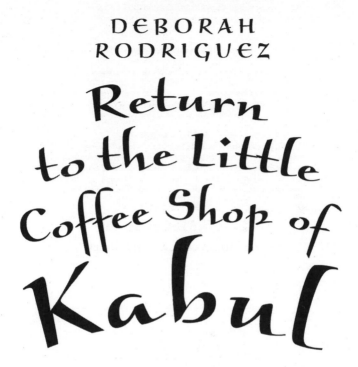

Return
to the Little
Coffee Shop of
Kabul

sphere

SPHERE

First published in Great Britain in 2016 by Sphere

1 3 5 7 9 10 8 6 4 2

A CIP catalogue record for this book
is available from the British Library.

ISBN 978-0-7515-6146-3

Printed and bound in Great Britain by
Clays Ltd, St Ives plc

Papers used by Sphere are from well-managed forests
and other responsible sources.

MIX
Paper from
responsible sources
FSC® C104740

Sphere
An imprint of
Little, Brown Book Group
Carmelite House
50 Victoria Embankment
London EC4Y 0DY

An Hachette UK Company
www.hachette.co.uk

www.littlebrown.co.uk

John Asahara, a wonderful man full of wisdom, love, and kindness.
You are an inspiration to many.

"Where there is ruin, there is hope for a treasure."

—RUMI

Prologue

"*Are you blind, you stupid girl? Do you want to get me killed?*"

The boy picked his bike out of the gutter and shook his small fist at her, but she just kept running. Her sneakers grew heavy with the mud underfoot and she struggled to keep her pace as she hurried through the narrow streets of the city. Around her, everything seemed to be moving in slow motion—the men pushing their carts piled high with pomegranates and cantaloupes, the covered women walking in pairs, leading their children by the hand, the mass of fat-tailed sheep being urged along with a sharp stick—but inside, her heart was racing so fast she thought it might burst.

She flew around a corner and elbowed her way through the crowds of people gathered near the outdoor food stalls, the smell of garbage and kabobs hitting her like an avalanche. All of her senses seemed to be turned up high—car horns blared, bicycle bells clanged, vendors shouted out their prices, generators whirred. How lucky she was that nobody seemed to bother with her, a frantic girl rushing through the streets with her hands covering her ears. But of course they wouldn't. No man would dare to put a hand on her in public, and the women would all be too wary to get involved. Yet she continued to jerk her head around like a frightened bird, her eyes on the lookout for anyone who might be following.

Past the shops with their sagging awnings and crumbling façades she fled, weaving in and out of the traffic that was becoming heavier the closer she got to the business center, where the glass and steel Kam Air building rose up from the sidewalk like a giant faceless robot. She grasped at the head scarf slipping back on her silky hair, and nearly tripped over a burqa'd beggar sitting in the middle of Qala-e-Musa Road, a baby resting on rags at her side, the only visible part of her body the one bare hand reaching out to the passing cars. But the girl had to keep going, had to move faster.

As she approached Shaheed Square she quickened her pace, leaping over the potholes that made the roads nearly impassible. Suddenly she felt her left foot slide out from under her and heard a cry as her hip hit the ground. She sat stunned for a moment, the mud oozing through her fingers and soaking her long blouse and jeans through to her skin. Two men walked their bikes in a wide circle around her, and ahead she could see another man in a white cap getting a shave on the street corner. Neither he nor the street barber holding a razor in one hand, keeping the man's face steady with the other, even blinked. It was as if she were invisible.

She stood and, without bothering to wipe away the filth that covered half her body, continued to run. Now the streets had become a little wider, the traffic lighter, the high walls lining the roads making her picture herself as a rat in a giant maze. She moved as quickly as her feet would take her. She was almost there.

But as she approached the guardhouse, her chest heaving with exhaustion, a small movement across the street attracted her eye. Through the window of a white Toyota, she saw a man pulling something black over his head. The chokidor must have noticed as well, for all at once the air was filled with activity. A car door slammed, the guard yelled and reached toward his gun, and the girl slipped through the gate and dashed toward the coffeehouse door.

1

The Starbucks latte she'd downed on shore an hour earlier threatened a comeback as Sunny gripped the metal rail of the seesawing ferry, her fingers turning an unnatural shade of blue against the peeling green paint. A boat? Really? Why on earth nobody had bothered to build a bridge between civilization and this godforsaken island was beyond her, as was the reasoning behind Jack's decision to buy there. *But*, she could almost hear Jack saying, *no passing judgment until you've seen it with your own eyes.* That is, she thought, if you're even able to see it through all this fucking fog and rain.

She remembered the time Jack had first told her about the place, back when they were both living in Kabul. He had just returned from one of his missions to the south, one in a string of many Sunny couldn't seem to get a handle on. All he had really told her about his job was that he was a skilled negotiator, but she already knew that from personal experience, as he always seemed to get his way with everything before she even realized what was happening. It was a Wednesday night, the night when all of Kabul, at least the UN, embassy and NGO workers, the missionaries and journalists who were still bold enough to venture out that late, would gather at her coffeehouse to hear one of the speakers she'd brought in to draw business. The place was buzzing with Dari, English, French, and Italian, filled to the rafters despite the bitter cold that refused to stay outside where it belonged seeping through the windows and barging in full force every time the door opened.

And then in came Jack, all chin and smile, plopping himself down in his usual spot like he was the one who owned the joint instead of her. "*Salaam dost e man,*" he warmly greeted Bashir Hadi, her barista, cook, and self-proclaimed protector. "Two glasses of your finest, kind sir!" he added. Bashir Hadi smiled and gave the nod to Yazmina, who ducked behind the counter and returned with a ceramic teapot concealing what he had to know was the usual crappy Chianti Sunny managed to dig up only by scouring the Chinese brothels—the last places in town to have even a drop, thanks to the Propagation of Virtue and the Prevention of Vice committee. Yazmina greeted Jack shyly, lowering her piercing green eyes as she poured the watery red liquid into the two demitasse cups she had hooked over her slender fingers. As Sunny rushed past his table, anxious to get everyone settled in time for the talk, she felt a tug on the back of her jeans. "Sit, woman! It's time to enjoy the fruits of your labor." Sunny tried to swat Jack's hand away, but his grasp on her belt loop was firm, and down she went.

"Bully."

"Happy to see you too, baby." She glowered at him in mock indignation. He knew how much she hated to be called baby.

"Ah," he said, rotating his cup in a circle until its contents had spun themselves into a tiny red whirlpool, then lifting it to his nose. "A fine vintage. Perhaps a '97, or maybe something a bit more recent, like an '05?" Jack took a slurp and swished the wine noisily around his mouth as if it were a swig of mouthwash. Sunny rolled her eyes.

"It'll do," he said as he set the cup down with a thud. "But mine will be better."

"Yours? What, did you get your hands on some black market Merlot or something? Hand it over, mister." Sunny stretched out her arm.

"No. I mean mine. Really mine. Someday, I promise you, you're gonna sit back and enjoy a bottle with the very name of yours truly slapped across the label."

"What, there's gonna be a Jack's Big-Mouth Red?"

"Ha-ha. Very funny. You'll be sorry. Now you'll be lucky if I share any of it with you. And mark my words, it's going to be a helluva lot better than this rotgut."

"Big deal. Even I could toss a bunch of grapes into that mop bucket over there and stomp around a little bit, and it would be an improvement on this crap."

"No, my dear," he said, leaning back precariously in the heavy wooden chair, "I'm serious. You just happen to be talking to one of the proud new owners of Screaming Peacock Vineyards, Twimbly Island, Washington, USA."

Twimbly Island. There came a point in their relationship when she thought if she heard that name one more time she'd scream. *You'd love it*, Jack had told her over and over, going on and on about its golden sunrises, its miles of driftwood-strewn beaches, the snow geese, the eagles, the great blue herons, the orcas heading inland for the winter, so close you could almost touch them from shore, as he tried his damnedest to work his magic on her. She remembered how relaxed he had seemed each time he returned from a visit to the island, and could just see how his steely blue eyes had warmed up whenever he fantasized about making a life there. So she'd force herself to smile politely and just listen, summoning up any latent traces of a skill she'd struggled to master throughout her entire lifetime.

It wasn't until after they finally packed their bags and sadly left Kabul behind that Jack's fantasy became a possibility, one that freaked Sunny out as much as everything else was freaking her out at that point. For her, oddly enough, Kabul had been the only place that felt like home, and she had planned never to leave. But things had changed over the six years she'd been living there. Friends were gone, places were shuttered, and the deadly missives launched by the increasing number of returning Taliban were now becoming too frequent, and too close to home, to ignore. Jack had his concerns about foreigners becoming targets, but beyond that, he felt strongly that it was high time to give Afghanistan back to the Afghans. *We treat them like idiots*, he had said. *And you know, and I know, that Halajan, Yazmina, Bashir Hadi, even Ahmet are not idiots*, he added, speaking of those who worked with her, those who had become as close to family as it got for Sunny. *We Americans infantilize everyone not like us.* You've got to love a guy like that, who sees a world beyond his own concerns, who will do the right thing just because it's the right thing to do.

And love him she did, so much so that before she knew it she had followed Jack back to Ann Arbor, Michigan, where his son was just starting college, and where he had landed a job as an international security advisor for a large NGO.

Worst. Decision. Ever. What had made Sunny think that she could go from Kabul hotshot to Michigan housewife just like that? Was she nuts? No, she was in love. And as the old woman Halajan, who owned the building where the coffeehouse stood, had once told her, *reason is powerless in the expression of love*. She—courtesy of her favorite poet, Rumi—sure got that one right, Sunny thought. But it wasn't only Sunny who was having trouble adjusting. She knew that Jack felt like an overweight pet-store hamster trapped in a communal cage in his corner cubicle. The only missions he took now were down the hall to the break room for coffee and candy bars, which, in her opinion, he seemed to be doing way too often. He was miserable, and seeing as how his son was now so busy with his own life, between his classes and his new friends, after a year of sticking it out Jack proposed to Sunny that they hit the road. His destination of choice? Twimbly Island.

But the winery was Jack's dream, not Sunny's. So they made a deal. They'd take a time-out to explore, to travel the world and try things on for size. No decisions for one year. They'd both keep an open mind. No pressure. And if nothing spoke to them after that one year, they'd give Twimbly a try.

They spent twelve months hopscotching from country to country, city to city, house to house, taking advantage of all the friendships they had made during their years in Afghanistan. Jack saw tons of possibilities, but each and every opportunity Jack put forward, Sunny pushed back. A bar in some quaint seaside town in Maine? Too boring. An adventure travel company in Peru? No hiking, llamas or Sherpas for this girl. A civilian boot camp in South Africa? No dice. She'd sooner jump off a cliff blindfolded and naked than deal with the ticks and testosterone that would come with that job.

Twelve months turned into thirteen, then fourteen. But being the gentleman that he was, Jack kept his word and continued to indulge Sunny's restlessness, even though he felt it was crucial that they start living a normal life, and the sooner the better. He'd seen way too many friends and colleagues who had become so addicted to living in war zones that they were now painfully restless and uncomfortable living anywhere else, and Jack told her he feared he was starting to see inklings of that in both of them.

After wearing out welcome mats from Cairo to Caracas, Sunny finally conceded to at least considering the winery, or so she told Jack. He'd been so patient that she felt it was only right to agree to take a look at the place. After one last fling, that is. Jack had been aching to go on a heli-skiing trip to Whistler with a bunch of his buddies, and graciously invited Sunny along. "I'm good," she'd responded, opting instead for a solitary long weekend exploring Santa Fe. They would meet in Seattle, and from there it would be off to the island.

Now she stood alone as the dock disappeared from view. For Jack's dream had evaporated on the side of a mountain when his heart gave out at eight thousand feet, causing hers, upon receiving that devastating call in the desert below, to shatter into a million little pieces.

Sunny swatted at the tiny rivulets of fog and rain dampening her cheeks, a gesture all too familiar from day after day of bawling at the drop of a hat. She felt like crying now, as the ferry barreled into the misty abyss. Would it have all looked better with him by her side? she wondered. "Damn you, Jack," she said out loud as she pulled the tote holding the flimsy cardboard box containing his ashes a touch closer. She was almost grateful he wasn't there to witness the stupid little hissy fit she was having with herself. The care he'd shown by placing her on the deed for the winery, despite his ex-wife's legal maneuverings, now made her feel ashamed of her own selfishness. If only she had said yes to the place earlier, Jack might have had a chance to live the life he had wanted so badly. How she hoped Jack's spirit wasn't watching over her at this moment, that he'd never have a clue about her plans to rid herself of the place as quickly as possible. She'd spent the months since his death in a fog, not unlike the one that was now wrapping its fingers around the approaching shoreline, and all she could hope for was that selling off her share to Jack's partner, Rick Stark, might offer a shred of closure. And maybe even a scintilla of clarity.

Sunny had never felt as lost as she did now, bobbing up and down in this dismal sea, as grey as the sky above. The path ahead seemed to be twisting into one giant question mark. Deep down she knew that, as much as she wanted to, she shouldn't go back to Kabul. Jack's predictions of escalating danger, particularly for foreigners, seemed to be coming disastrously true. She'd just read of yet another kidnapping, this time a French aid worker, and not long before that word had come of a US diplomat killed by a suicide bomber while delivering books to a local school. But none of that meant she might not still go back. She'd left the coffeehouse behind for Halajan, her son Ahmet and his wife Yazmina to run in partnership with Bashir Hadi, with wishes for their success and gratitude for their unflagging support, and for a friendship that meant more than anything in the world to her. Though it didn't seem as though she was really needed, she had no doubt that they would all welcome her back with open arms, as was their way, should she ever decide to return.

But for now here she was, on a boat. Headed toward Jack's dream. Without Jack. She took a deep breath and jammed her nearly numb hands deep into the pockets of her down jacket, where the latest letter from Halajan remained crumpled inside. *Don't grieve,* the old woman had quoted from Rumi. *Anything you lose comes round in another form.* Well, Sunny thought, I'm good with that. As long as it doesn't come around as a shitload of fog.

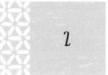

2

Bashir Hadi was hard at work, rubbing the copper espresso machine until it sparkled with the orange and green glow of the coffeehouse walls surrounding it. The aroma of fresh lemon from his worn rag blended with the sweet scent of chocolate chip cookies baking in the oven, enough to make anyone's stomach purr with anticipation.

Outside, the temperature was dropping, but inside they were safe and warm, busy with the chores that needed to be completed before the Thursday evening rush. *The calm before the storm*, Sunny used to say. Hopefully tonight would bring the kind of storm they wanted—a crowd that would fill every table in the place—and not the kind that appeared to be brewing in the cloudy sky above. It had become difficult enough to keep the customers they'd worked so hard to get while Sunny was still there, what with the increased measures required by the UN, embassies, and NGOs to ensure the safety of their workers.

Yazmina was grateful to Bashir Hadi for convincing first a stubborn Sunny, then later Ahmet and the rest of them, to increase the security. The wall, which now stood tall and defiant beneath Sunny's magnificent painting of a thousand doves set against a cobalt sky, was the first step, the one that got them UN compliance, that gave sanction for UN personnel to frequent the café. Which they did, until the rules became even tougher. So then came the blast film for the windows, to keep the glass from shattering into hundreds of deadly shards, as well as a safe room for customers to run to upon word of a coming attack. The shipping container they had installed up against the front gate, to serve as an extra checkpoint and a place to deposit weapons, had helped gain more customers, as had the addition of a second *chokidor*, a young man who was hired to stand guard inside the coffeehouse during busy times. But even with all that, there was nothing they could do about the growing number of foreigners leaving Kabul each day, and there were some nights when their own voices seemed to echo off the walls as they straightened vacant chairs and wiped down the empty tables, trying their best to appear busy.

Despite the chatter they'd heard from others in the neighborhood who had come to resent the foreigners' presence in their country, at the coffeehouse they were always welcoming to those who had remained, those who had come to treasure the place as one of the last of its kind in a changing Kabul. But honestly, where else could these people find such good cappuccino and even better conversation? Sunny had worked hard to make the coffeehouse a special gathering place for those far from home, a place filled with laughter and warmth and aromas that clung sweetly to your clothes long into the night. Its reputation was something they were all grateful for, and something Yazmina was determined to preserve, no matter what. Thank goodness tomorrow would be Friday, the start of the Afghan weekend, and the day they would—*inshallah*, God willing—be making extra money from holding their weekly bazaar in the courtyard out front.

Friday! Yazmina pushed herself up from the wooden chair where she had settled in to fold a pile of soft purple napkins. So much still to be done.

"I am fine," she assured Bashir Hadi when she noticed his slanted dark eyes narrow with concern. She placed her hands on her slightly rounded belly and gently rubbed, the warmth from her palms seeping through the thick cotton of her *shalwaar kameez* and onto her skin. So far no sickness with this little one, not like the last time. She remembered how hard it had been to try to keep hidden the sudden waves of nausea, and the mound growing from under her clothing, for so long. Seven months— from the day Sunny had taken her in until the day when her daughter Najama was born—of concealing the truth from almost everyone around. That her husband was gone, killed by a land mine while walking his goats, was no protection from the shame, or worse, that would have been inflicted upon her had her secret come out. When no husband was present, everyone was a suspect, and the pregnant woman considered a whore.

How things had changed for her since then, how different she was from that scared mountain girl, on the run from the men who had taken her from her home as payment for a debt owed by her uncle. The girl she was then would have never dared dream of all this; the coffeehouse, a home filled with laughter and joy, a new husband whose heart had grown large enough to allow him to see past the old ways and embrace her dead husband's child as his own. Even Kabul had come to feel like home, the staggered muezzin's call to prayer that was broadcast from the highest minaret of every mosque now a welcome background to the sounds of daily life, instead of a noise that made her jump right out of her skin, and the crowds of people of all colors and clothing now as familiar a sight as the goats that brayed on the hillside back home.

"Najama! Pay attention, *qandom*, my sweet one. Don't you want to learn to read?" Across the room, Halajan struggled with the fidgety little girl squirming on her lap. Yazmina smiled at her mother-in-law's wrinkled brown face, remembering how eager the old woman had once been to learn to read herself, and how grateful she had been to Yazmina for her help.

"Listen to your nana," she said, using the name Sunny had given Halajan after Yazmina had married her son Ahmet. How fortunate she was to have this woman as her mother-in-law, so unlike those she had heard of who beat and scarred their sons' wives for bearing girls instead of boys, or those who starved and abused the young girls sold into marriage with their sons.

Yet she had not always held so much love in her heart for Halajan, whom she had at first seen only as a stubborn busybody with a tongue as quick as a serpent and an attitude to match. How shocked she had been by the thoughts the woman stubbornly held onto, and shared with the world so unashamedly. Of course, she was still all those things, but now Yazmina understood better. Halajan, as well as her husband Rashif, came from a different time, a time that she and Ahmet had never witnessed, a time when ideas were not cause for punishment, and when women could be doctors or lawyers without being considered immoral. Yazmina had also come to admire her strength and her fierce loyalty. Halajan would do anything to protect her family, the café, her home. And hidden underneath that grey chador, along with the baggy denim pants and defiantly short grey hair she kept concealed from the outside world, Yazmina knew there was a heart that was softer than the baby-fine pelts used to make President Karzai's sheepskin hats. Just to observe the way she looked into the eyes of her husband Rashif was enough proof of that. How lucky she felt to have this new family to fill the dark hole left by the loss of her own parents, so many years ago now.

Yazmina placed a fresh kettle of water on the *bokhaari*, pausing to savor the heat from the burning wood inside as it softened her limbs one by one. If only Layla were here. It had been one month since she had tearfully kissed her little sister goodbye, with equal measures of hope and fear. Sunny's friend Candace had convinced them that a stay in America would be good for the girl, and had generously called upon her connections to obtain a student visa. How could Yazmina say no? She longed for the world for Layla, so who was she to keep it from her? Yet she counted the days until her sister's safe return to Kabul.

Across the room she saw Halajan's eyes light up as the door to the coffeehouse opened. In came Rashif, accompanied by a blast of cool air so strong that he scrambled to shut the door behind him.

"You are early!" Halajan said, clearly delighted. Najama slid off her lap and ran to embrace the short man's knees in a tight hug. He, in turn, magically produced a piece of toffee from the pocket of his brown *korti*, handing it to the child with a kiss on the top of her head.

"Are they still there?" He nodded toward the passageway that led to the house where he lived with Halajan. Yazmina knew he was eager to join her husband and the other men, that he had closed the tailor shop early for this very reason. After all, Rashif had been the one to push Ahmet in this direction, the one who had first encouraged him to open his eyes and form his own ideas, who had convinced him to loosen his grip on some of the old fundamentalist ways. Sitting among Ahmet and his friends from the university, discussing new ideas and new ways of doing things, surely must bring back memories of Rashif's own early days as an activist. If only it were not so risky, meeting like that in a time and a place where anything that went on behind closed doors was cause for gossip, or worse.

"They have been in there for hours already. Please tell Ahmet he is needed here in the coffeehouse. It's getting late." But before she had finished her sentence, Rashif was already out the back door.

"Let them be, *dokhtar*." Halajan rose to begin setting the tables. "If our country is to find its way forward, we must make room for thoughts to simmer a little. Talk can be a powerful weapon, because one day it will lead to action. We must use patience. Our struggle has been a long one, but stumbling forward is better than plunging back."

Yazmina knew better than to argue with the old woman. Although she could hear Rashif's voice in Halajan's words, she knew how proud she was of her son's virtuous nature and his ability to allow change in himself, even if it sometimes seemed to come at a pace as slow as a mule's. But deep down he was clearly his mother's son, her modernist ways seeping in through the blood they shared.

Her thoughts were interrupted by the ringing of the phone. There was a girl at the gate, reported Daoud, the *chokidor* who was on guard. Zara, she said she was called. She was asking for someone named Omar. Perhaps someone should come to see what this was about?

"I will go," said Yazmina, seeing Bashir Hadi bend over to open the oven door in an attempt to rescue his cookies from burning. She pulled her pashmina shawl around her. "*Bya*, come Poppy," she ordered the German shepherd that Sunny had left behind. She waited as the old dog rose from her spot by the warm oven and stretched, first her front legs, then the back. Though she wasn't much of a watchdog anymore, Poppy merely being there was enough to make many people think twice about their actions.

When Yazmina saw the visitor standing alone by the gate, she understood why Daoud had hesitated to let her enter. Women in burqas were not a common sight at the coffeehouse. And with the chatter about threats of suicide bombings against places where foreigners gather, conducted by men disguised as covered women, one had to have suspicions about what that burqa might be hiding.

But as Yazmina drew closer she could see by the shivering narrow shoulders and the feet—small and slender even in their sneakers—that this was truly just a young girl. "Come inside, little one," she said softly. "Let us get out of this cold."

Yazmina saw Bashir Hadi's face turn stiff with alarm as she entered with the covered girl. Halajan stood defiantly and drew Najama tightly into her arms. For one long moment, the coffee-house remained silent.

The girl must have noticed as well, for suddenly she flipped the entire burqa up and over her head to reveal the blue denim jeans and yellow T-shirt underneath. "Please," she said, "I am sorry to disturb you. I am only looking for my friend Omar."

"I'm sorry, *khwaar jan*, dear sister. There is no Omar here."

The girl lowered her dark eyes toward the floor. "But I know he is here. I have followed him here before." Then she looked back to Yazmina. "All I am asking is to speak with him."

Yazmina thought about the young men gathering at Halajan's house. This Omar must be one of them, one of the students who crossed through the passageway in the wall each Thursday afternoon for their weekly discussions. But still, one couldn't be sure, nor could one be sure of who this girl Zara was, or who might have sent her here.

"I tell you, there is no one here by that name."

"But I am his sister," the girl pleaded.

"I thought you said he was your friend," Halajan shot back.

The girl looked down at the floor again, clearly embarrassed.

"Is he in danger?" Yazmina glanced at the back door, thinking of Ahmet and Rashif in that roomful of men.

Zara shook her head. "No. No danger."

Halajan lifted Najama into a chair and slowly approached the anxious girl. "You must fly away home, young one." She placed her hands on the girl's shoulders and turned her toward the door. "Your love life has no business here."

The girl turned back to face Yazmina and Bashir Hadi. "I am sorry to have disturbed you. Please accept my apologies."

Yazmina watched with a little knot in her stomach as Halajan escorted Zara to the door. There was something not right with this girl. She could not help but think of herself when she was not much older than that age, scared and alone with nobody to turn to and nowhere to go. She hurried past Halajan and followed the girl out into the courtyard. "Wait!" she called, catching up to her under the budding branches of the acacia tree. Zara turned, and when she did Yazmina recognized the look of desperation in the girl's eyes as her own. This must have been how she had appeared to Sunny that first day when they crossed paths at the Women's Ministry, where Yazmina had fled from the men who had taken her from her uncle's house. "I know you are upset."

"It is nothing. I am fine," the girl insisted, continuing toward the street.

"Please." Yazmina stopped her with a hand on her upper arm. "If there is something I can do to help you, you must tell me. Are you in some sort of trouble?" Yazmina glanced down at the girl's middle.

The color rose in Zara's cheeks as her eyes widened. "No! Of course not!"

"Have you been bothered, or threatened?"

The girl shook her head and wrapped her arms around each other.

"Has someone hurt you?"

Again a silent no.

"Well then, what could be so bad to make you appear as though you're carrying the weight of a hundred bricks across your shoulders?"

The girl remained silent, her eyes turned toward the ground.

"Do not be ashamed that you came here," Yazmina assured her. "I understand how difficult things can get sometimes. If there is something I can do to help you—"

Yazmina could see the girl's lower lip start to tremble before she spoke. "It is my parents," she said, her words rushing out like water from a spigot. "I know they are arranging a marriage for me. I saw two women pay a call on my mother. I hear my uncles and aunts talking. I know the proposal to my father will come soon."

"But that is a *good* thing, *khwaar jan*," Yazmina assured her. "You are not a child. This is the proper way. Do not be afraid."

"I'm not afraid." The girl wiped away a tear with the back of her sleeve.

"Well, what is it then? Are your parents not good parents, do they not want a good life for you?"

"Yes, they are good parents. I love my parents. And I do not wish to disobey or dishonor them."

"So what is the problem?" Yazmina brushed strands of the girl's long silky hair away from her face with her fingers.

"I don't want to be married," Zara answered, a little too adamantly.

Yazmina nodded slowly. "Ah. It is because the man is mean? Or old? Or ugly?"

The girl shook her head. "I do not know yet who the man is."

"So perhaps he is a good man. Like my Ahmet."

The girl hesitated slightly before finding her answer. "But I want to study."

Yazmina nodded, and tried to imagine herself in this girl's position. She was married at fifteen to her childhood friend Najam. There had been no questions in her mind, no thoughts of studies up in the mountains of Nuristan. She had been happy in her marriage until the day Najam had died, killed before he even had a chance to see his daughter Najama come into the world. But life was different here in Kabul, and the rules seemed to change with every passing wind.

"Perhaps your parents will understand," she suggested.

The girl shook her head. "Not this time. This man is a wealthy man. His mother arrived with a servant, in a big car. My parents have turned away offers that have come before, but I know this one is different. I hear my family whispering, I see my aunts and uncles looking at me as if I were a prized sheep picked for sale at the bazaar."

"It is clear your parents are caring. They are choosing well for you."

Yazmina saw Zara's shoulders suddenly heave. "But my heart belongs to someone else," she confessed, with a sob so loud it echoed off the courtyard walls.

Omar, Yazmina thought to herself. Halajan was right. She embraced the girl and held her trembling body close. "Quiet now. You must calm yourself. This is not the end of the world." She could practically feel the girl's pain shooting out from beneath her skin. But still she must do what was right.

"You need to stay away from this boy," she said softly into the girl's ear, which only made her cry more. "It is the way things are done, little one. We all know that. It is tradition."

But tradition or not, for now this girl was suffering. Perhaps Yazmina could not do much to change the situation, but what she could do was offer her friendship. She knew all too well how it was to feel helpless and alone.

She waited for Zara's cries to subside, then took her hand and walked her to the gate. "Be strong, *khwaar jan*," she said with a hug. "Sometimes things work out in ways you could never imagine. But if you need me, I am here for you. Remember that." The girl quietly thanked her, furled the burqa up into the air and over her head, and left.

Back inside the coffeehouse, Yazmina hurried to hug Najama. She prayed her daughter would never have reason to feel as sorrowful as that poor girl did, but who knows what life might bring? She was worried for Najama's future, especially now, when everything around them seemed so uncertain.

Halajan had returned to her chores. "You worry too much. That girl will be fine. The children these days, they are full of drama. Everything is a crisis. This is a matter of puppy love, you will see. Getting involved in others' troubles will only bring us trouble," the old woman said. "And trouble," she continued as she stroked the wall beside her to ward off bad luck, "is the last thing we need in this place."

3

The wheels of the rental car spun fruitlessly in the mud as Sunny made a left turn onto the steep driveway. She turned off the ignition and sighed, relieved to no longer be driving. The twenty-minute trip from the ferry landing had felt more like an hour, the pines obscuring the view on both sides, hemming her in like giant wooden prison bars. If there was a soul to be seen living behind that curtain of green, she sure couldn't spot them. Only two cars had passed her after she made the first turn up the hill, one a battered truck with lumber hanging out of the back, the other a Subaru with bikes on top. A faded directional sign, similar to those she had seen along the road that seemed to be pointing to nowhere, showed the way up the drive to the house, but it was clear that the only way to go would be by foot. Sunny glanced down and said a quick goodbye to her grey suede Uggs, shut the car door behind her, and began the hike up between the gnarly vines, cursing Jack every step of the way. She stopped only briefly to catch her breath and shake her head at an abandoned firetrap of a barn halfway up, and then continued, the wet ground providing a thwacky percussive soundtrack with each step she took. It reminded her of her least favorite season in Kabul, when the winter rains would turn the muddy, flooded streets into a navigational nightmare, and the thick sludge would seep in through every crack and crevice imaginable.

At the crest of the hill, a rickety mongrel of a house stood framed by a dull midday sun that was still struggling to be seen from behind the clouds. Sunny narrowed her eyes and cocked her head sideways at the structure. What the hell was it? Raised Ranch? Cape Cod Classic? Mid-Century Monstrosity? The place looked like a poorly constructed jigsaw puzzle, with every piece jammed together regardless of size or shape or color. It was all disintegrating shingles, lopsided angles, and a front porch straight out of *The Waltons*. She stood in disbelief, hands on hips. "Hello?" she called out in her booming voice, hoping that Rick, after getting her message that she'd arrive around midday, might be there to meet her. But of course nobody answered.

She had just started back down the driveway when she heard someone call out from behind her. "Hey! Hold on! Hello! Wait!" She turned to see a skinny young man in ripped jeans and rubber boots rushing toward her. "Can I help you?" he shouted across the soggy lawn.

"I don't know," she shouted back.

"Sky," he said as he came to a halt in front of her and wiped his palms on his jeans.

Sunny smiled politely and squinted toward the clouds above.

"Sky," he repeated, holding out his hand. "That's my name."

"Oh!" She held out her own hand. "Sunny."

The boy raised two pierced eyebrows.

"No, that's me. My name is Sunny."

"Of course," he laughed, revealing a metal stud glistening in front of his teeth. "My bad. I should've known. Nice to meet you." He clasped her hand between his own tattoo-covered ones and shook. "You just got here?"

"I did. I told Rick I was coming. Maybe he didn't get the message." Sunny's eyes wandered from the barn to the house and back again. This was so not what she had imagined, not even on her worst days.

"Well, you want to look around?" the young man asked eagerly, shifting from foot to foot.

"Don't have the key."

"No worries. Nobody on the island locks their doors."

She followed him as he trotted toward the house, admiring how his long, shiny brown curls bounced with every step he took. *To be that young and lovely*, the forty-two-year-old in her thought, struggling to keep up.

"But if you do want a key," Sky said as he reached the back door and bent to lift up a worn straw mat, "here's our secret hiding place."

"That's original," she said with a smirk as she tucked the key into the back pocket of her jeans.

The ripped screen door screamed in protest as Sky pulled it open and stepped aside to allow her to enter. They were in the kitchen; at least, she assumed it was the kitchen from the slight glow coming from the green phosphorescent hands of the frozen clock on the electric stove. The room was so dark she could barely make out the shape of the old Frigidaire in the corner, with its rounded corners and hinged handle. Sky flipped the switch by the door, but nothing happened. "Sorry," he said, raising his eyes to the ceiling. "I've been meaning to bring in some light bulbs."

As Sunny's vision began to adjust to the dimness she was able to take in more. The dead flies legs-up on the window-sills. The crusty glasses in the sink. Sky watched silently as she took a sorry inventory. *Thank God Jack isn't with me* was her first thought, trying to imagine the lengths she'd have to go to in order to cover her disappointment with this place. There was no way she could be that good an actor.

"My bad again," said Sky, bowing his head a little. "I would have cleaned the place up a little if I knew you were coming."

"You work for Rick?"

"Oh, no." Sky drew back his chin and shook his head a little. "Haven't seen that guy in ages. He lives all the way up island, near the military base. It's Jack I do work—I mean, used to do work—for. Just keeping an eye on things for him, stuff like that. Really great guy."

The sadness that had been shadowing her for the past few months suddenly tightened its grip. Sunny swallowed and struggled to blink back the tears that she knew held more power than she did. Sky lowered his eyes, then politely turned away to pretend to fiddle with the light switch. Sunny stood in place, concentrating on her breathing. "Yeah, pretty great," she finally managed to utter, the three words coming out in a little croak.

Sky turned around and placed a hand gently on her shoulder. "We all miss him, you know."

Sunny nodded, envious of this boy's memories of Jack on this island when she had none. If only she could have pictured his head bent over the newspaper at the kitchen table, or remembered his crackly laugh bouncing off these walls, maybe it all might have felt different.

She dragged herself through the kitchen door toward the rest of the house. The bedrooms and bath told pretty much the same story as the kitchen did. Dingy sheets covering the sparse furniture, a moldy shower curtain, rusty faucets, a peeling linoleum floor, and a plastic bucket half filled with stale, brackish rainwater perched on top of the toilet lid. The whole place had the aura of an old sepia photograph, all brown and yellow and dark, and Sunny found herself practically holding her breath as she passed from room to room.

The living room seemed slightly more promising. At least it was big enough for entertaining, if one was so inclined. Which she wasn't. She ran her fingers along the slats of the dirty white shutters that lined one entire wall of the room, and plopped herself down on the worn couch, where she was greeted with a cloud of dust up her nose. "*Achoo!*" she sneezed once, then again, and then five more times in a row, as was her way. Waving away the multiple blessings Sky was politely offering, she returned to the kitchen for a tissue from her purse, and checked her messages. Still no word from Rick. She circled the room until she finally found a spot where one little bar appeared on her phone, and hurried to send a message to the number he had given her. *It's Sunny. I'm here, but won't be for long. Call me.* God, how she wanted this day to be over.

But when she returned to the living room Sunny let out a gasp so loud you could have heard it all the way back on the mainland. Sky laughed. He'd unhooked the shutters, revealing one of the most stunning views Sunny had seen in her entire life. The sun had made a brief appearance above, and below, the turquoise waters of Puget Sound shimmered like a sequined evening gown.

She had to admit, for one quick moment, that Jack's description of the beauty of the Sound, at least when the sun shone, had been spot on. She'd give him that. But still, what had made him think she'd actually want to make a life here? For one thing, it was way too quiet, except for what was beginning to sound like a crazy woman on a rant next door. And for another thing, it was too wet. And woodsy. And isolated. What had he been thinking? She rubbed her temples, trying her damnedest to wrap her head around this place, to see what Jack saw, besides that view. And why wouldn't that woman stop screaming, for God's sake?

Her answer came in the form of a frantic peahen hustling a trail of little ones across the lawn. The worried mama circled around her chicks like a tightly wound-up toy. But the sound Sunny heard wasn't coming from her. It came from the branches of a maple tree, where the peahen's peacock mate was screeching out a full-scale warning to the barking ball of matted fur loping toward his family at breakneck speed. A fat orange cat lay in wait by the bushes, licking his chops.

Sky rapped on the window with his knuckles. "Bear! Bad dog! Leave it!"

Sunny covered her eyes but watched through spread fingers as the birds scurried away and the cat slithered under the porch. That's when she saw an ancient Asian man in a faded baseball cap waving a crooked stick in the air with one hand while flinging handfuls of dust right and left with the other. He looked like a demented fairy godmother as he crossed the property at the rate of a tortoise, either belting a song or arguing with himself, Sunny couldn't tell which.

"That's your next-door neighbor," Sky said.

Sunny followed him outside, skirting the puddles that were blending into one giant lake across the soggy grass. Sky joined his hands in front of his chest and made a slight bow. "*Youkoso irasshai mashita.*"

The man stood there silently under the tree, hat in hand, slowly turning his stony gaze to Sunny, who frantically and awkwardly bent down, replicating Sky's gesture. You have got to be kidding me, she thought as she took in the sight of this strange man, from his miraculously spotless brown moccasins to his denim-on-denim outfit to his cropped full head of white hair. When she finally straightened to find herself eye to eye with him, the smooth, unlined face behind the wire-rimmed glasses surprised her. Not a single wrinkle, except for those ears. The two lobes hung long and low, and to Sunny looked like a couple of sheets of paper someone had crumpled up only to later realize they were something that was actually needed. And those eyebrows! You could practically braid them up and twist them into little buns they were so long and thick.

"*Benvenuti in paradiso*," the old man said loudly, gently taking her hand and raising it to his dry warm lips. "I am Giuseppe," he added, the three words tinged with an accent Sunny couldn't quite pinpoint. "Around here, just Joe."

"Pleased to meet you," she said, surprised by this Japanese guy's Italian but relieved at his English. It had been starting to feel like her early days at the coffeehouse, when the confusing jumble of tongues had made her brain spin like a top. "Sunny."

He turned and tilted his ear toward her mouth.

"Sunny!" she repeated, louder this time.

"Ah, that I know," he nodded. "The remarkable Sunny Tedder, straight from Jonesboro, Arkansas via Kabul, Afghanistan and other points unknown. And you are even more *bellissima* than I ever imagined." Joe scattered the remains of his birdseed across the lawn and tossed the stick into the air for the dog.

She could feel the color rising in her cheeks. "Nice dog you've got there," was the only response she could think of, this time delivered at a volume equal to his.

"My dog? Bear? Oh no." He shook his snowy head. "Not my dog. Your dog. Jack sprung him from the shelter a ways back. I've just been watching him. He's a good dog, aren't you, Bear-boy?" he yelled toward the dog, who was too busy turning the stick into a pile of toothpicks to answer. "He's quite a scoundrel, that dog. I tell you, once he—"

"And the cat?" Sunny squinted her eyes and wrinkled her nose, not sure she really wanted to hear his answer.

Joe nodded. "Sangiovese? Yours as well."

"Typical Jack," she muttered out loud, her shoulders dropping with annoyance.

The old man wagged a gnarled finger in her face. "*A caval donato non si guarda in bocca.* Don't look a gift horse in the mouth, they say. Or a cat, for that matter."

Oh no, she thought. Not another Halajan, with the quotes. Joe's shameless cackling at his own joke quickly turned into a hacking cough. She grabbed his arm and gently patted the back of his worn blue shirt.

"Don't be fooled by this one's charm," Sky warned. "He's a tough old bird. Before you know it he'll be getting you to bring him his newspapers and clean his house for him."

"Not to worry. I'm not planning on staying here."

Either Joe didn't hear her, or pretended not to. "Young man, you give away my secrets," he chided. "I suppose you've also already spilled the beans about our little project." He lowered himself slowly onto a wooden bench surrounding the maple, patting the spot beside him as an invitation for Sunny to sit, which she did. At the bottom of the sloping lawn, the Sound stretched out like a smooth, welcoming blanket, as if it were a totally different body of water than the choppy dark sea she had crossed just an hour before. She checked her watch. Only about two hours left to connect with Rick before she had to catch the last ferry out. But Joe had embarked on some long story to which she'd barely been listening.

"Of course," he was saying, "all of the winemakers on the island buy their grapes from the mainland. The vines you see in front of their places? Mostly for show."

"Wait, what? You mean nobody makes wine on this island?" Sunny thought she must have misheard the old man.

"Oh, they make wine," Sky, crouching down on his haunches in front of them, explained. "They just don't grow their own grapes. It's too difficult here, in this weather, on this land."

"You mean Jack bought half of a winery with no grapes?"

"This place hasn't made any wine for years." Sky reached out to scratch the dog behind the ears. "Rick said he was waiting for Jack to come back before he put anything more into this place, before he brought in any more grapes."

"Well, now I guess he'll just have to do it on his own." Sunny noticed the two men's eyes meet for a split second. "So those vines in the front are simply for decoration? Do they even get grapes on them?"

"Ah, that, kiddo, is where young Sky and I are doing our magic, with Jack's blessing of course. You see," he said as he slowly sat back and leaned against the tree, "when I settled over in Italy, after the war, I grew my own grapes, I made my own wine. My Sylvia, bless her soul, came from a family famous for their Chianti. For forty years I had my own little patch of land, where I made just enough to last me and all my friends from harvest to harvest. Ever since she died, and I came back home to here," Joe pointed to a low white house visible through the trees, "to help my brother, I have dreamed of trying again. And what you see over there," he said, pointing in the other direction, "will be the first vintage of Screaming Peacock Vineyards' rosé."

Sunny followed his last gesture to the sad, empty vines she had walked through earlier. "I thought you just said it was too hard to grow grapes around here." Jack had to have been delusional when he made this decision, she thought. That long scar across his head from the blast he'd experienced in Kabul was proof enough that his brain had seen a lot of scrambling over the past few years. How else could she explain this normally rational man's faith in this place?

"You know, this is not such a bad place," Joe said, as if reading her mind. He coughed into his sleeve. "Sure, it can be lonely," he continued without missing a beat, dismissing the thought with a wave of a hand. "And yes, it can rain enough to drown a bullfrog, but things could be worse. Me," he said, pointing at his chest with both index fingers, "I was away from this area for sixty years. A long time to stay away from where you were born and raised, right? And when I came back? It was very difficult. Joe, I said to myself, this is not home anymore. Why are you here?" He flung out his hands, as if he were asking himself the question all over again.

"Now my late brother, may he rest in peace," Joe paused to look up at the sky and back down again, "he would tell you this is the best place on earth. God's Green Acre. My brother, he was a happy man. Always content. Believed in live and let live, forgive and forget. Much more than me." Joe sighed. "But he was right about one thing." He bent and struggled to scoop up a handful of moist dirt from the ground below. "It is good here, the land. If you treat it well, treat it with respect. It's like a temperamental woman," he continued without taking a breath. "Like my Sylvia was. Show her some tenderness, listen to her, attend to her needs, but always make sure to leave her longing for just a tiny bit more, and she'll give you whatever she's got, and then some. But deny or ignore her or try to make her be something she's not, and she'll shut down faster than a possum getting a whiff of fox." Joe squinted toward the vines and shook his head. "Jack understood that."

She had to laugh a little to herself at that. Who was this funny old man who looked Japanese but spoke English like an Italian, who talked with his hands as much as his mouth? And didn't he ever stop?

"So you know what they say in Italy, right? *Bisogna accomodarsi ai tempi.*"

Sunny looked at him blankly. Suddenly she felt exhausted.

"Gnaw the bone which is fallen to thy lot," Joe continued. "Make the most of what you have," he explained, with an encouraging pat on Sunny's knee. "You'll hear my story soon enough, and I will learn yours. We'll have plenty of time to talk more and get to know each other better."

Sunny forced a smile. Inside, she was feeling a little sorry, knowing that wouldn't be the case.

4

"Have fun. Be safe. And remember what Yazmina said: not too many sweets. And no soda! And be careful not to . . ." The door of the old brown Mercedes slammed shut before Ahmet could say more. Halajan was anxious to get moving, knowing that the drive could take forever, a trip that should normally last no more than twenty minutes. They should have left earlier, and would have, had she not been forced to wait for Khalid, the *chokidor*, to arrive at the coffeehouse in his own sweet time to give them a ride. Traffic in Kabul had become a nightmare thanks to the barricades that could turn a through road into a dead-end street without warning, and the thing they called the ring of steel, which was really just a fancy name for the checkpoints guarded by the newly appointed police—those pimply-faced boys with goggles pushed up on their helmets, knives strapped to their body armor, flashlights attached to their rifles—trying their hardest to appear as tough as the international forces that came before them.

"Just turn and go around that truck!" she yelled impatiently from the back seat. He drives like an old woman, Halajan thought. How she longed to grab the steering wheel from Khalid's hand. You could bet your life she wouldn't be so meek and courteous as he was being, not if she could drive.

It was a full hour before he finally dropped them off at their destination. Najama tugged at the bottom of Halajan's green chador, pulling her with a four-year-old's determination toward the statue standing guard at the zoo's entrance. The bronze lion glimmered in the early spring sunlight, his face proud and defiant.

"Do not worry, little one. We will go say hello to our old friend Marjan, as always."

The girl ran ahead as Halajan struggled to keep up. The story of the hero lion was one of Najama's, and Halajan's, favorites. Of course, she had not shared all the details with her granddaughter. Like how, after the mujahideen had driven the country into violence and chaos, there was no one left to feed the animals in the zoo, and many of them died of hunger. Or how the deer and ducks met their ends on the dinner plates of the hungry fighters, and about how the others—tigers and bears and monkeys, all those who were considered *haraam*, forbidden—died of neglect or stray bullets. But Marjan, the lion; now *there* was a fighter, as proud and tough as the Afghan people themselves. As the story went, it was when the fighting had reached its peak that an idiot warrior with something to prove had slipped into the animal's cage, seeking to tease him. But the *mujahid* was no match for the lion, who gobbled him up in an instant. The next day, the dead man's brother came seeking revenge by throwing a hand grenade straight at the lion's snout. Though blinded and scarred by the attack, Marjan refused to give in, and instead lived on through two more decades of war and turmoil into old age, finally coming to rest in a grave in the flower garden at the rear of the zoo. No, Halajan thought as she watched the child gently stroking the bronze cat's majestic mane, Najama would hear those gruesome details on her own, soon enough.

Yesterday's clouds were gone, leaving behind a sky as blue as the deepest of the Band-e Amir lakes high in the Hindu Kush mountains. The crisp morning air had not been enough to keep away the flocks of families seeking a few hours of peaceful escape behind the zoo's high, sturdy walls, or the young couples walking and talking together, safe from the judging eyes and wagging tongues of others.

Halajan dug deep into her pocket for the coins needed to enter the aquarium. The girl skipped ahead through the blue doorway, Halijan hustling to join her inside, where she found Najama standing transfixed behind the low chain separating the people from the ugly brick walls holding the tanks. The look on her granddaughter's face—that mix of curiosity and delight that seems only to appear on the very young—was well worth the price of entry. Though Halajan had to wonder what it was about a stupid fish swimming in circles through a forest of plastic plants that could bring so much joy. Halajan, she preferred the snakes.

Outside, Halajan held tightly to Najama's hand as she pushed her way through the crowd, past the cascading fountain to the pit where the big bears lived. Along the enclosure's stone wall, a trio of women in blue burqas drew back with a start as a brown bear reared up onto his hind legs with bluster and command, as if he were a fat warlord waving around an AK-47. Najama squealed with delight, then spun on her heels, anxious to see more. The two of them wove their way down the stone pathways past the pens of listless gazelles and wolves, past a lone lioness pacing back and forth across a small patch of dirt, past a cage full of nasty-looking vultures pecking relentlessly at one of their own.

Though the zoo had made many improvements since its years of wartime neglect and its near-extinction under the Taliban, it was still nothing like the modern marvel it had been upon its opening back when Halajan was still in her teenage years, when things had been so different. The zoo had been the pride of Kabul, a wondrous oasis built along the banks of the flowing river, surrounded by the city's winding hills. The generous King Mohammad Zahir Shah, the last king of Afghanistan, had even donated a pair of snow leopards from his own private collection at Kaaraiz e Meer, outside of Kabul. No, this sorry excuse for a zoo was not the zoo she had known. But still, they were trying.

"Look at Mr Showoff." Halajan led the little girl to an empty space between the tall fir trees, where a peacock stood in full bloom, his eye-spotted tail a shimmering fan of sapphire and emerald. "I think the poor bird is looking for a wife," she said to no one in particular. Well, she thought, even single he is at least better off than the ones for sale in the narrow alleyway of the Kaa Forushi bird market, sitting day after day in their wicker cages, unable to spread their wings.

Najama stood mesmerized by the bird's splendor, so vibrant against its dusty brown surroundings. "Nana! I want a pretty bird! *Luftan?* Please?"

"*Inshallah.*" God willing. Halajan smiled and herded the girl forward toward the next lonely animal, a single pig rooting in a pen of patchy grass, his pale snout blackened with dried mud, oblivious to the curious crowds eager to see the only pig in Afghanistan, where, under Islamic law, he was definitely considered *haraam*. But what was even more fascinating than the peacock or the pig to little Najama were the bright yellow and blue and green cars of the spinning ferris wheel in the distance. Halajan fiddled with the purple ribbons holding the tips of Najama's thick braids in place, and did her best to ignore the girl's pleas. She would just as soon jump straight off the top of Mount Noshakh naked than allow herself to be spun and tossed like that, locked like a pigeon in a painted cage dangling eight stories above the ground.

"Look over there, Najama!" She turned the child's attention toward a crowd that had suddenly gathered around the monkeys' cage. As the two of them maneuvered their way closer, through a sea of brightly colored chadors and of a mob of dark cropped heads, Halajan spotted a short man in blue jeans tossing bits of kabob through the small open spaces of the wire fence. Everyone, young and old alike, was screaming with laughter at the little creatures as they competed for the tiny morsels, diving over each other and into the waterless moat in a routine fit for a circus. Halajan clicked her tongue. "Do these people not see?" she asked her granddaughter, pointing to the white metal sign with a big, red circle and backslash covering an illustrated hand with morsels tumbling out of it. "Do they not pay attention to the announcements?" she said, looking up to the loudspeaker above. "*Do not feed the animals.* Perhaps they cannot read, but are these people idiots?" Yet the monkeys continued to reward the crowd with their antics, encouraging more and more participation from their own side of the fence, until the floor of the cage was littered with food and garbage. The animals greedily picked their way through the contraband loot. When one curiously unwrapped an entire piece of chewing gum, popped it in its mouth and started to chew like a sassy teenager, the crowd roared. "Ach," cried out Halajan in disgust as she grabbed Najama and turned to leave.

But the laughter around them had suddenly become a chorus of wild hollers and shrieks and whoops, and all at once the crowd was on the run, in pursuit of one tiny brown monkey who had somehow managed to escape from its jail. The men and boys were scrambling and pushing and leaping over each other—just like those monkeys—to claim the honor of being the first to capture the poor thing. One threw a soda can into the monkey's path, and another followed, until the sky had become a sea of flying cans.

Halajan had seen enough.

She pulled Najama away from the spectacle and headed quickly back down the walkways that led to the zoo's exit to sit and wait for Khalid. Have these people not learned anything? No, this was not the Kabul she knew, the one where respect and dignity mattered above all else. What had become of her city? Hers was not the Kabul where people acted worse than animals. Hers was not the Kabul where men felt free to piss on the streets regardless of who was nearby, where mothers fed their children opium and rented them out to others for a day of begging, where spectators gathered daily on a bridge to watch men suffering and dying from heroin addiction on the muddy riverbank below, as if it were a movie for their entertainment.

She let out a huge sigh. How she longed to get home, to be out back in the little courtyard, alone, where she could pull off her itchy head scarf and light up a smoke, and dream of the old days, and the pride she had once felt for her city and its people. How she prayed that feeling would one day return. And how she hoped that that "one day" would come soon, *inshallah*.

5

The kitchen floor was finally beginning to reveal its true self, layer by layer, as Sunny relentlessly drove the sponge mop back and forth and back again. She paused to brush away the strands of wavy brown hair that had escaped from the clip on top of her head, and stretched backwards with a groan. The crappy mattress had done a number on her last night, a penalty she accepted as the price she had to pay for missing that last ferry. And with barely enough cell service to make a call, searching for a hotel or inn or B&B on this island would have been a nightmare. Figures. And today? If it weren't for getting hopelessly lost in that green maze of towering pines that made every road around here look exactly alike, causing her to be two hours late for her appointment with Rick, she'd be watching TV in a cozy room at the Seattle Hyatt with a glass of red wine and a room-service pizza on its way.

Rick Stark. On first impression she had been admittedly charmed. He was tall—taller than Jack—and carried himself with the air of a man who knew exactly what he wanted, the type whose every gesture was smooth and deliberate. She'd seen plenty like him before. In fact, there was a time in her life, or perhaps even two, when she would have welcomed a guy like that into her bed with open arms. But she hadn't felt that way about anybody in a long time. Not since Jack.

Rick had been the only customer in the coffee place when Sunny poked her head through the shiny silk banners hanging from the doorway, and as she entered he turned his head toward her, cellphone glued to one ear, and waved her over. She shook out the damp feathers clumped inside her puffy jacket, draped it over the back of a chair, dropped her leather knapsack onto the floor and sat, taking in the room around her as he continued with his conversation. The place felt like a flashback to the sixties; batik panels suspended from above, a Haight-Ashbury street sign over the bar, a poster of Chairman Mao—his profile tilted optimistically upward—behind the bakery counter, walls plastered with bumper stickers demanding that the ocean be protected, the earth be loved, the planet be saved. Sunny wondered why Rick had chosen this place to meet. He didn't look at all like he belonged here, with his slicked-back hair, buttoned-down shirt and shiny black shoes.

"What'll you have?" he asked with a smile as he put down the phone and scraped back his chair.

"Well hello to you too. Cappuccino, I guess?"

"Wet, or dry?" he purred, as if he were offering something dirty or illicit.

"Um, dry, I guess?" She had no clue. She'd gotten used to the whole venti or grande, regular or soy, caf or half-caf thing that had happened since she'd been away, but wet or dry? How the hell could a coffee be dry?

40

Rick returned with a hefty ceramic cup filled with a creamy brew, the aroma of which brought back fond memories of times long gone. Sunny settled back into her chair with a little sigh.

"Good, right? Twimbly's finest." He leaned forward and rested his forearms on the table, his own cup clutched tightly between his hands.

She took a little sip. "Mmm. The best I've had since my own, at the coffeehouse."

"Ah, yes, the famous café of Kabul. Jack never stopped talking about that place."

Sunny had to laugh to herself, thinking about how she had felt it was actually Twimbly Island that Jack never stopped talking about.

"Must seem pretty quiet around here to you." Rick checked his watch. "Not much happening, unless you're into whale-watching or kayaking."

Sunny nodded as she blew lightly into her cup.

"Of course," he continued, "come summer, things do pick up a little." He launched into a rapid-fire inventory of the island's statistics and attractions—population 62,300, thirty-five miles of spectacular countryside from tip to toe, world-class cycling, canoeing, bird-watching—ticking them off one by one as if he were guiding a tour.

Sunny was determined to keep her own impressions of the place to herself. "Well, Jack certainly did love it here," she heard herself say.

Rick stared into his cup and laughed a little. "True. True. That guy loved everyone, everything, and every place. Sometimes made me wonder if he could tell shit from Shinola. Excuse me for a second," he said, reaching for his phone, which had begun to buzz like an angry bee. Sunny bristled a little at his last comment as she watched Rick's fingers peck at the screen. "I'm sure you'll find plenty to do around here once the weather improves," he continued without raising his head.

"Oh, I'm not planning on being here that long. Nowhere near that long."

Rick paused and lifted one eyebrow up toward her. "Really?"

"Not in my plans." She wiped a drop of milk from the table.

"Huh." His head bowed back down to the phone. "So I assume you'll be heading back to your Kabul coffee shop?" he asked as he returned to his typing.

Sunny started to shake her head, the echoes of Jack's convictions still bouncing around in her brain. But Jack was gone. And with him went the last connection she had over here, in the States, with Kabul—those shared memories that had kept it all alive for her day after day. "Not sure," she heard herself answer. Saying those words out loud for the first time made her realize just how much she missed her old life. She had never felt as alive as she did in Afghanistan. More seemed to happen in just one day there than happened in a lifetime anywhere else.

"So what can I do for you today?" Rick asked, his eyes still riveted onto the little screen.

Sunny sat forward and tucked her curls behind her ears. "I want to make a deal with you. Jack's half, my half, to you. Market value. Clean and simple."

Rick slowly put down the phone and turned his toothy smile back on her. Then he cleared his throat. "Well, that's certainly an interesting proposition," he said after a beat.

Sunny was about to ask him about the property's last appraisal when the phone rang again. Once more Rick apologized but took the call, heading outside to the parking lot while he talked.

She could see him through the café's window, pacing back and forth in the mist. Sunny checked her watch, pissed that missing the last ferry had now clearly become a certainty. All of a sudden the guy didn't seem so attractive to her anymore.

"So let me ask you something," Rick said as he came back in and blotted the moisture from outside off his face with a napkin. "What makes you so certain you want to sell?"

"What am I going to do in a place like this? This was Jack's dream. Not mine."

"But you don't know where you're going?" Rick narrowed his eyes.

Sunny shrugged her shoulders.

"Well, what do you think Jack would want you to do?"

"Jack's not here."

"Just saying." Rick tilted his head back and drained his cup. "Another?" She shook her head. Rick shouted out his own triple shot order to the sleepy guy behind the counter. "You don't think he'd rather see you tucked away safe and sound here on Twimbly than running around Pakistan or Tajikistan or whatever Stan strikes your fancy next?"

Sunny didn't know whether to laugh or cry. Under the table she could see Rick's legs dancing their own little jig. Cut this guy open and he'd probably bleed caffeine, she thought.

And then Rick said something she hadn't expected. "Well, personally, I think *I* know what Jack would have wanted. And me? I want to do right by him. So here's what I'm willing to do." He leaned forward and folded his hands together on the table. "My half, to you. Market value minus twenty per cent. For cash, that is."

Sunny was stunned. "You want to sell?"

"For Jack," he said solemnly. "For you."

She drew back as he slid a clammy hand over hers. "You mean you're not going to start up the winery again?"

"It wasn't exactly a part of my plans. I'm really too busy to do it justice. And now . . ."

"Well it wasn't exactly a part of my plans either," she protested.

"It's quite a good deal I'm offering. You really should think about it."

"I could think about it until the cows come home and it wouldn't change anything."

Rick sat back again and drummed his fingers on the table.

"So, wait," Sunny continued slowly, as if speaking to a five-year-old, "if you want to sell, and I want to sell, why don't we just agree to sell the whole mess to someone else?"

Rick lowered his dark eyebrows and slowly shook his head. "I'd rather not do that to Jack."

"I don't get it," she answered a little too loudly. "Don't you think Jack would want what I want?"

"What I think, sweetheart," he said as he ran his hand back over his shiny dark hair, "is that you might not know what you want. And maybe you didn't know Jack like I knew Jack."

It was then that Sunny truly began to sense something else at play behind this guy's wide smile. How dare he? *Sweetheart*? And no one knew Jack better than Sunny knew Jack. Like how kind and respectful he was to everyone, regardless of who they were or where they came from. Or how deeply he felt for those in need. Or how quick he was with the perfect wisecrack to lighten a dark mood or brighten a cloudy day. Suddenly she began to notice more about the man sitting across from her. Wasn't his hair just a little too perfect? And his shoes, so shiny she'd bet he could simply glance down after a lunch and check those big old teeth in them. Why on earth had Jack chosen to be friends with this guy? She knew they had met years ago when Jack had briefly been stationed at the base up-island, and that Rick was the townie who had taken him under his wing and introduced him to life on the island. But seriously, to remain friends all these years, and to go into a partnership with a guy like him? Ah—but there was where Rick had been right. Jack had been friends with everybody. She bent to retrieve her knapsack from the floor and stood.

Rick stood along with her. "You're going?"

"Gotta run," she answered, her words sliding down the scale in mock apology.

"Well, think about my offer. Though I suppose we could sell the place. One of those dickhead developers who are ruining the island would snap it up in a nanosecond. But really? The way I feel about it? I honestly think we should remember how much the place meant to Jack."

She turned to face him, her eyes narrowing into tiny slits, as if squinting might actually help her see this man more clearly. "You know what?" she finally answered. "Why don't we both just think about it for a day or two? I'm sure we can figure this out somehow." And with that she flashed him her own wide smile, grabbed her jacket, and walked out the door.

Asshole, she thought to herself now, thinking back on the conversation as she took in the sight of the shabby kitchen around her. Now what was she supposed to do? Maybe he was right. Maybe she should honor Jack's wishes. But then again, maybe it was just a tactic to get her to lower her asking price. Which, of course, she could do. But the thought of letting that creep manipulate her in such a way, when he was supposedly Jack's friend, made her sick to her stomach. Regardless, she supposed she should offer to meet with Rick again to discuss the possibilities in more detail. But the next time she'd make sure to allow enough time to get lost en route. No way was she going to let herself be stuck for one more night than necessary on this fucking island, with nothing better to do than scrub the damn floors.

6

Zara woke to the smell of cooking eggs coming from the kitchen. How early her mother must have risen today. She stretched and stifled a yawn, careful not to rouse her little sister Mariam breathing softly and evenly on the *toshak* beside her. Still half-asleep herself, Zara's foggy thoughts turned to the lazy Friday ahead, when she and her sister would first help their mother serve the morning meal, and later partake in their own midday prayers as the men went off to the mosque. And then she remembered, the dread filling her veins like a crippling poison. Any day, even this one, could bring a proposal, and along with it the end of her life as she knew it. There would be no more waking with her sweet sister by her side, no more of her mother's warm breakfasts, or the touch of her hand as she smoothed Zara's hair into a tidy braid. Gone would be the days of burying herself in her schoolbooks, the feeling of satisfaction from a difficult problem solved or a question soundly answered. There would be no more giggling and gossiping with her girlfriends as they hurried between classes. And there would be no more Omar.

Zara bolted upright, her bare feet landing on the rug beside her with a thud. If only her worries had all been a bad dream and things could still be just the way they were. But now she felt as though she were working against a giant ticking clock, trying to turn back its hands to a time before the specter of a proposal had reared its ugly head.

As she readied herself to join her mother in the kitchen her thoughts went to a day not long ago, a day when her future seemed as bright as the golden sun above, a day made all the more so delicious by its secrecy. A Wednesday, it was. She and Omar had agreed to skip class, borrow a friend's car, and escape for a picnic together at Qargha dam, about thirty minutes outside of the city. How badly they'd wanted to have some precious time together to talk, to sit and share their hopes and dreams for as long as they wanted, with nobody around to judge or tattle or condemn. Of course, even with no one who knew them anywhere in sight, the outing would have still aroused suspicions, would have caused heads to turn and questions to be asked about a young man and woman out alone, just the two of them, together. So rather than risk any complications that might come from that, she'd enlisted the help of her sister, to whom the promise of a break from school for a day by the lake was more than enough to ensure silence.

"Your smile seems to be saying a million words that your tongue leaves unspoken," Omar had said to her as they walked along the pebbly shore, shoes in hand.

Ahead of them, Mariam hopped along the water's edge, the lower half of her long black school uniform turning even darker with dampness. "I'm just imagining," Zara answered.

"Imagining what?"

"Oh," she giggled a little, "just thinking of the day when we will be walking on a beach with a child of our own."

"You are dreaming big dreams, my heart."

"And why not? Isn't that what life is about? Capturing your dreams and turning them into what is real?"

"And what else is in those dreams, might I ask?"

"You know. Everything we have already talked about. First, we will get our diplomas. Then we will do some studies in another country, maybe Germany or even Australia. I will become a famous lawyer, and you will become a celebrated journalist. And we will have three children—two boys and a girl—who will all grow up to be strong and handsome and kind, and who will always remain devoted to Allah and to their loving parents."

Omar laughed. "I see you have it all worked out. If only life were so."

"And why would it not be so? My parents have been supportive of my studies. They are proud of my ambitions. And they have not been in a hurry to marry me off to some skinny cousin or an uncle once removed who barely reaches my shoulder. We are lucky."

"Maybe we are lucky. But we must also be realistic. I am only a student who has to work two jobs just to get by, who lives in a house crowded with cousins. Your parents will not want me as a son-in-law either. My family is not important or rich—we're simple farmers from the Panjshir Valley. We have practically nothing."

"Then I will change their minds for them. You will see." Zara picked up a flat, smooth stone and flicked it across the lake's glassy green surface, watching until it disappeared behind a trail of foam. She lifted both arms toward the blue sky and twirled under the midday sun, the hem of her *kameez* slapping against the legs of her jeans. Omar laughed as he reached out to steady her, the quick, illicit touch of his hand like a burst of flame through her sleeve. Zara smiled, and hugged herself in her own embrace, happy with the world and everything in it.

But she also remembered that later that day, after the three of them had been seated on the terrace of a waterside restaurant for lunch, a strange feeling had come over her, an unease that seemed to have appeared out of nowhere. It began when they were digging into their *chopaan kabobs*, as the first hot pieces of charred lamb were pulled from the sticks and popped into their hungry mouths. The hair on Zara's arms had suddenly stood at attention, as if a stiff breeze had blown up off the lake. But the edges of the bright tablecloths remained still, and the water's surface appeared as smooth as a mirror. Zara's eyes scanned the tables around her, many still sitting empty under full place settings laid out by the hopeful owner. Even on such a beautiful day the tourists were still staying away, Zara thought, scared off by the memory of the horrific attack that had occurred at the Spojmai Hotel right next door, less than one year before. Dozens had died after being held hostage for hours. Others had escaped by jumping into the lake, clinging to a stone wall throughout the night as they waited to be rescued. The Taliban had claimed responsibility, just as they did for every attack that brought big headlines, whether they actually were the ones who did it or not. But whoever had stormed the hotel with their grenades and machine guns, Zara—like the rest of the Afghans dining peacefully around her—knew they wouldn't return. They had sent their message. Perhaps it was the ghosts from that day that were the cause of her unease, Zara thought, as she pulled her scarf tighter around her shoulders.

They remained on the terrace, warmed by the afternoon sun, as Mariam savored a bowl of *sheer yakh*, scraping gently at the mound of ice cream with her spoon as if she could make it last forever. Zara pushed the new pair of fake Ray-Bans up higher onto the bridge of her nose and allowed herself to relax, her focus switching to a pair of yellow paddle boats, shaped like swans, gliding toward the dam. The lake sparkled with a million tiny pinpoints of light, as if mocking the dull brown mountains around it.

After Omar had paid the bill and they'd started across the patio for one last look at the shore before heading home, Zara was hit once again with a sense of apprehension. Her eyes darted from table to table with the fear that perhaps she and Omar had been spotted by someone who knew her family. But Zara saw no familiar faces. She turned to search the terrace of the hotel next door, and checked behind them, peering through the glass doors that led to the interior of the restaurant, but still no one seemed to be paying the slightest bit of attention to their little group of three. Even so, Zara just couldn't seem to shake the feeling that she was being watched.

Now, by the light of the morning sun streaming through the bedroom window, Zara thought she understood. On that perfect day, a day where promise floated through the lakeside air like a kite on a string, a day when anything seemed possible, perhaps that sense of menace had instead been the arrival of a dark premonition, the foreshadowing of the unwelcome turn of events that was soon to come.

"*Salaam*," Zara greeted her mother good morning as the woman scooped a bowlful of chopped tomatoes into the pan of eggs. Zara took out the plastic eating mat, carried it into the dining area, and unrolled it onto the floor. As she set out the plates and the thermoses of black and green tea, the rest of the household began to gather, her uncles and aunts lowering themselves to the floor to partake in their morning meal. Mariam was now awake and as chipper as a baby bird, chattering away as she fulfilled her job as the youngest in the household, pouring water over each pair of waiting hands and offering a towel to dry.

As she scooped up her breakfast with the warm naan torn from the flat loaf passed from person to person, Zara once again felt there were eyes upon her. But this time she was definitely right, and the little smiles on her aunts' faces and the looks shared among them turned the soft eggs in her mouth into a thick sludge that she could barely manage to swallow.

Perhaps she'd gather the courage to speak with her father today, she thought as she watched his strong fingers grip the cup at his lips. He had not yet said a word to her about a proposal, so there was still a chance it was not too late. Maybe what Yazmina had first suggested at the coffeehouse had been correct. Maybe her father *would* understand, and the whole matter would soon be forgotten. But then the rest of Yazmina's words echoed in her mind. *It is the way things are done. It is tradition.* And as the meal was finished, and the women stood to clear the dishes, and the call to prayer began to sound in the street outside, and the men hurried out the door to the mosque, Zara became leaden with the knowledge that her new friend had spoken the truth.

7

"Anyone home?" The kitchen door flew open with a bang. Bear bounded in and skidded across the damp floor, leaving dark, muddy stripes in his wake.

"Damn it, dog!" Sunny yelled, dropping her mop.

"It's just me," shouted Joe, scraping the bottoms of his moccasins against the wooden doorjamb. "But I come bearing gifts." He placed the plastic container in his hand onto the Formica table as if it were a delicate piece of fine crystal. "Cheese!" he said, as he removed his wet jacket and draped it over a chair. "The best homemade mozzarella this side of Campania." He kissed the tips of his fingers with a flourish. "*Mangia*."

Sunny picked up the discarded mop and leaned it against the stove. "Really? They have a good cheese shop on this island?"

Joe laughed. "That'll be the day. No, it's my cheese. *Formaggio di Giuseppe*. For you to enjoy. Try some." Outside the window, the grey afternoon was swiftly turning to night. Sunny reached into a plastic shopping bag and produced first a two-pack of light bulbs, and next, a bottle of wine.

"A woman prepared for everything. Now *that*, that is something I love." Joe offered his hand and helped her up onto the rickety chair, where she had to balance on her tiptoes in order to twist the fresh bulb into the socket. "Let there be light!" he exclaimed as he helped her back down.

"And, more importantly, let there be wine," she added, grabbing the bottle by its neck.

"Allow me," Joe insisted. He wrestled a red pocketknife from his jeans and sat. "So how was your day?" He flipped open a little corkscrew from the edge of the knife.

"All right, I guess. I met Rick."

Joe lifted his eyes to see a small cloud pass over her face. "And how did that go?" he asked, piercing the cork with the sharp tip of the metal spiral.

Sunny cocked her head sideways a little. "Well, not so good. Or, rather, at least not how I had pictured. You know, Joe, I'm just not sure what to make of that guy."

Joe hesitated, but for only a second. "Well, though it is none of my business, you know what they say." She looked at him blankly as he pulled out the cork with a pop. "*Guardatevi dai falsi profeti*. Beware of the false prophets, who come to you in sheep's clothing, and inwardly are ravenous wolves."

"And what's that supposed to mean, may I ask?" Sunny swatted the cat off the counter and reached for two juice glasses from the cupboard over the stove.

Joe shrugged his shoulders. "You know," he continued before allowing her the chance to ask more, "Jack was a big fan of my cheese. First thing he'd do when he landed on the island was come knocking on my door." Joe rapped his knuckles loudly on the table. "'So we meet again, my old friend,' he'd always say. Then I'd see his hungry eyes begin to scan every surface of my kitchen as if he were on one of his recon missions." Sunny laughed as Joe brought one hand over his bushy brows and turned his gaze from counter to counter. "Ha! Yes, he was certainly a fan of my cheese. And he was also a big fan of you too, kiddo." Sunny swallowed. He could see her chest rise and lower with a deep, silent breath. "And let me say one more thing," he pointed toward her with the knife, cork still attached, "it's okay to feel bad about losing someone. No matter how much time has passed. A day, a year, a hundred years. Doesn't matter." Joe paused to clear his throat. "After my Sylvia left this earth, I kept waiting for the day when my heart would no longer ache with memories, the day that would pass from morning to noon to night without a single, agonizing image of her sweet face appearing in my mind. Well, guess what?" He sat back in his chair. "It has not happened yet, and now I know it probably never will, at least not in my short future."

Sunny remained at the sink, a dishtowel slung over one shoulder. She shook the water from the glasses and handed them to Joe.

"Life, it goes on." He lifted the bottle and poured. "You find new things to keep you busy, new friends to help you pass the time, new ways to make yourself feel happy. And when life gives you lemons, you make wine." Joe laughed and raised his glass. "*Cent'anni.* A hundred years. And to my new friend Sunny Tedder—may she find her heart's content." They each took a healthy sip, then set their glasses down on the table. Joe carefully wiped the knife's blade across the leg of his jeans, peeled the top off of the plastic container, and dissected the cheese with the precision of a surgeon. Once done, he stabbed the tip of the knife into a soft slab and offered it to Sunny with a bow of his head.

He watched as she took her first bite. "Oh. My. God," she said, with her mouth still half full. "Are you kidding me, Joe? This is the most delicious cheese, no, the most delicious *thing*, that I have ever tasted." Her shoulders seemed to relax for the first time since he had met her, making her neck appear to grow inches longer than before. Sunny helped herself to more, her eyes slipping shut as she savored the milky treat. Suddenly they both jumped at the sound of a car door slamming outside.

"Company!" said Joe with glee as he scraped back his chair and struggled to stand. "Now who could that be?" He shuffled to the door and opened it to find Sky shaking off the rain like a dog fresh from a bath. Joe and the skinny young man embraced each other in a part hug, part handshake, part pat on the back, an elaborate ritual that ended with a fist bump, a routine they'd clearly perfected over time. "I tell you, one day my eyeglasses are gonna get caught in those things, and you, young man, you're going to cry like a baby," said Joe, pointing to the gaping holes in the boy's earlobes, stretched into shape by a pair of metal grommets. Joe rubbed at his own saggy earlobes, just imagining the pain.

Sunny and Sky greeted each other with a little hug of their own, looking like long-lost siblings with their matching mops of curly brown hair. "You know," said Joe, pointing out the window toward the darkening sky, "I just thought of it. Perhaps you two meeting is an omen. Sunny, Sky!" He laughed at his own joke as the two of them groaned. Joe pinched the front pockets of his shirt between his index fingers and thumbs and pulled the fabric away from his body, flapping his arms a little to dispel the dampness left by Sky's wet jacket. Then he cleared his throat.

"So tell me, Sky. What on God's green earth could you be doing here on a night like this?"

Sky shot him a confused look, which Joe answered with a swift jerk of the head toward Sunny, who was busy helping herself to more cheese.

"Oh," Sky finally responded. "Well, you see, I was just on my way home from my bartending job at The Dirty Monkey, and I saw the lights on from the bottom of the hill, and I wanted to make sure everything was all right with the house." He turned to Joe for approval. "And you're still here, Sunny?"

"Missed the ferry." She held up two fingers. "Twice."

Sky nodded his head slowly up and down.

"Sit, sit. Please," Sunny said as if she had just remembered she was in her own house. She stood and rushed toward her new guest to help him with his jacket, piling it on top of the already soggy mess that was Joe's. The two men sat as she returned to the paper bag on the counter. "My breakfast," she explained a little sheepishly as she lifted out a can of Mountain Dew and a box of Frosted Flakes. "And my dinner," she added, revealing a box of Triscuits, a jar of pickles, and a large bar of chocolate, which she artfully arranged on a couple of plates that she set down on the table next to Joe's cheese. Another glass was rinsed before she finally joined them. "Please," she said, filling Sky's glass. "Enjoy. Happy to have the company."

Joe watched Sunny's actions with a smile on his face.

"So how long will you be staying on the island?" Sky asked Sunny, the little silver bead hanging in front of his teeth sparkling with every word.

"I wasn't planning on staying at all."

"Well you should!" he answered with the enthusiasm of the boy he was. "There's so much to do. Fishing, hiking, skydiving, kayaking, paddle-boarding . . ." Sunny's expression remained frozen as the two men waited for her reaction. "Art galleries, boutiques?" Sky tried. Nothing. "And in the summer, it stays light forever. Like Norway. Hey, and the car show is next week!"

Joe helped himself to some more wine. "Sky is a one-man Chamber of Commerce. He should run for mayor."

"He reminds me a little of someone else," Sunny said, flashing Joe a subtle smile.

"I've lived here all my life," Sky continued. "Well, practically all my life. My parents moved us up here from Los Angeles when I was little. I wouldn't live anywhere else. Maybe for a little while for school, but that's about it."

"Sky is right," Joe agreed. "It is a beautiful island. Oh, and I almost forgot, we found your other key. The one to the barn." He nodded at Sky, who dug it out of his pocket and slid it across the table to Sunny. Joe watched as she zipped it into the pocket of her down vest. She reached for the bottle and topped off their glasses. This was good. Tomorrow—tomorrow he'd bring her a warm loaf of bread and a jar of his red sauce.

8

The vendors were already at work setting up their folding tables in the courtyard as the morning sun climbed its way into the cloudless Kabul sky. On the street, a jumble of vans and carts and taxis and cars were unloading bins and piles of goods, as both men and women approached with heavy bundles over their shoulders, dragging behind them the plastic chairs that would provide some relief throughout the long day of commerce. How the little bazaar had grown since they first started offering weekly space to those whose businesses had been hurt so badly by the restrictions imposed by the international organizations that would no longer allow their people to shop on Chicken Street, designating it as yet one more dangerous place in Kabul that was off-limits. But here, behind the safety of the high walls topped with razor wire, under the watchful eyes of the coffee-house's two *chokidors*, everyone was allowed to shop to their heart's content, in turn allowing the vendors, along with Ahmet and his family, to bring in a few more dollars to help make ends meet.

Yazmina greeted the women who appeared with their arms heavy with scarves and jewelry, and helped them arrange the cloths for covering their tables and string the clotheslines that would be used to display their wares. "*Salaam alaikum*," she repeated to each of them, after the customary three kisses on their cheeks. "How are you? How is your health? How is your family?"

Bashir Hadi was busy setting up his own table, where the coffeehouse favorites that Sunny had taught him to make—brownies, peanut-butter-and-chocolate-chip cookies, date bars—would sell like hot cakes. He hoped they would go particularly fast today, he had told them this morning, as he was anxious to get home to where his wife, Sharifa, was working all day to prepare the special dish of *mantu* for the family. He could practically feel the little pockets of ground beef exploding in his mouth already, the mint and garlic sweet and tangy on the tip of his tongue.

Ahmet stopped briefly to check in with Daoud, who was standing tall and firm by the coffeehouse gate, his eyes continuously scanning the busy courtyard like a beacon at sea. After the *chokidor* assured him that everything was running smoothly, Ahmet slicked back his hair and began his weekly rounds, sharing his own greetings with the eager men laying out their smooth lidded boxes, and the others hanging their heavy woven rugs. Against the far wall, a string of women's dresses caught his eye, sparkling under the sun like a rainbow. Even from where he stood, Ahmet could recognize the good quality, but these dresses were nowhere near as beautiful as the ones his Yazmina had created, by hand, for Sunny and her friends, and later for some of the wealthy Afghans who had clamored for her designs, back when the child and the coffeehouse had not taken up so much of her time.

He watched as his wife stood admiring a tableful of handmade dolls dressed in miniature embroidered dresses and *hijab*, with long, dark stitched lashes shooting out from their almond eyes like the rays of the sun. Like little Yazminas, he thought, suddenly struck by the glow that seemed to be surrounding her like the halo of an angel, that warm light that comes only from a woman with child.

It wasn't long before the courtyard began to fill with the foreigners who showed up each week, strolling the perimeter, fingering the beads and admiring the chunky bracelets of silver and lapis, testing the strength of the wing-shaped kites, their obvious hunger for a bargain matched by the vendors' eagerness for a sale. Ahmet knew it would be a good day. He rubbed his hands together and smiled, and headed across the courtyard to escort Yazmina back inside the café, where she could sit and get some rest. How excited he was for this child, so much so that he sometimes felt the urge to shout his joy from the rooftop. But of course, out of honor and modesty, he would not share the news of Yazmina's condition with anyone, not until her belly became obvious through the heaviest of clothing, leaving him no choice. For in Afghanistan, to discuss a wife's pregnancy was to acknowledge engaging in the act that made it so, and that was something just not discussed. Outside the family, only Bashir Hadi had been told, and that was only because Ahmet did not want his wife working too hard.

By late morning Ahmet could see that things in the courtyard were starting to wind down. Only the most serious shoppers remained, their hands heavy with plastic bags, and a few of the vendors had started packing up.

"*Khob asti laalaa?*" How are you, big brother?

Ahmet turned to see his young friend Omar, surprised by both his presence at the coffeehouse on a Friday and by the traditional *perahan tunban* he wore, instead of the usual jeans he chose for their classes and meetings on weekdays.

"Hello, my friend, to you as well." The two men embraced and clasped each other's hands in greeting.

"I've come to buy some of your delicious cookies for my family, but they are already gone. Next week I will have to get here earlier."

"Well, it is good to see you anyway." Ahmet nodded toward the coffeehouse door. Omar headed inside and straight to his usual table by the wall, near the back. Ahmet followed with two cups of hot *chai*. "So," he asked as he pulled up a chair and sat, "how are your studies going?"

"Very well, thank you. Although sometimes it's difficult, with my duties at my uncle's shop, and my other job at Roshan selling phones."

"Yes," Ahmet answered, his eyes taking in the coffeehouse. "I understand."

"I'm sure you do," Omar agreed.

"Ah, but we're lucky, are we not?"

"That we are, my friend." Omar blew lightly on the surface of his tea. "That we are."

Ahmet crossed his legs. "There are many good people there at the university," he ventured, attempting to remain casual with his stream of talk.

"Many."

"And many pretty girls, am I right?"

Omar nodded.

"By the way," he said as he raised his cup toward his lips, "my mother tells me there was one who came by here yesterday, looking for you. Tall, silky hair, light complexion . . ."

Omar's eyes lit up a little. Ahmet raised his eyebrows and took a sip of the steaming liquid. Omar quickly composed himself, and sat up straight in his chair. "Perhaps it was my classmate Zara. We are working on a project together, and I missed her in class yesterday, because of my job."

"Well she must have missed you too. Apparently she was anxious to speak with you. This must be a difficult project."

"Yes, yes. Quite difficult."

"Apparently."

The two men sipped in silence for a moment.

"So you will be able to work it out, this project, after the weekend?"

"I hope so," said Omar with a sigh.

"So this Zara, she does not need to come looking for you at the coffeehouse again?"

Omar shifted in his seat, his cheeks reddening a bit at the mention by somebody else of the girl's name. Ahmet couldn't help but think about how uncomfortable he had once been because of his own feelings for Yazmina, how the mere sight of her slender wrists would cause him to become weak in his knees and forget his duties, how his thoughts of her had challenged everything he thought he knew about the way things must go between a man and a woman. And now, how happy he was to have her as his wife, to look straight into her deep green eyes without fear or shame, to lay down next to her smooth, warm body at the end of each day. He felt sorry for the young man in front of him. But still, there were customs that had to be followed.

He cleared his throat before he spoke. "I'm sure her parents would not be happy to know of your Zara coming to see you outside of school."

"She is not 'my' Zara," Omar answered quickly, too quickly to be believed. "And I'm sure her parents are aware that she is working on a project. That is all."

"You must be careful to respect our ways, Omar. Nothing good can come out of a relationship where the parents don't approve."

"I understand that, my friend." The boy dug in his pocket for a buzzing phone. Ahmet winced, knowing that in a good family, an unmarried girl with a phone in her hand was something a parent would rather not see. And if a girl was found to be texting or talking with a boy, well, the shame that could bring on the family would bear some serious consequences.

"Just be careful, little brother. Our world may be changing, but some traditions must still be respected. You must go about things in the proper way, for the sake of all. You cannot jeopardize your future, nor Zara's."

Omar shook his head. "Don't worry about me, big brother." He tightened the ends of his checkered *keffiyeh* around his neck. "Life is good. And with a little luck, it will only get better."

"*Inshallah*," Ahmet responded.

"*Inshallah*," Omar echoed.

After seeing his friend out the door, Ahmet poured himself another cup of *chai* and sat back down to rest for a moment. The conversation had troubled him, bringing up thoughts and emotions old and new, making him feel as though his mind was being twisted and turned and tossed around like one of Poppy's rubber dog toys. He thought of his wife's sister Layla, who was not much younger than this girl, Zara, must be. What will it be like when she returns from America and goes herself to the university? He could only hope that the girl would have enough sense, and enough pride, to not get mixed up in this sort of situation.

He remembered how incensed he had been just a few years before when he had discovered that his own mother had been receiving letters from Rashif, to whom she had not yet been married. A widow, an old woman, trading in words like that. *You are my dearest*, one letter had said. *My loved one is a mile away and yet a lifetime*, read another. But, really, had any harm been done? Hadn't Rashif come forward like a gentleman to ask Ahmet's permission to marry his mother? And to see how those two were together, like a pair of lovestruck teenagers. It was as if their relationship was always meant to be. If only he could understand better, if only these things were made clearer. He sighed and rubbed his hands up and down his forehead, as if that might help make it so. But his thoughts were interrupted by the sound of *azzaan* calling for *Jummah* prayer, so he buried the debate away for another day, and instead concentrated on rushing to the mosque to join the rest of the congregation in their Friday ritual.

9

"Fuck me," Sunny said out loud as the man in the neon vest leveled his flattened palm in front of the hood of her Toyota. They'd waited forty minutes in line already, just to miss the ferry by one stinking car? She turned off the engine with a sigh, and helped herself to a handful of chips from the half-empty bag beside her.

"*Col tempo la foglia di gelso diventa seta*. It is time and patience that changes the mulberry leaf to silk."

"I don't understand how you can stand it here, Joe. I mean, really? One whole day just to get to a dentist appointment?"

"It is one whole day that I get to spend with a beautiful woman," he answered with the same charming smile he had used to sweet-talk her into driving him off the island and into Seattle. *I have an appointment overtown, off the rock*, he had said. The rock. Perfect. The same thing they call Alcatraz, she'd thought at the time, right before Joe gave her hand a little squeeze and said, "I would be honored if you'd accompany me."

Sunny could read between the lines. She figured that, at his age, Joe didn't drive, or preferred not to. She could certainly take a few hours to help the old man out, though she didn't really feel she had any choice in the matter. He was not an easy person to say no to. But no matter what, it would probably do her good to get off the island, to give herself a chance to clear her mind.

The two weeks she'd ended up spending on Twimbly so far had been a true test of her nature. On one hand, there was something forbidding about the place. Streets with names like Forsaken Lane, Phantom Court, and Rocky Road, all of them leading down to Worthless Bay. Then there was the sign for fresh eggs that she passed all the time, that had another sign right under it that read "Out of Eggs", no matter what time of day it was. And the dark restaurant with the signboard whose thick plastic letters announced "Chef Hurt. No Meals." She shuddered to imagine that kitchen mishap. And on Saturday, those women shrouded in black like a coven of witches, or widows in mourning, lining both sides of the road over in the town of Chittleham. It wasn't until she'd almost passed them by that she noticed the anti-war signs in their arms. But when she'd rolled down the window to offer a cheery thumbs-up, she became freaked by the stern, frozen expressions that made the women look more like zombies than peace activists.

On the other hand, there were also those people who were a little *too* friendly for her taste. Did she really need to swap her life story with the gas station attendant before she'd even had her first sip of coffee? Or hear every little detail about last night's choir performance at the community center while her bags were being held hostage by the checkout girl at the Red Apple?

The worst was that woman in Meyersville. Sunny had decided to cheer herself up a little with a new top, or maybe even a jacket. Every shop window seemed to be filled with the same things—big, flowy dresses, layers of vests and scarves, chunky loose-knit sweaters—not exactly her go-to style, but maybe if she looked she'd find something more along the lines of her jeans and T-shirts.

She picked a store at random and reluctantly opened the wooden door. A little bell rang, and a stringy woman with a long, loose grey ponytail greeted Sunny from behind the counter. "Hi," she chirped. "I'm Raven. What can I help you with today?"

"Just browsing." Sunny smiled and turned to the racks lining the small shop's walls.

"We have some beautiful new shrugs from Peru that I can show you, if you're interested."

"No thanks. I'm good." She had to admit, though, that some of these clothes were actually okay, when you got up close. Sunny tossed a few items over her arm.

"Let me take those for you." Sunny jumped, startled by Raven's voice just inches from her ear. "And I'll bring in a few others I think you might like."

Sunny emerged from the little curtained cubicle wearing the first top. As she smoothed the pleats over her hips, she could see Raven in the mirror behind her, wrinkling her nose.

"Um, no. Not for you."

Personally, Sunny had thought she looked pretty good. Okay, maybe the shirt was pulling a little at the seams, but still. She pursed her lips and rolled her eyes at the mirror.

"Sorry, I just tell it like it is. I see it as a service to my customers. After all, if they can't trust me . . ."

The next outfit didn't get a much better reception. "No, no stripes. Here, just try some of the things I brought in," Raven said, reaching for a green linen tent dress hanging from a hook. Sunny knew she'd look like a Christmas tree in that thing, but nevertheless did what the woman told her.

Again, a no. "A girl like you needs sleeves."

Sunny could feel the color rising in her cheeks. She was so tempted to tell Raven where she'd like to shove those sleeves. It almost made her miss shopping in Kabul, where she'd try to disguise her foreign status (and the resulting price gouging that would come because of it) by covering herself with a burqa. Of course, neither the shops nor the market over there had even the tiniest space for a girl to try something on, so she'd had to measure herself shoulder to shoulder with a string, which she carried with her everywhere to ensure, if not a proper, at least an approximate, fit.

It had been a long two weeks. Even the stunning view of Puget Sound that had captured her heart so suddenly that first day had failed to reappear, leaving in its stead a dreary outlook of grey, so evenly dull that you couldn't tell where the sea met the sky. But she did have to admit one thing. The evenings were becoming something that she actually found herself looking forward to. The old house had somehow become a kind of gathering place. Joe would "just happen to be wandering by" right before the sun went down, and Sky would stop in after work to "check on the vines", which, to her, seemed to be doing just fine on their own, thank you very much, waking slowly from their long winter nap with little fuzzy buds swelling from their branches. Together she and Sky would drag in a few logs from the pile on the porch to build a fire, and the kitchen would soon fill with the warm, cozy smell of burning wood. Sky would bring wine from one of the vintners on the island, which the three of them would rate on a scale of one to ten. Joe would proudly present them with whatever masterpiece he'd spent that day concocting in his kitchen next door: pasta fazul, spaghetti bolognese, chicken cacciatore, each dish a delight for the senses. And Sunny would bring it all home with her world-famous cookies.

And they'd talk. And talk. Actually, mostly Joe would talk, but sometimes one of the others would manage to get a word in edgewise. Sky told them he'd started to fill out his applications for the winemaking program at the community college in Yakima. Sunny shared some of the funnier stories about her time in Kabul, like the one about her crazy friend Candace appearing at Yazmina and Ahmet's wedding with a live sheep in the back of her SUV. The perfect gift for a bride and groom, she had been told. And the time when the coffeehouse was about to be raided for alcohol, and Bashir Hadi had the brilliant idea to hide everything in Poppy's doghouse, knowing how that would be the one and only place a swaggering Afghan officer would be too scared to look.

She turned to look at the man in the passenger seat next to her. She had to admit she'd never come across anybody quite like him before, and she'd come across her fair share of characters in her travels. The new men in her life, she thought with a laugh. An old Japanese American Italian, who had to be at least twice her age, and a metal-studded island boy young enough to be her son, a thought that suddenly made her shudder. Ah, and let's not forget Rick. Now there was one man who was truly pursuing her, like a fox after a rabbit. Since their meeting he'd managed to reach her once by phone, and had left several messages, which would pop up like crazy whenever she'd find herself within range of a cell signal. She didn't feel too compelled to answer, as neither of them was budging on their position. But he was the one putting on the pressure, and she was sick of him trying to lay a guilt trip on her. Because, truth be told, sometimes she'd lay awake at night feeling a little bit like a traitor for abandoning Jack's dream. Especially those nights when she missed him so badly she could swear her heart actually physically hurt. Those were the nights she'd grab her phone from the nightstand and punch up the last communication they had with each other, the one she'd read over and over so many times she knew it by heart.

Hey you, he had typed from the ski cabin in Whistler.

Hey you yourself.

What r u doing?

What, r u ten?

LOL.

Stop, she had begged him. *I miss your face.*

Soon, baby. I miss your ass.

Stop calling me baby!

K.

K?

That means okay. Don't you know anything?

I know plenty, mister.

How's Santa Fe?

Lonely. Can't wait to see you.

Two days. Twimbly.

Yep.

You'll love it as much as I do. Promise.

If you say so.

I say so. Be there.

With bells on, she had replied. *And not a stitch more.*

But even after those tough nights and all the uncertainty they churned up, by the damp, cold light of day she still couldn't imagine herself surviving on this island. And though she wasn't quite sure where she wanted to go, or what she wanted to do, she did know that wherever and whatever it was, she was going to need some money to go there and do it. In the meantime, at least she wasn't paying for a hotel room. And when she thought about how much karmic debt she was avoiding by not relying on the kindness of friends with couches, a little while longer on the island didn't seem like such a bad idea. Except, she thought as she heard the car engines around her *finally* come to life, at times like now.

Two hours later, from the comfort of a thinly padded vinyl chair bathed in flickering fluorescent light, Sunny gave up on the thought of finding that clear head a visit to the mainland had promised. She checked her watch for the tenth time in twelve minutes. What was he doing in there, getting a full set of veneers or something? She stood and stretched her arms above her head and released an enormous yawn that echoed across the still room.

From behind her desk, the receptionist paused from stamping envelopes to shoot Sunny a look. She'd noticed the girl earlier, when she and Joe first came in. How could you not, with that hair that looked like an upside-down skunk, one half a dazzling white, the other as black as night. Now the girl swiveled slightly in her chair, away from Sunny, and went back to her work. Sunny pulled her phone from her leather knapsack and snapped a close-up from behind.

Found the perfect new do for you! she texted to Candace, thrilled for once to have an actual cell connection, which she then took advantage of to read, listen to, and delete even more messages from Rick. A quick look at the news sites was enough to tell her she hadn't missed a thing—the world was still pretty much a mess. She checked her watch again. "What the hell is going on in there?" she asked herself, but apparently said out loud.

The girl shrugged her shoulders without turning around. "Dr J. likes to take time with his patients. He thinks it shows that he cares."

"Yeah, and if I know my friend Joe, he hasn't stopped flapping his jaws long enough for the doc to get even the tiniest peek inside his mouth."

The girl continued with her envelopes. Sunny yawned again. "I'm gonna go get a Coke. Want one?" She headed toward the office door.

Now the girl swiveled sideways in her chair and placed her right hand on her heart in a gesture Sunny recognized as definitely not American. "Thank you, but I'm not thirsty right now."

Sunny stopped in front of the desk. "Where are you from?" she couldn't help but ask. She was curious. She'd seen that same type of body language all over the world, just not here.

The girl raised her eyebrows and sighed, obviously annoyed by the question. Sunny decided not to push it. "So what's it like working here, um, I'm sorry, what was your name?" she asked instead, in a lame attempt to engage the girl in a little conversation.

"What's it like?" the girl responded incredulously. "And my name is Kat."

"You know, like do you get any interesting cases?"

"In a dental office?" The girl once again turned back to her work.

"Or does anybody famous ever come in?"

"*Deawaana,*" she muttered under her breath.

"Excuse me? Did you just call me crazy?" The word *deawaana* was one of the first Sunny had learned in Kabul.

"No, I—" the girl fumbled.

"Wait, how do you know how to speak Dari? Why, you're Afghan, aren't you?"

"I'm an American," the girl answered abruptly.

"Okay. But you, or your parents, or you and your parents, were born in Afghanistan, am I right, Kat?"

"So?"

"Well, I'm from there too!"

The girl looked confused.

"I mean, I lived there for six years. Right in Kabul."

"Why? Did the military make you go? Or were you CIA?"

"Me? Oh no, I had a coffeehouse. An amazing little place."

Sunny dragged a chair over to the counter and, forgetting all about her Coke and her boredom and Joe and his teeth, began to pour out her story—how she had escaped small-town Arkansas for the adventure that was Kabul, how her then-boyfriend's money allowed her to start up the café, how proud she was of its success, and how very much she missed the place and all of its craziness. It felt good to share her memories with this girl, and even though the poor thing hadn't asked and had no choice but to listen, Sunny couldn't help but believe that behind that mask of boredom there was a tiny spark of yearning to hear what she had to say.

10

The warm smell of baking bread greeted Halajan as she headed down Qala-e-Fatullah road toward the string of colored bulbs blinking in the dawn light. "*Salaam alaikum,*" she said to Fattanah, who sat behind the open shopfront window handing out slabs of golden flatbread to a dwindling line of hungry customers.

"*Wa alaikum as salaam,*" the woman answered back, her gaptoothed smile always a welcome sight. Over her shoulder Halajan could see a handful of cross-legged women on the bakery's raised floor, silhouetted by the brick oven's glow, their sleeves rolled up high on their sturdy arms as they weighed and kneaded and pounded and rolled the lumps of floury dough into the long oval discs she picked up early every morning for the coffeehouse. Back when Sunny was there the bread had been the hard French kind that all the foreigners seemed to like so much, delivered from Carte Se, a whole forty-five minute drive away. But Halajan, she preferred Fattanah's soft, chewy *naan*, and also preferred to pay her money to these women who worked so hard to support their children. She'd never forget the day the Taliban shut down the widows' bakeries, where bread was baked by women left without male relatives to support them, to be sold to other women like them at a price they could afford. Even though bakeries run by women had a long tradition in Afghanistan, under the Taliban the only jobs women were allowed—in women's hospitals, women's prisons, or at the security checkpoints in airports—were those made necessary by the Taliban's own rule, the one that forbade non-related men and women from mixing. The bakeries had been a lifeline for many desperate women, the only thing keeping their families from starvation. For a while the Taliban let them be, but it wasn't long before the women endured threats and beatings that came with orders to shut their businesses down. But now the bakeries were back, and though this one sold bread to everyone, Fattanah made it a point to hire widows to do her baking.

She thanked Fattanah as she exchanged her coins for a stack of *naan* taken fresh from the fire on a long wooden paddle, and headed back home where, behind the bright turquoise gate and the towering wall, everything was still quiet. Only Bashir Hadi was visible to her through the windows as she crossed the patio to the coffeehouse's front door.

"*Salaam.*"

"*Sob bakhair.* Good morning to you, Halajan." He paused and propped his mop against a chair, the low morning sunlight bouncing off the wet floors. "Let me take that from you."

Halajan handed him the bundle of bread she'd carried wrapped in a bleached-out head scarf, and started down the hallway toward the back door, just as she did every morning, her plastic shoes clack-clacking on the marble tiles and Poppy trailing close behind, just as *she* did every morning. In the privacy of the tiny courtyard, Halajan untied her head scarf and leaned back against the concrete wall, her wrinkled face turned toward the sky. Poppy groaned and stretched out in a sunny corner to warm her aching bones.

"You and me both, girl. We're not as young as we used to be." Halajan remembered the day Jack delivered Poppy to the coffeehouse. She had screamed. But, as usual, Jack had done a good thing. Poppy had earned her weight in gold just from being by Sunny's side, and now by keeping a wary eye on all those who entered the coffeehouse, as rheumy as those eyes were. Halajan missed Jack, so handsome, so tall, like a movie star. And so brave, the way he swooped in to rescue Layla when she was in danger of being taken from her home in the mountains, just as her sister Yazmina had been. But what she loved most about Jack was how he made her laugh, the way he'd say things to her about Sunny—right in front of her face—in the rapid-fire Dari that Sunny could never understand. And Sunny, too, she missed. Sure they'd fought like cats and dogs, and Sunny could be so annoying with that laugh that was as loud as the horn of a truck stuck in traffic, but still. Like they say, *there is a way from heart to heart.* And it was true. After all they had been through together, they had become as close as family. Not to mention the credit Sunny deserved for all the improvements she had made on this house Halajan had rented to her for her café. The three humming generators drowning out all signs of life around her were proof of Sunny's determination. If they had remained out in the front courtyard where they had been, the coffeehouse never would have had the success it did.

She hitched up the elastic waist of her sagging blue jeans and reached deep into the pocket of her long sweater, feeling around for the hard metal tube Sunny's American friend Candace had given her the last time she had passed through Kabul. An electric cigarette. Whoever thought of such a thing? But Candace had urged Halajan to give it a try, thinking it might help her quit her secret habit. Halajan had no desire to stop smoking, but Candace had also mentioned that since there would be no smoke, there would be no evidence, and that made some sense to her. Her insides filled with the fruity vapor as she took her first drag of the day, the sight of the fake orange glow at the tip of cylinder almost making her laugh out loud. Next time she'd try to remember to put her Marlboros back in her pocket.

Candace. Halajan shook her head just thinking of the woman. There was another one who at first had made her hackles rise like an angry cock. Even Sunny hadn't seemed to like her much when they first met in Kabul, until they found out they were both from the southern part of their country, perhaps, Halajan thought, the same tribe. But Candace had changed, no longer the Princess Candace who used to charge into the coffeehouse in her high heels and bangled arms, demanding the best table, tossing her fancy coat carelessly at whoever was standing guard by the door. From what Halajan could see, Candace had become a more serious person, one who had learned how to put her big mouth and deep pockets to work for people who had neither voice nor money. Halajan marveled at the way that woman could make things happen like magic, like conjuring up an instant throng of customers clamoring for Yazmina's designs after she saw how clever the girl was with a needle. And like pulling the tangled strings of Afghan bureaucracy to give Yazmina's sister Layla the gift of a stay in America. But also the things she did for people she didn't even know, finding the money needed for food and supplies and bribes to help women in prison for what they call moral crimes—the crimes of refusing to be forced into sex with those who have paid for it, for being victims of rape or of abusive husbands—women imprisoned for making their own decisions in personal matters. Her latest work was creating a network of safe houses to help those who had managed to get out of prison, and for those in danger of being put in one. Halajan always looked forward to hearing what Candace was up to, and was glad her work brought her through Kabul so often.

The shadows from the branches of the pomegranate tree in the center of the concrete courtyard grew shorter as the sun rose in the morning sky. By now the tree struggled to bear fruit, and what little it did manage to produce was small and sour. The tree had to be as old has Halajan herself, growing tall in this spot from the days when the property was just an empty lot, a place where she and Rashif would play as children. How could they have ever imagined, back then, where their lives would take them? It had been no surprise, so long ago, that their young love was not meant to be, and that they had both been married off to others by their families. But finding each other again after so many years, after they had each been widowed, was almost a miracle. Six years they spent with barely a word between them—even the slightest acknowledgment in public was strictly forbidden by tradition—the only communication written in ink on the pages of the letters Rashif slipped into her hand every Thursday at his shop in the *Mondai-e*. She'd quickly hide the envelopes in the folds of her chador—if the letters fell into the wrong hands there would be a terrible shame brought upon her family. Her collection grew to hundreds of letters, all remaining unread until the day Yazmina innocently came across one of them, and then discovered Halajan's other secret: Halajan couldn't read. She smiled now, just thinking of the words she'd first heard in Yazmina's voice. *I am dreaming of seeing your eyes*, Rashif had written, and had called her *my dear*, always signing off with *Love, your Rashif.* And now they were married. That, she thought, was the true miracle. It was the influence of Rashif himself, and the love of Yazmina, that had lured her son Ahmet off his strict traditionalist path, opening the door for Rashif to become her husband. For in Afghanistan, a woman whose husband dies leaving her with a son can only remarry if her son, the eldest male member of the family, arranges it.

And that had been just the beginning of the changes in Ahmet. Before Rashif and Yazmina had come into his life, it seemed as though his only ambition had been to remain as the *chokidor* for the coffeehouse. Halajan had encouraged him over and over to become something bigger, to go to Germany, perhaps, to join his older sister Aisha at the university there. But Ahmet had made it his mission to protect and take care of her, like the good Afghan son he thought he should be. How proud she was that he was now finally going to the university here in Kabul, and even prouder that he was starting to open his eyes, and his heart, to a world beyond that of the fundamentalists.

Yes, she thought as she stopped herself from instinctively tossing the false cigarette to the ground to crush it out under her shoe, all in all life was pretty good. She still worried about the future of her country, and what it might bring to the lives of her family, but not too deep inside she felt the stirrings of hope. For she knew that in Afghanistan, though nothing was easy, nothing was impossible either.

11

There were days when Sunny thought that the spectacular view she had seen through the living room windows that first day on the island had been a mirage. Joe had told her to be patient, although, of course, his advice was delivered via an Italian proverb and an endless explanation that followed. It was true that sometimes, if you sat still long enough and were lucky enough to be at the window at exactly the right moment, you might catch a quick peek of the snow-capped mountain across the water before it would disappear again behind the fog. But that was about it.

Patience. Sometimes Sunny thought she'd skipped straight from chaos to inertia, without ever stopping for the patience phase. There were days when she felt as though her entire self was being tested by the situation with Rick. He wasn't budging, sticking firmly to his notion that the place should be held onto in honor of Jack and his dream. Yet he still refused to accept Sunny's offer for her half of the property, even though she'd caved a little and dropped her asking price by a tad as an incentive.

She leaned back into the couch and dug deep into a carton of mint chocolate chip ice cream. Bear lifted his head and eyed the spoonful with longing. This dog must eat better than I do, it occurred to her, remembering the little plastic bags of roasted chicken and rice Joe had left with her when he'd dropped Bear off for the day, claiming he had something he needed to do, although she couldn't imagine what. There *wasn't* anything to do in this damn place. Even Sangiovese, the cat, looked bored, his tongue scraping rhythmically across its paws in an endless, needless bathing ritual.

She didn't even want to think about how long she'd let herself stay on the island. The days just seemed to pass, and she'd wake each morning still there. Doing nothing. Nothing to do. She had tried, one Tuesday when it hadn't looked too damp out, to take a walk, hoping it might help clear her head a little. She'd stood frozen at the bottom of the driveway, her eyes turning left, right, left, then back again, each direction reflecting a mirror image of the other, with nothing but a flat, dark corridor of thick pines stretching out as far as she could see. She finally chose a left, for no particular reason, and began to walk.

At first it had been okay, and she started to think that perhaps this walking business might be something she'd try every morning; that is, until she settled things with Rick and left the island for good. But after about ten minutes of not seeing anyone else out there walking, or biking, or jogging, or driving for that matter, she started getting a little spooked. A couple of times she found herself spinning around to see who was following her, only to realize that the footsteps she heard had been her own. And the wildlife she'd hoped to spot during this attempt to become one with nature? All dead. Smashed squirrels and squished snakes and crushed slugs and flattened worms. Roadkill all around. At one point the sound of a plane overhead seemed to offer a welcome sign of life, but when she looked up it literally disappeared into thin air as the grey sky swallowed it whole. A ghost plane. After what seemed like an eternity of silence, she began to wonder if something had happened, if some terrible disaster, some apocalyptic event, had occurred, leaving her unaware and alone and left out there to die. She grabbed the phone from inside her pocket. No service, of course. Then she turned around and hurried back to the house, doubling her pace.

What was with her, scared of her own shadow? Where was the Sunny who, much to Bashir Hadi's, and Jack's, dismay, would leap at any chance to throw on a head scarf and hit the unpredictable streets of Kabul on her own, so anxious to breathe in the smell of fresh *naan* coming from the bakeries and soak up the sights of the bearded vendors on Chicken Street as they haggled over the price of an "antique" sword or a lambskin hat? And when did she become such a lump? she wondered as she scraped at the bottom of the carton with the spoon. She never used to be like this. Hard work was something she'd always been drawn to, reveling in the challenge of a tough task and picturing the rewards she knew would follow. The coffeehouse was proof enough of that. She was proud of her accomplishment. And that feeling she used to get just from standing back and listening to the hodgepodge of languages, from seeing men and women from around the world, all so far away from everything familiar yet feeling so at home in her, Sunny's, place? Nothing could beat that.

Her last Skype session with Yazmina, from the vegan café down in town, had been a little tough. Seeing the jerky image of the Kabul coffeehouse in the laptop screen had made her feel as though it were a set of a movie, like it wasn't, and had never been, real. The place looked good, with a few slight changes that had been made here and there—some new curtains, cushions, tablecloths—but it did seem a bit quiet for a Thursday evening. Yazmina had spoken quickly and breathlessly in her improving English, her face seeming to glow as she shared with Sunny her wonder at little Najama's cleverness, her pride at her husband Ahmet's involvement with others determined to help build a better Afghanistan, and her worries about what trouble that might bring. But she was clearly busy, and before Sunny had a chance to inquire after Halajan and Rashif, or Bashir Hadi, or to ask about how Yazmina's sister Layla was doing in Minnesota, Yazmina had to go. Sunny had signed off with a feeling of envy she wasn't proud of.

Bear stood and stretched, then padded over to the couch where Sunny remained seated and rested his chin on her thigh with a sigh. "You said it, boy." She stroked the brown fur on his head and stared out into the grey. There was no question about it. It was time to get out of Twimbly. It was time to settle with Rick. It was time to get a plan—a vision that was hers, and hers alone. And if it involved going back to Kabul, so be it. So long as she came up with a plan. It was time to get off her sweet ass and put it in gear.

But this place didn't seem to be helping much with that. She'd felt muddled and soft ever since she had stepped off that ferry. It was as though the island had cast an evil spell on her, one that made her lazy, and hungry, all the time.

Yes, decisions needed to be made. But maybe not right this moment. Candace was coming to town. And she was bringing a surprise.

12

The blue dome capping the faded walls of the Shah-e-Do Sham-shaira mosque loomed before her, the edifice nearly blending in to the dusty hills beyond and clear sky above, save for its stacked white columns and high, arched windows. Halajan rushed past, through the gaggle of old men stooping to feed the pigeons, her eyes straight ahead, defying anyone who might wonder at a woman traveling alone in the center of the city.

The streets were jammed with traffic, horns blaring and tailpipes spitting out enough fumes to choke an elephant. She covered her nose and mouth with the bottom of her scarf and turned left onto the narrow bridge that spanned the Kabul River, its once verdant banks and flowing waters now a mud-caked trench littered with garbage and filth. Once safely on the other side, she paused for a moment to catch her breath, then continued left toward the *Mondai-e* bazaar, past the vendors on the streets surrounding the market, many crouched next to the blankets spread at their feet, others leaning on their wheeled carts as they sipped their *chai*, waiting for a taker for the fabrics and undergarments and sugarcane juice they offered. These were the ones, she knew, who were not allowed to be selling, who had not paid for the right to have their space. But that didn't seem to stop anyone from buying. As Halajan was about to make the right turn into the passageway that would lead her to her destination, she heard a small voice at her side. "Rabbits, *maadar kalaan*? Do you need some rabbits today, grandmother?"

She turned to see a grinning boy no older than ten, his clothes in tatters and his face smeared with dirt, offering a birdcage heaped with a squirming pile of brown fur. But as she bent closer for a better look, the boy's smile suddenly collapsed, his eyes widening with fear. Out of the corner of her own eye she spied a blue-shirted policeman waving a stick. The boy lifted his arms to cover his face before the first blow fell. Halajan heard his cry and quickly stepped in front of him, raising her head to look the menacing man squarely in his steely eyes. This time the stick stopped in midair. Halajan's look narrowed into a squinting dare as she remained frozen in place, waiting for the rage to leave the man's face. Then she turned and began to slowly walk away, one eye remaining behind to make sure it was understood that there was no sale underway, and no reason to harass. The boy smiled and waved. Halajan quickened her step. Najama didn't want a rabbit anyway. No, it was a peacock Halajan was after. And today, she was in the mood for a deal.

Through the tight alleyways she wound, first left then right then left again. She knew her way well, from the times she had been here as a girl, with her father. The lane grew smaller as she continued—another left, then a right—until the sounds of the street were completely drowned out by the twitters and trills and caws bouncing off the crumbling mud walls. The Alley of Straw Sellers, where men had gathered for many generations with birds for sale, lay straight ahead.

Halajan squeezed her arms close to her body as she entered the heart of the market, where in some places it was not even wide enough for two people to pass without touching. Seeds and husks sailed through the close air, stirred up by the flapping of hundreds of wings.

It did not seem all that long ago to her that the birds of Kabul had been silenced by the Taliban. In a place where even the poorest of homes followed the old royal tradition of keeping songbirds, the bird sellers at the *Market Kaa Forushi* had been thriving. But to the fundamentalists, there was only one song that mattered—the song of the Koran—and everything else was deemed a distraction. They swarmed through the bird markets and into people's homes, opening cages and forcing the birds out into a hostile world, one the birds were not prepared for, where many met their fates in the mouths of hungry cats and dogs.

Now there were plenty of people keeping birds again. For even on the darkest of days, in a home with little money to spare, the song of a bird is an invitation to dream. And besides, how much trouble could a bird be anyway? thought Halajan. As Sunny used to say about Yazmina, they *ate like birds*.

Today in the market there seemed to be more socializing than selling going on; the men and boys crouched close to their stalls, sharing a laugh or a smoke or a cup of *chai*. But as Halajan walked past their chatter suddenly seemed to come to a halt, silenced by the sight of a woman trespassing through their male world.

That made Halajan itch for a bargain even more. Was her money not good enough? And what was the problem? she thought as she stopped for a moment to scan the alleyway behind her. She could not see even one other customer interested in purchasing their wares. Halajan took a deep breath, inhaling the cloud of cigarette smoke around her, and continued deeper into the dark maze.

She passed the dog kennels empty of dogs but crowded with chickens and roosters and ducks, and circled around to the place where men kept their prized *kowks* and little *budanas* in airy wicker cages, to be let out only for show. Here the birds were treated like kings, coddled and fussed over from Saturday to Thursday, with hopes that Friday morning would bring riches from the men placing bets on their fighting prowess. Though from what Halajan remembered being told, even then the birds were scooped up and shielded from clawing talons before any true battle could occur. They were far too valuable to let any real harm come to them.

Deeper and deeper she went, through the jumble of cages filled with canaries and finches belting out their birdsong in the dark alleyway. Some looked a little worn, others seemed scrappy. Halajan thought how confused they must all be from the darkness. You would hardly know what time of day it was, if it weren't for the slivers of sunlight breaking through the narrow slats of the tin roofs above. But it was the caged doves that made her the saddest, with their hopeless dreams of flight stirred daily by the coos of their luckier brothers and sisters soaring through the late afternoon Kabul skies.

Finally she came upon the peacocks. Halajan planted herself firmly in front of a toothless vendor who sat on his heels, sipping his tea. The man barely raised his eyes.

"How much?" she asked without bothering to stop for the usual formalities.

"Twelve thousand."

Halajan laughed. "The cost of half a year's rice just for one little bird?"

"That is my price." The man stood and turned away from her, busying himself with a leaky bag of seed.

"You must be a very rich man, to turn away at the smell of money."

The man shrugged his shoulders and continued with his task.

"Twelve thousand afghanis for a bird that does not even sing. And that one over there, the one missing the feathers on his wing. How much is he?"

The man turned toward the bird and hesitated. "Ten thousand," he grunted.

"For a scraggly old bird? You should be paying me to take him off your hands."

"He still has a beautiful tail. One with colors that will fetch a hefty sum."

"Okay. So then what about the white one? Who would want a peacock with no color?"

"The albino peacock is very rare. Very prized. That will cost you thirteen thousand."

Halajan turned to leave, feeling insulted by this greedy man who seemed to have no sense. She pulled her scarf tighter around her neck and began to walk away.

"Fifteen hundred," came a voice from behind her.

She turned back toward him and planted her feet firmly on the ground. "Fifteen hundred for what?"

He reached his hand into a cage that held three small birds, retrieving one that he separated from the rest without hesitation. "Fifteen hundred for this one."

Halajan looked down at the little brown bundle of feathers. "Ach. You call that a peacock?"

The man nodded. "It is a she-hen."

"How can you tell?" she asked, eyeing the others in the cage with suspicion.

"The feathers on the wings. They are darker brown. It is a girl."

"So you are trying to sell me a peacock with no tail?"

"She is all you can afford. She is not as prized as the male birds."

"Of course not," said Halajan with a scowl. Not even in the bird world do women have any value. The little bird remained silent and still in the man's rough hands. She was no bigger than a teakettle.

"You must take it or leave it. I don't have all day, old woman."

Of course you don't, thought Halajan, as she stood contemplating the helpless creature in front of her. What kind of surprise would this be for Najama? No matter how long the girl might wait, there would never be a beautiful tail appearing from the behind of this bird. How would she ever explain this choice that was destined to end in disappointment?

The man bent down to return the bird to the cage.

"Wait!" Halajan commanded. "Twelve hundred and you have a deal."

"Thirteen," he said as he straightened back up.

Thirty minutes later she was back across the river, a domed cage wedged up against her skinny legs, waiting for a bus to carry her home. Three buses had passed her by before she had been able to locate where the normal stop was. It wasn't like it used to be. Even during the Russian times there were proper bus stops, where the buses would pull over for passengers to get safely off and on. Now it was a free-for-all, with no signs anywhere, and the decision to stop purely at the whim of the driver.

Finally one of the little green buses came to a halt in the street in front of her, and Halajan hurried to keep up with the others rushing to board, the birdcage banging against her side. She handed the attendant her ten afghanis and managed to secure the last available seat in the women's section—the one directly in front of the men's, the seat most women avoided so as to not be forced to deal with harassing touches from behind. But Halajan didn't care. If anyone wanted to bother with this grandma, go ahead. Sometimes it was good to be old, she thought as she took note of the women around her, their gazes lowered to avoid the leering stares and unwanted pursuit that happened so often when a young woman traveled by bus. Unable to simply use a smile as a way of flirting with a girl, with the hope of a smile in return, a boy would instead choose to follow her, knowing her daily habits, and where she would be when.

Halajan lifted the cage onto her lap as more people crowded the bus. So many stops! And so much traffic. At this rate she would never get home. The peahen seemed impatient as well, its peeps and squawks growing louder and more frequent with the driver's every step on the brake.

"Shush!" whispered Halajan as she bent forward to check on the bird. It did look a little out of sorts, with its feathers puffed up and its eyes drooping shut. Finally the bus broke free of the traffic and was able to pick up some speed. Halajan steadied the cage with one hand and held fast to her seat with the other as they bounced up and down over the ruts and potholes below, counting the minutes before she could get off of this damn thing. The bird's peeps and squawks were turning into more of a screech, and now, just like the men were glaring at the women, the women were starting to glare at her. "Quiet!" she hissed to the peahen. But the screeching wouldn't stop. The bird did not look well. Perhaps it is carsick, Halajan thought, just as a dribble of thick liquid escaped from its beak.

Halajan turned her head toward the window to avoid the stares of the women being cast upon her like sharp stones. How she envied the men in their cars below, free to come and go in privacy as they pleased. She closed her eyes and tried to concentrate on the surprise ahead. Najama would be happy as a trout in a mountain stream when she saw her peacock. There would be no reason to tell her the truth about the peacock being a girl, at least not until the bird was grown. And by then, *inshallah*, the two would have formed a special bond, and all would be forgiven.

13

The peacocks had been at it since before sunrise, the horny males belting out those fake screams of ecstasy that were their secret weapons for luring a mate with their supposed prowess. Men, thought Sunny as she poured her first cup of coffee. Through the kitchen window she could see Joe out on her lawn, already perched in his usual spot on the wooden bench under the maple, sipping espresso from a tiny ceramic cup, Bear curled up with a stick by his feet. She grabbed a sweater and crossed the dewy lawn to join them.

"That screeching is going to be the death of me, I swear it, Joe. Worst alarm clock ever."

"And good morning to you too, kiddo. I trust you had a good night's sleep, at least until you were awoken by our lovely birdsong." He tapped his cup lightly against hers and took a sip. "But then I'm sure you are familiar with the story of the peacock and the nightingale, aren't you?"

"Nope," she yawned. "But I'm sure you're going to tell me." Sunny sat back against the trunk of the tree and closed her eyes as she waited for the coffee on her lap to cool.

"Well, you see," he began, "in the story, the peacock goes to the goddess Juno to complain that she had not given him the song of the nightingale, a song wondrous to every ear, while he became a laughing stock each time he opened his mouth. Juno consoles the peacock by pointing out his beauty and his size." Joe held both his arms out wide to illustrate. "The peacock then asks 'What is the use of beauty, with a voice like mine?' 'Your lot in life has been assigned by the Fates,' she tells him. 'Each must be content with his own particular gift.' In other words," Joe leaned back next to Sunny, "take care not to strive for something that was not given to you, or you will waste your life being disappointed by what you don't have."

"And I suppose there is a message for me somewhere in there?"

Joe just shrugged his shoulders, then drained his cup.

"Well I still can't stand those birds."

"I'm sure Rick would be more than happy to come take care of them for you if you asked him."

"What do you mean take care of them?"

"He shoots them." Joe placed his cup on the bench and positioned his arms as if they were holding a rifle. "Kaboom!" he said as he pulled the imaginary trigger. "I've seen him do it plenty of times."

Sunny cringed at the thought. "Jeez! What's with that guy?"

Joe shrugged his shoulders again.

"He's such a strange one, Joe. And I wish he'd stop honking on me to buy him out. If he wants to sell, and I want to sell, we should just sell, right?"

"Rick may be an unpleasant man, but he's not a stupid man. I suspect he has his reasons. Like they say, *Chi ha una retta coscienza possiede un regno.* His own desire leads every man." Joe lifted both feet and placed them gently on Bear's soft brown behind. "So, maybe you should buy him out."

"Why on earth would I do that? What would I do with a place like this? Not to mention where I'd ever get the money from," Sunny snorted. "You're looking at practically my entire bank account right here." She swept her arm over her head. "That is, if you shut one eye and block out half of it."

Joe laughed. "Well, you know what they say. Where there's a will there's a way."

"You know I have no will. And you also know that I don't want to stay here forever."

"Who said anything about forever? Forever is a long time, kiddo. Trust me. I know."

"This isn't the life for me, Joe. Can't you see that?"

"I see all sorts of things."

"Well, maybe you do. But you can't see what's in my head. Sometimes I can barely make out what's going on in there myself."

Joe shrugged his shoulders. Sunny had a sudden urge to shake the old man. "Besides," she continued, "even if I did have the money to buy Rick out, then what? I just sit here on the top of this damn hill and get fat? How would I live? I know how hard it is to get work on this island. Not that I'm even considering doing that, mind you. Not on your life."

"So you say."

"Okay, old man." Sunny put down her cup and folded her arms in front of her chest. "What are you getting at?"

Joe sat up straight and rubbed his hands together, his eyes bright with excitement. "Okay. Fine. You want to work? You can work. Now, here's what I've been thinking. First we spiff up the place a bit. Not too much. Not too slick. We want it to look authentic. A little landscaping, maybe a couple of parking places. Perhaps a fountain over there." Sunny followed the path of his bony finger. "Then we're all set to go. Weddings in the vineyard. A cheese shop in the shed. And in the barn? A tasting room. Wines from all over the state. My cooking. Your hospitality. We'll kill 'em, kiddo!" He clapped his hands together like a boy at his first circus.

Sunny leaned forward, propped her elbows on her knees, and planted her forehead in her hands. "Not gonna happen, Joe." She let out a huge sigh. Bear slid out from under the bench and planted a lick on her nose.

"I'm just saying."

"Yeah, well, I'm just saying no."

Joe shook his head, then took her hands in his own. "You know, Sunny Tedder, there are times in your life when you have to take advantage of what fate has given you, just like Juno said to that whiny peacock. And also just like what I said to myself when I had to leave here, but then found Italy. You are so busy striving for what's not yours that you don't appreciate what is. You had Jack's love, and you always will. It lives in this place, and it lives in our friendship as well. What is no longer yours is the life you had at that coffeehouse in Afghanistan. But that doesn't mean you can't use your gifts, and find your happiness, somewhere else. Trust me. I know."

Sunny wondered, not for the first time, what Joe wasn't telling her about his own past. No doubt he'd talk about it, in his own time. For now she simply looked down at the muddy ground and rubbed her forehead, and silently cursed the lump that was forming in her throat. "You're *killing* me, Joe. Do you always wake up like this?"

"*Chi dorme non piglia pesci.* Those who sleep don't catch any fish."

Sunny swallowed and stood. "Please, stop with the proverbs already. And while you're at it, stop complicating my life. It's complicated enough as it is."

The trouble had all started eight days ago, when Candace showed up.

"Have I had a week!" Candace said in typical fashion as she blew through Sunny's kitchen door like the bombshell that she was. Sunny stepped back and couldn't help but smile. The Candace Show was in town. She'd missed her old friend who at first glance looked, not old, but at least her own forty-something years for once. It was as though she had finally settled into her face, instead of keeping up a constant battle with it. It suited her.

"What happened to you?" was Candace's second line. Sunny looked down at her own baggy sweater and expanding thighs. But before she had a chance to get angry, she heard another voice behind her.

"*Salaam*, Sunny jan."

She slowly turned to see a tall, green-eyed young woman in a long pink tunic and matching scarf, with pants that covered a pair of legs that seemed to go on forever. The girl stood in the doorway, looking so much like her older sister that Sunny had to blink twice. "Layla?"

The girl stepped forward and kissed Sunny three times on the cheeks.

"Oh my God! Layla! Look at you!" She held the girl by the elbows and checked her out from head to toe, shocked at how much she had changed from that skinny twelve-year-old Sunny had left behind in Kabul. "Come, please. Come in." She took the suitcases from Layla's hands and shoved them into a corner. "What an amazing surprise!"

Candace leaned on the counter as Sunny pulled out a chair and gestured for Layla to sit. "I can't believe it's you! You came all the way here with Candace to see me? How is Minnesota? When do you have to get back to school? How long are you two going to be here?"

Layla sat back in her chair, eyes wide, as if Sunny's questions were a speeding train coming straight at her. She turned, confused, to Candace.

"Give the girl a chance, Sunny."

"Well, how long can you stay?" Sunny directed the question to Candace this time.

"Me? I, unfortunately, have to be out of here ASAP. Headed to DC. All the money people are in town." She began to count off her obligations on her fingers. "A big fundraiser, some meetings with donors . . ."

Sunny tried to hide her disappointment. "Well, okay then, so we'll just have to make the most of our time together. I'll show you guys everything—"

"But Layla," Candace continued, "Layla would be happy to stay a little longer. Right?" She turned to the girl, who simply shifted her beautiful eyes back and forth between the two women.

"But I thought—"

"It is *so* nice of you to offer, Sunny. Things have been a little difficult for Layla in Minnesota. You know, adjusting and all? Her host family turned out to be not as sensitive to Afghan ways as they should be, especially the teenagers in the house. You know how kids can be. It's been hard on the girl, and she's been begging to go home. But Yaz and I have agreed that she should try to stick out her stay, if any solution could be found. So I thought to myself, who would be more sensitive to Afghan ways than Sunny Tedder herself? So here we are!"

"But I'm not staying," Sunny protested. "I can't—"

"Well, how long *will* you be here?"

Sunny had no answer.

"It's settled then." Candace grabbed an apple from the counter and rubbed it against her sleeve. "Layla will stay as long as you do."

"Why can't she stay with you?"

"Please." Candace shook her head as she swallowed a bite. "My life is no place for a girl like Layla. Airport to airport, back-to-back meetings, a new hotel room practically every night, crappy room-service meals, and then every morning getting up and starting it all over again."

"But my life isn't either! I have no home, I'm not settled."

Candace looked around the kitchen, her eyes stopping on the fresh-cut chrysanthemums on the table, the cookies cooling on the counter, the cat curled up atop the heating vent under the door leading to the living room. "You look pretty settled to me."

"But I'm not a mother." Sunny could hear her own voice cracking. "I don't have the faintest clue what to do with a teenager."

"Well I'm not a mother either, in case you haven't noticed. And really, what's there to do? You feed them, make sure they have clean clothes, and try to keep them out of trouble." She tossed an apple to a startled Layla. "Easy-peasy! Oh, and she needs to be studying English. Not that she doesn't already do pretty well with it, from hanging around the coffeehouse and lessons in Kabul. But it's part of the deal for the visa. And no worries about money, I'll pay."

For one quick moment, every infuriating thing about Candace that used to trigger Sunny's ire came flooding back like a sudden storm. But seeing the poor girl, so far from home, so far from everything she knew and everyone she loved, was enough to make Sunny keep her mouth shut. She'd manage for the short time she'd remain on the island.

And like a fairy godmother, with a wave of her wand, Candace was gone.

Now, from her seat on the bench beside Joe, Sunny watched as the girl emerged from the house, wrapped in a blanket from head to toe.

"*Salaam,* Sunny jan," Layla called out with a sweet smile.

"Good morning to you too, sleepyhead," Sunny called back.

"*Ohayō,*" Layla said to Joe with a little bow as she reached the bench, using the Japanese greeting he'd already taught her.

"*Buongiorno, bella,*" Joe answered back.

Sunny sighed. Better start looking for an English teacher, she thought to herself.

"Just look, Sunny," said Joe as he graciously extended his arms to offer Layla a seat on the bench, "you have wanted so badly to be in Kabul? Now the Fates have brought a little Kabul to you."

Upon waking earlier that morning, Layla had stretched her arms up over her head and yawned. How lazy she felt beneath the puffy blanket Sunny had insisted she sleep under. It must be very late, she assumed by the light coming from behind the curtains. She was not used to the silence that came from having a room of her own. Of course when she was very little, growing up in the mountains, she had slept in the same room as her entire family, their beds pushed up against the stone walls, away from the hearth in the center of the room where her mother would prepare their meals, and where they would all eat. There were two other rooms below, but those were used to hold wood and grain, not sleeping people. In Minnesota, she had shared a room with Brittany, her host parents' daughter, who was the same age as she was. Layla had never seen any room like it before. It was as if Brittany were a princess in a pink palace, her bed draped with pink gauze hung from above, a thick pink carpet covering the floor, a sparkly pink chandelier dangling from her ceiling. The only thing the girl lacked, in her opinion, was the grace of a princess. Layla fought to mask her shock each morning as they dressed, Brittany trying and discarding outfit after outfit of skirts that barely covered her private parts and shirts that clung to her breasts like the skin of a grape. And the secret parties that would happen when Brittany's parents weren't home, when boys and girls would wrap themselves around each other and rub their bodies together in what they called dance, some of them sharing alcohol and cigarettes they'd brought hidden in their purses and knapsacks. But the worst was the argument Layla had witnessed between Brittany and her mother. Who knew what had caused it? Probably something unimportant, but it escalated quickly and before Layla knew it Brittany had stormed up the stairs and slammed her bedroom door, shouting "I hate you!" at her poor mother, who simply turned and went back to the kitchen. Layla had at first wanted to hide, embarrassed and ashamed by the disrespect shown by this girl. Yet soon those feelings became clouded by a coldness growing inside her, a sense of despair for a world where the elders were not treated with the honor that was their due.

But here at Sunny's house all was peaceful and quiet, and Layla's dreams had been plentiful. Some she remembered with a smile. Like the one where she had been in the small back court-yard of the coffeehouse, playing ball with Poppy and her little niece Najama. The Kabul sun shone from overhead, the shadow from the pomegranate tree long and slender. The old woman Halajan was standing against the wall watching them with a smile, her breasts hanging loose and low, her head scarf pushed back, and her leathery face turned upward toward the sun like a turtle reaching from its shell. The dream had been so vivid she could almost smell the cigarette smoke that gave away Hala-jan's secret every time she entered a room. She missed the old woman, with her sharp wit and keen eye. She missed everyone, and everything, back home.

Her other dreams were not so good. Layla had never been able to shed the nightmares about the men who had taken her as revenge for her sister's escape, the memories of those days before Jack had come to rescue her. She had been only twelve years old then, but sometimes it seemed like yester-day. Yazmina had been gone for four months when the same big black SUV that had snatched her away from their uncle's home returned, this time for Layla. The snows had melted, the roads were clear, and the men were determined to get what they came for. But before they got far with her, long before they could reach Kabul, where she would have been sold to the highest bidder to be his third or fourth wife, or forced into a life of slavery or prostitution, this strange Western man dressed in a *shalwaar kameez*, with eyes that sparkled like blue ice and a voice that spoke with calm authority, appeared like a hero in a Bollywood movie and whisked her away and into the arms of her beloved sister. There had to be a special place in paradise for a man like him, she was sure of it. If it weren't for Jack, she might have never seen Yazmina again. And if it weren't for Sunny, her sister might never have even survived. She made herself a quick promise to try very hard to like it here, to make it work, to show appreciation for all Sunny and Jack had done for her family.

And then there were the dreams of peacocks. She had to laugh a little. Why on earth would she dream of peacocks, silly animals she hadn't given any thought to since she was a child?

She stood and turned to face her image in the mirror on the back of the bedroom door, and unfastened the single black braid that hung to her waist. Her shiny hair flowed down thickly over her shoulders, like the cascading waterfalls in the mountains back home. I wonder if Sky will be coming today, she thought as she made one slow stroke with the brush, then another, just as her sister had taught her. Such an odd boy, with those holes as big as plums in his ears, and silver jewelry inside his mouth. She shivered a little just thinking of how that must feel. And those tattoos! At home they would be forbidden, and any boy who would dare to have one would be certain to keep it hidden under his sleeve. And yet, there was something about Sky's gentle eyes, and his sweet smile, and the way his funny curls bounced up and down when he laughed.

"Stop!" she said out loud to herself, yanking her hair practically out of its roots with the brush. What was the matter with her, having thoughts like this? Of course she had not spoken to the boy, other than to say hello, and had only watched him when she knew he wasn't looking. But then, when he was in the same room with her it was as though someone had taken her by the shoulders and spun her around and around, then left her to stand, her head remaining dizzy and light. Nonsense, she quickly told herself. Perhaps it is merely coincidence. Perhaps there is something here on this island that is making her ill. She checked her forehead with the back of her hand and, satisfied that there was no fever, quickly rebraided her hair, wrapped herself up in the blanket that hung on the back of the chair, and went to say good morning to Sunny.

14

The afternoon sunlight bounced off the windows of the low cinderblock building, giving the school an eerie, fiery glow. Zara shifted impatiently from foot to foot on the gravel below, anxious for the silence inside to burst into the clamor of giggles and screams that meant class was dismissed, and her sister Mariam ready to be escorted home. Her stomach growled loudly, like a tiger. The knowledge that the news of a wedding could be handed to her at any time was making her ill. She had not eaten in days.

Her stomach turned again as she thought about the conversation that had occurred with her father when he told her he'd been discussing a proposal for her. At first, after she'd gotten up the courage to tell him she still did not wish to marry, she thought everything might be okay. Her father had laughed, throwing his head back in that way she had seen so many times before when she and her sister were very little and did something to amuse him. At the time she had laughed a bit herself, more out of relief than anything else.

But with his next words she felt her heart sink down to her shoes.

"Of course, my daughter. I understand. Of course you are reluctant to leave the comfort of your family, the home you have known since you were born. But you are grown now, and this is a man of my tribe, our tribe. A man of means, with a house, a car; a man who has made a fine offer for you. You will overcome your girlish jitters. You will see. Even your mother was at first nervous and afraid to marry, and see now how ridiculous that was. It will all be fine."

"But please, *baba*, I want to continue with my studies," she protested, knowing that her love for Omar must remain a secret, that her father would consider love a silly reason, one that had no bearing when it came to making a match.

"You have done well with your studies, daughter, and I am proud of you. But you must marry someday. It will be a good marriage. And perhaps it will be possible for you to continue at the university even after you are wed."

Zara could tell by the look on his face that her father did not fully believe the words that were coming from his own mouth. And when he added the thought that they should not insult a man like this man, the whispers she had heard around the house and the stories she had heard about others all came together, and she began to picture just how things had occurred.

After the man's mother had paid that first call on her mother, no doubt unannounced yet welcomed in for tea, as any caller would be, after she had peppered Zara's mother with questions about Zara, and impressed her with whose daughter, whose wife, whose mother she herself, was, after she assured Zara's mother that their families were of the same tribe—third cousins in fact—only then would the two women become open with each other about the purpose of the visit. Next would have come a visit to both her parents from the man himself, accompanied by his mother, and perhaps an aunt. At the end of the conversation, if her parents were satisfied with the proposal being made for their daughter, they would have expressed their willingness to accept by bringing out the *khuncha*, the silver tray decorated with flowers and ribbons, to offer the traditional *shirini*, sweets, to the man's family. If they had done that, it would mean the bond had been made.

"You gave them the sweets."

Her father did not reply right away.

"You did, didn't you? You passed the *khuncha*."

Again her father did not answer.

"Please, *baba*. Do not make me marry this man."

Zara held her father's gaze firm with her own pleading eyes. For a moment he seemed to soften a bit, his brows and shoulders heavy with the weight of the situation. But she feared things had already gone too far, and had doubts that he would ever change his mind.

Not a word more about the proposal had been said since that day. She had still not seen Omar in class, and she was too worried to send him a message with her phone, fearing her parents might see. Now she pulled her head scarf tighter around her neck. As she looked down to check the time she saw a shadow pass over her phone's glass surface. She raised her eyes to see a looming figure dressed all in black, with a pair of thick, wire-framed glasses resting on the tip of her nose, standing before her.

"The principal wishes to speak with you," the woman said with an expressionless face.

Zara's heart filled with dread. This principal, Faheem, was a man who ran the school with an iron fist, a fist that was said to turn quickly into a groping paw once watchful eyes were diverted. Her friend Shafia was not the only one who told tales like this. So far Zara had managed to keep her distance.

"My mother is not here with me. Is my sister all right?"

The woman simply turned and headed inside, expecting Zara to follow. Had Mariam misbehaved in class? She was usually such an obedient girl. But whatever this man had to say, Zara knew better than to take it too seriously. His professional reputation was that of an incompetent man, one who greedily considered position and favors as his right, like so many others in Kabul these days. It was clear to everyone that he benefited from a source of money over what his job allowed.

Faheem's coal-black eyes, and the tight little smile he wore as he stood behind his immense desk, told her more than she wanted to know. To Zara's dismay, he ordered the woman to go bring her little sister from her classroom once the lessons were over, leaving the two of them alone together in the room. Zara wondered how much this woman was paid to allow something so improper to take place. "Please, sit." He pointed Zara to a wooden chair positioned across from his desk, but she remained standing, the smell of cigarettes and musk clogging her throat with a stale sweetness. Faheem slicked a wisp of unnaturally dark hair across his forehead and asked, "May I offer you some *chai*?", his voice like honey.

Zara shook her head, her eyes pointed out the window toward the empty schoolyard. "Just some water, please," she croaked, her throat suddenly as dry as the desert floor.

Faheem clapped his hands twice, summoning a skinny young man who seemed to appear out of thin air. "Water for my guest!"

he barked at the quivering boy, who quickly ran out through the open door to do as he was told. Faheem turned back to Zara. "So," he folded his hands in front of his chest, "how is your family?"

"My family is well."

"Your father, he is fine?" he asked with a smile that revealed a mouthful of yellowed teeth.

Zara nodded, puzzled by the politeness of this man who was usually so stern.

"He is in good health, then?"

"My father is in fine health," she answered, squirming a little at his probing.

"That is good to hear." He nodded slowly up and down. "So there is no reason he cannot leave the house?"

"No," Zara answered, confused.

"You see, he and I have some important things to talk about."

"Is my sister in some sort of trouble?"

Faheem laughed, causing a drop of spittle to escape down his chin. He wiped it away with the back of his hand. "No, no trouble. It is not your sister I am waiting to discuss."

"If you have dealings with my father then you must speak with him and not me." Zara lowered her eyes to the floor, where the man's shiny black shoes glistened from their spot under the desk, despite the dullness of the bulb flickering above.

"You know, my little bird, you should let me see that pretty face of yours, and not turn it away from mine."

Zara flinched at the sound of his words. She felt as though his eyes were boring a hole right through her clothes. Faheem started toward her from around the desk, his steps slow and deliberate. The hair on the back of her neck rose like that of a cat. Just then the boy returned with her water.

"And where is my Coke?" Faheem roared. "Can you not do one job right, you stupid donkey?" Faheem dug deep into his pocket and flung a handful of coins toward the boy, who scrambled to gather them up. "And while you are at it, bring me back some cigarettes, and not those cheap Chinese pine ones they sell around the corner." Zara wanted to yell out to the boy, to beg him to stay, but when Faheem deftly pushed the door closed behind him with his foot, she steeled herself for the ordeal ahead. But nothing could have prepared her for what came next.

Faheem now stood facing the window, one arm bent at the elbow as he stroked his beard, a patch of hair as black as that on his head, a shade that matched nothing in nature. "I hear that you are a serious girl, one who likes to study." He turned back toward her.

"That is true," Zara answered in a small voice, for one second thinking that maybe she'd been mistaken, that this man, a school principal, might be preparing to commend her for her diligence. She reached for a sip of her water.

"But you know," he continued as he paced the room, "it is the role of a wife that is an honored one." He stopped before her, so close now that she could smell the sour breath escaping from his mouth. "A girl like you," he said, "would be lucky to have a man as handsome and rich as me to take care of all her needs."

Zara placed the glass back down on the edge of the desk, her hand trembling.

Now Faheem ran his manicured hands slowly down the sides of his shiny Western suit, as if he were a prince preparing to address his kingdom. "And a family like yours, a family of no consequence, would earn great respect through your marriage to a man of my stature. It is a mystery to me why your father hesitates to give me his answer."

She grabbed the edge of the desk as the strength left her legs. An avalanche of despair descended on her. This could not be true, what he was saying. But why would he lie? A million thoughts flooded Zara's brain. Not once had she heard this man's name mentioned in her household, unless it was talk about his school. She knew nothing of any other connection of his family to hers.

"And you, what do you have to say, my bride? I'm sure they've taught you to speak your opinions at the university. Have you no answer for that?" He reached for the glass and turned it to plant his mouth for a sip from the exact spot where hers had touched, then licked his thick lips as though tasting her for the first time.

She had no words. How she wanted to yell and turn and run, as loud and as fast and as far as her feet would take her. But instead she heard a small, shaky voice coming from her. "I don't want to be a wife. I just want to continue my studies."

Faheem laughed again, louder and longer this time. "Do not be foolish, little one. I can give you more than a college degree will ever bring." He reached out toward her, his soft doughy hand slowly brushing the hollow of her cheek, sliding down along the side of her neck, coming to rest at the top of her collarbone.

Zara froze at the sting of his touch, her face burning with shame. Never in her life had she been treated in this manner by any man. She pushed his hand away.

Faheem reddened with anger. "You are a feisty little one, aren't you?" he hissed as he grabbed her wrist. "No matter. I will see to that, once we are wed."

"I will never marry you!" she heard herself say before she had the chance to think, as she struggled to break free of his grasp.

Faheem held tight to her wrist. "No matter what you say, you are already mine. The deal is as good as done. Your father would not dare to say no. Not to someone like me."

It was then that she felt the tears dropping off of her cheeks and onto the floor.

"And be aware that I always take great care to keep track of what is mine." Faheem pointed the first two fingers of his free hand at his own eyes. "My eyes are everywhere." He dropped her wrist as if he were discarding a morsel of meat not to his liking, and returned to his chair behind the desk. "The way you let your head scarf fall back while you are at the university," he hissed, "and the clothes that you wear there. Why do you dress like a whore? Is there someone you are perhaps trying to impress? Is that what all this nonsense is about?" He leaned back in the chair and drummed his fingers together.

Zara stood shaking, silent, refusing to answer.

Suddenly the front feet of Faheem's chair hit the ground with a thud. In an instant he was back at her side, ripping the purse from her shoulder. He thrust his hand inside and pulled out her phone, holding it high above her head, out of her reach. "I am watching you, my child. I know where you go, what you do. I know who your friends are. And if there is someone else, I will find out who." He threw the phone into a drawer and slammed it shut. "Patience is bitter," he laughed, "but its fruit is sweet. And I am sure, my child, that yours will be sweet fruit indeed."

15

The dark water churned in the wake of a giant container ship heading north to Alaska, a flock of gulls keeping pace above. Sunny stood outside the back door of the house and watched until long after it disappeared from view, then checked her watch. She was trying to make herself scarce during Layla's session with Kat, knowing that her inability to keep her own mouth shut while the two of them were conversing tended to make Layla's progress a slow go.

The idea to bring Kat—whose real name she now knew was Katayon—over to the island to help Layla with her English a few times a week had come to her in a cartoon light bulb moment. Where else would she ever find a Dari-speaking person in a place whose only diversity seemed to come from the variety of trees or brews of coffee? Kat had been a bit of a tough negotiator, but in the end Sunny's promises of sun-filled afternoons on the island had won out over the tedium of the job in the dentist's office. Now she felt just a little bit guilty, as the breeze off the water made bumps rise on the skin on her arms, making her look like a naked chicken. She pulled down her sleeves and headed across the lawn to the barn.

The two girls seemed to be hitting it off okay so far, but it was difficult to tell by just a couple of weeks. The exuberance she had once so admired in Layla seemed subdued by the stress of life in a strange country, or perhaps simply by the stress of being a teenager. The girl was way quieter and more withdrawn than Sunny had remembered. And Kat? She couldn't quite figure that one out. On the outside, she appeared all tough and feisty, yet Sunny could tell there was more going on behind that defiant exterior. And, for two girls born in the same country, could they be any more different? The look on Layla's face when she first saw Kat's black-and-white hair was priceless. And she supposed that Kat must be equally perplexed by a girl who insisted on keeping her head covered at all times, even inside the house. But for Sunny, hearing the two of them chatting at the kitchen table made it feel like home, especially when Layla started rattling off questions in Dari. But Kat would have none of that. *English only in this house*, she insisted over and over.

Sunny dug into her jeans pocket for the key Sky had given her so many weeks ago and forced it into the heavy brass padlock that hung from the barn door. She struggled to make the key turn, jamming it left and right over and over without success. Then she picked up a rock and banged at the lock with all her strength. No dice. It would be easier to just huff and puff and blow this place down like the big bad wolf than to get this door open, she thought as she stood back and eyed the weather-beaten structure. She cupped her hands around her eyes and leaned forward to peer between the shrunken wooden slats, but was unable to make out much in the dark. She jiggled the key in the lock again, now more gently. This time it opened.

The outside light streamed in through the door behind her as Sunny stood with her hands on her hips, surveying the scene. The barn was a hell of a lot bigger than it looked from the outside, and was jam-packed with equipment from front to back and side to side. The wall to her right was completely obscured by what she assumed to be winemaking apparatus—vats and barrels and bins—and the left looked like a cemetery for dead gardening tools. But it was the back of the barn, where heavy beige tarps had been neatly and carefully draped over a huge mountain of something, that intrigued her most.

For a moment Sunny fought her natural urge to snoop. But then again, for now all this stuff—well, at least half of it—was still hers, wasn't it? Despite Rick's badgering, and both of them offering to drop their respective selling prices even more, they still hadn't reached an agreement about what to do with the place. And she was the one living there, after all. Maybe she'd only look at half the stuff. And now Rick was suggesting that she pay him "a little good-faith money" just for her and Layla to continue living in the place, as to him, he said, it looked as if she was really planning on staying. Fuck him, she thought as she headed to the back of the barn. She'd uncover it all.

She pulled her brown curls into a knot on top of her head and pushed up her sleeves. The first tarp slid off in a cloud of dust that danced across the slivers of sunlight piercing through the gaps in the roof above. But all that appeared was an old TV set with a cracked screen. Her shoulders slumped with disappointment. Under the next tarp she found an empty birdcage that had some potential, for something, someday. She dragged it away from the pile and put it aside. But the next item she bent to uncover caused Sunny to let out a little gasp, for peeking out from under this tarp were the heavy carved wooden legs of what could only be that furniture from Nuristan that she had always loved so much, and that Jack had always referred to as termite bait. And indeed it was a gorgeous table, and one that she recognized as her own from where it once stood in the front corner of the coffeehouse. A wave of homesickness washed over her as she ran her palm lovingly over the smooth walnut surface and breathed in its rich, dark smell. But what the hell was Jack doing with her table? As she whipped off the coverings of more items in the pile she began to get the picture.

At first she couldn't contain her excitement. Sunny squealed out loud at the sight of the bowls and cups from the potters in Istalif, so blue they seemed to glow even in the darkness of the barn, the lustrous *suzani* bedcovers, hand stitched for generations by Uzbek women in Afghanistan, the silk embroidered pillows that had brightened her outlook even on the darkest of nights. And there was the rug, one of many she had purchased at "the carpet mall of death", as Jack had called it due to the fact that the Russian-built cinderblock building was five stories high with all four walls facing an interior parking lot—a lot with only one narrow passageway for both entering and exiting. A security nightmare. He had, in a moment of weakness, given in to her begging one Sunday afternoon, and had accompanied her there for a spree. He ended up sitting there patiently for hours, gentleman that he was, as she sipped tea with the merchants and spent half his paycheck.

But then it hit her. Jack had obviously made a huge assumption about their future, her future, no doubt planning to sweeten the Twimbly pot by bringing over the things that might make her feel content. And she was pissed. She couldn't deny how happy it made her feel to be reunited with her favorite belongings, but now she'd have to start from scratch if, or when, she moved back to Kabul. *Thanks a lot, pal,* she thought as she pictured a smug little smile plastered on his face, which only made her miss him that much more.

She was halfway through her rummaging when she found, taped to the underside of a squat wooden table, the envelope with her name on it. The sight of Jack's impeccable handwriting took her by surprise, making her feel almost as if he was speaking to her from the grave, or from that box of ashes she hadn't yet had the heart to part with. She ripped it open, hoping to hear more. But there was no note inside, only a small brass key.

She made a mad dash around the room in search of anything with a lock, flinging the dusty tarps around as though she were executing judo throws. It was when she came across a short, rectangular object sitting in the farthest reach of the barn, with four points poking up at the canvas from each corner, that she stopped. This one she had a hunch about, and when she lifted the tarp with pinched fingers, as if uncovering a priceless portrait, she knew she was right. It was a piece she recognized from a trip she and Jack had taken to Bamiyan, an object so beautiful it practically took her breath away—a hand-carved wooden dowry chest, no doubt once owned by a wealthy nomadic woman. Sunny had to laugh, wondering if Jack thought he was being funny, mocking her own inability to settle down. In the old days, a woman would have taken to the road with these chests filled with things like linens and jewelry, medicinal herbs, clothing for their future children, and family documents. But what could be inside now? Sunny rubbed her hands together with anticipation as she slipped the key into the lock and tilted the top of the chest back on its hinges.

She slammed the lid shut as quickly as she had opened it, her heart pumping a million beats per second. Bundles and bundles of hundred dollar bills, more cash than she had ever seen in one place in her entire life. Enough money to feed an entire Afghan village for years. Her mind raced with confusion. Why the hell would he be keeping this kind of money in cash? And in a barn? Sure, there were plenty of other men she had met in Afghanistan whom she could imagine getting into this kind of thing, but Jack? Even with all his unexplained absences, she'd never once suspected him of being anything less than one hundred per cent above board. He had stood out like a cowboy in a white hat among a sea of black in Kabul, where there were plenty of foreigners who were seduced by the easy money that came from selling drugs and weapons. But still, however he had earned all this, why on earth couldn't he have just put it in the bank?

Suddenly the answer hit her like a smack in the head. The money had to be Rick's.

She reached again toward the chest, her hand trembling as she slowly lifted the lid for a second look. She hesitated to actually touch the money, shuddering at the thought of what shady services it might have bought, or whose unguarded pockets it may have come from. But when she noticed a slip of white paper poking out in the center of the chest, she couldn't help herself, and plunged her arm deep into the stacks.

"Damn you, Jack!" She flung back her arm and with it came a wad of bills that went flying across the barn, slipping from their wrapper midair and showering down like confetti on New Year's Eve. But she had to laugh at herself for falling for such a lame prank. She should have known better. She could tell instantly by the too-smooth feel of the bills that they were fakes. And she knew just where Jack had gotten them.

She'd seen the moneychangers on the street corners of Kabul checking for counterfeit currency plenty of times, squinting to assess the color, holding the bills up to their ears to hear how they sounded. The ones piled high in the trunk had the consistency of cheap computer paper, but the color, she had to admit, was pretty authentic.

She grabbed the white paper that continued to cry out to her from beneath the stacks, and unfolded it to once again see Jack's handwriting.

Gotcha! But it is no joke that I love you, Sunny. Stick with me, baby, and we'll share a long, beautiful life of riches, just the two of us, together.
xoxoxoxoxoxoxox

Sunny slumped down onto the dusty floor, the feel of Jack's strong arms wrapped around her surrendering body all too fresh in her memory, the image of his crinkly blue eyes when he laughed enough to make her chest ache with longing. The nerve of him, calling me baby, she thought as she wiped a tear from her cheek. And there she remained—thinking of Jack, wanting Jack, missing Jack—until the sunlight's pattern had shifted across the floor toward the other end of the barn. Then she stood, brushed herself off, and forced her mind to turn toward finding a solution for getting all this stuff out of this shithole before the grime and mildew could take its toll.

16

The faded posters plastered across the walls of the dark room told of countless calamities—falling stones and dangling electrical wires, cars plunging headfirst into water or slipping down steep mountains, ominous black arrows twisting this way and that. One simply showed a very large exclamation point, screaming out its warning from the middle of a white triangle with a border as red as blood.

But Halajan wasn't alarmed by the signs. She had learned what each and every one of them meant by heart, along with all the other rules and regulations for driving a car. She had been enrolled in the driving school for nine weeks already, and had only three more to go.

At first it had felt strange to be the oldest person in the class, the only one who could truly remember the days when a woman behind the wheel of a car was not such a rare sight, a time when a woman could even drive a public bus as a job. The others must have wondered what an old fool like her thought she needed with a driver's license. But her age was forgotten the day she volunteered to give the teacher, Anisa, a break by offering to take a turn reading the manuals out loud to the class of women who, like so many other women in Kabul, could not read a word.

Now the others would wait outside for her and Najama to arrive each morning, greeting Halajan with kisses and showering the little girl with trinkets and sweets to keep her quiet in the classroom while they all tried to concentrate on their studies. Halajan's favorites were Bita and Tamra. Bita, whose husband had been crippled by a roadside explosion, was determined to drive in order to save the hours she spent each day travelling around the city by foot, taking her children to and from school and shopping for her family's needs. The driving school was the first school she had ever attended. Young Tamra told of being taunted by boys for her desire to drive a car. Lucky for her, her father and brothers were proud of her strength, and supported her wishes.

Halajan loved coming to the school, waking early to dress and feed herself and Najama, slipping out before Yazmina could find chores for her to do and before anyone had the chance to ask where they were going. They'd take the bus to the city center, just the two of them, past the armies of children on their way to school, the girls all in black, save for their little white headscarves. The first few times when the two of them had reached their destination the driver just kept going, despite Halajan rapping on the windows and shouting out her request to get off. There were no ropes to pull or assistants to help, like there were in the old days. She and Najama had had to practically run to get to the school on time. But by now the driver had come to know them, and treated them both like royalty, pulling right up to the curb without even being asked. Halajan and her granddaughter would descend into the cool morning air to walk the last two blocks that took them past the vendors arranging their carts for a day of commerce, Najama giggling as she and her nana dodged the bucketfuls of water being tossed from each storefront by the shopkeepers fighting a losing battle with the dust that invaded from the street.

After greeting the other students at the door of the school, Halajan would lead Najama inside to say hello to Anisa. Now *there* was a woman. The only female driving instructor in all of Kabul and not scared of a soul. She had been driving herself since the fall of the Taliban, taught by her kind and open-minded husband, who was a taxi driver. It was his sympathy for the women who were stuck without transportation—those who could not take a taxi because they were not allowed to speak to men other than those in their family, and those who were made uncomfortable by the stares and harassment they would often receive on public transportation—that had led him to encourage her to share what she had learned with others. The threats they had faced after opening the school, and the taunts Anisa still received when behind the wheel—male drivers trying to force her off the road and young boys pelting the car with pebbles and stones—only seemed to make her stronger. Halajan had witnessed it for herself, just last week, when Anisa had taken the class out, two at a time, in the Toyota Corolla for their first drive. As they pulled up to a stoplight, the two men in the car to their right had called out in singsong voices, "*Jaan jaan*, how much is it to Taymani?" Before she knew it, Anisa had leapt out of the car and marched straight over to their open window, hands on hips. "Come now, little boys, do you really think you can afford this ride?"

Halajan hadn't been able to stop herself from laughing on and off throughout the rest of the lesson.

There were plenty of driving schools in the city that were run by men, and women could, if their fathers or husbands and the schools themselves allowed, go there if they chose. But having a woman instructor made it easier for many, as the gossip that ran like sewer water through the streets of Kabul would be less. Of course, Halajan was too old to be the target of such gossip, not that she would have cared anyway. She had chosen Anisa's school to show her support for this woman who she hoped would lead the way for many others to come.

And even though Anisa took her job as a teacher very seriously, she did allow Halajan and the other women in the class to have their fun. The best was when they would take turns sitting in the middle of the room on the stack of plastic chairs, their hands resting on either side of an old steering wheel that was connected to a skeleton of a car. There, in the privacy of the classroom, they would pretend to be kings of the road, shifting the unconnected gear knob quickly and with a firm hand, spinning the steering wheel sharply back and forth as if speeding up a mountain road, banging on the pretend horn at any imaginary person who dared to get in their way. Even little Najama would be given a turn, propped up by pillows and books to help her reach the controls.

Halajan loved every day at the school, and knew she would miss it terribly once the course was completed. But today's lesson was giving her reason to pause.

She stood near the door, her ropy arms crossed beneath her sagging breasts and her wiry brows drawn into a knot. The grease-stained carpet in front of her was covered with nuts and bolts and wrenches and the guts of an engine, or maybe two, that looked like they had been vomited straight out of the hood of a car. Today's lesson was to be in the basics of automobile mechanics.

Halajan rolled up her sleeves and prayed for the hours to pass quickly, hoping that, with a little luck, she'd soon be back on the bus with Najama at her side, reciting their story to each other as they did every time.

"And where did you go with Nana today, Najama?"

"We went to the magic city!"

"That's right, we went to the magic city." Halajan smiled at the little girl's enthusiasm about the place they had dreamed up together, a make-believe city where anything could happen, and where nobody but Nana and Najama were allowed to go. Her stories about their adventures were so fanciful that nobody dared interrupt her to press for the truth.

"And what did we do there, in the magic city?"

"We captured the dragons!"

"Okay, we captured the dragons today. Yes we did, little one. And maybe we saw the prince dancing as well, right?" And they'd repeat it again, Halajan feeling slightly guilty at drawing her granddaughter into her own lies. She wasn't sure how her husband would feel about her learning to drive. Rashif might worry a bit too much about her safety, fearing the kind of attention a woman driving a car would get in this city. Jack had brought in Poppy the dog for that very reason, to protect Sunny when she insisted on driving by herself. But Halajan did know how her son would react. Even with his opening mind and expanding views, he still remained stubborn in many ways. Sometimes he seemed like a child just learning to walk, taking two steps and tumbling before getting up to try again. No, she would keep this her secret until after it was done. She would fight any battle she might have to face to get behind the wheel once she had the license firmly in her hand. And there would come a time when she and her grandchild would share a laugh about their trips to the magic city, should Halajan live long enough to see that day, *inshallah*.

17

"Hey, guys, give me a hand, would you?"

Kat opened the kitchen door to see a heap of blankets with Sunny's legs attached. The pile landed on the floor with a thud and a cloud of dust.

"You're not going to believe what I've found, out in the barn." Sunny seemed out of breath, and though her eyes appeared a little wet and puffy, her cheeks glowed like a burner set on high. "You *have* to see this. Come on, you two lazybones, hurry!" Layla closed the book on the table before her and tilted her head at Kat, who gestured for her to come along.

Now what, Kat wondered, as she watched Sunny shifting back and forth from foot to foot with impatience. Never before had she come across a woman so unpredictable. One minute she'd be all bossy, like the time she had come to ask Kat to teach Layla. Kat hadn't even had a chance to think it over before it was all settled. But the next minute she'd seem sort of sad and confused. Sometimes, when Sunny didn't know she was watching, Kat would see her sitting on the living room couch with Bear's head resting on her lap, looking out over the water with a glassy stare, as if she were in a trance or something. Right now she just seemed kind of excited.

Kat liked Sunny, and was finding the job to be actually okay, despite the fact that she hadn't uttered a word in Dari for so long. But Kat made a point of keeping her conversations with Layla to English as much as she could, anyway. When Sunny asked her why, saying something about how she would love to have the house filled with the sounds of Afghanistan, Kat claimed a dislike for the sound of the language which honestly, to her, seemed so rude and abrupt when compared to English. The word please was not used much. In Dari it wasn't *I think you should go now*—it was *You go!* You didn't say *Please shut the door*, *Shut door!* was perfectly acceptable.

Layla was a quick learner, soaking up new words as quickly as Kat threw them out there. Such a smart girl. How could she still be so stuck on the old ways, even over here, away from home, where nobody was watching? The three kisses thing every single time she said hello, the way she still preferred her hands over a fork. And that unibrow! Kat knew that in Afghanistan plucking your brows could only mean you were getting ready for marriage, but still. Kat often struggled to keep herself from pointing these things out to Layla, but she knew enough to keep her mouth shut. It wouldn't be polite to insult the girl. Though Layla didn't seem to have many boundaries when it came to Kat. She literally followed her around like a little puppy, taking Kat's hand in her own and forever peppering her with questions about her life. Some Kat answered. Others she left alone.

Pretty much everything was good about working on the island, except for the commute from her uncle's house in Seattle. But Sunny understood that, and had invited her to stay over whenever she wanted, which she had done a couple of times so far. Meeting Joe that first night had been a trip. He made Kat laugh, with his bushy eyebrows and big old ears, and she loved the way his arms would fly around nonstop when he talked.

And then there was Sky. She could barely think of his name without getting all goose-bumpy. Those eyes, so bright and twinkly, and those lips, so quick with a smile. He was just so damn hot, with his ripped jeans and tight T-shirts, not to mention all that metal and those awesome tats. And he was so, so sweet! He seemed like the kind of guy who would save a stranded kitten from a rooftop, or help an old lady across a busy street, or surprise a girl with a hundred roses on her birthday. She wondered if he had a girlfriend. But if he did, why did he seem to spend so much time with a loud, middle-aged woman and a random old man? Maybe she'd remain late working with Layla this afternoon, and ask to stay the night again.

The two girls followed Sunny across the lawn and through the open doors to the back of the barn. There Sunny stopped and turned with a huge grin across her face. Layla suddenly dropped to her knees and gathered a pile of bedcovers up to her nose. "Oh, Sunny jan!" she gasped between inhalations. Then she stood and danced through the maze of furniture, caressing the wood as if it were the back of a cat, squeezing the pillows close to her chest. "*Boy-e-watana maita!*" It is just like home!

"I know, right?" Sunny joined in and the two of them dove deeper into the stack, their squeals of delight binding them together like a pair of squawking blue jays.

Kat suddenly felt as though someone had kicked her in the stomach, hard. She turned and hurried out of the barn, the pounding in her ears keeping pace with the quickening rhythm of her heart. Halfway across the lawn she stopped and lowered herself down onto the thick carpet of grass, and closed her eyes against the brightening sky. In, she breathed, and out, willing herself to that place inside where she would go so often, the place that would swallow her memories whole and leave her with a mind as blank as an empty wall.

It could have been ten minutes, or it could have been thirty, before she was startled by the sound of a throat being cleared in that fake way people do to get your attention. She opened her eyes to see Sunny standing above her with a hand on her hip, her head cocked to the side.

"What?" Kat shaded her eyes with one hand.

"Don't you just love this stuff? Isn't it beautiful?" Sunny held out a string of lapis in one hand.

"It's okay, I guess."

"Have you ever seen anything like this before?"

Kat nodded as she stood and brushed off her jeans.

"I'm sure your mother must have brought some of her own things over from home, right?"

Kat shrugged and turned away, eager to hide her eyes and the tears threatening to burst with her secrets. She hated it when she got this way, powerless against the rush of feelings that could take over in a split second. All she wanted was to be able to honor her mother by showing the same strength she had shown Kat when she brought her to America, alone, nine years ago, and that she had shown again in her fatal attempt to stand up to Kat's father, seven years later. Kat had hidden the details of the truth from everyone she knew, telling them simply that her parents were dead. The real story was too horrifying for anyone to really understand, including herself. What kind of a world was it where a man's blame for his own problems turns into a hatred for a way of life he doesn't even try to understand, where his religious beliefs become so twisted that they push him to the point of murder?

They were five years into their life in Seattle when the day came that she and her mother had finally been granted citizenship. They stood before the judge in his chambers, her mother weeping with relief at the sound of his rubber stamp as it came pounding down onto their papers. "Finally," she whispered to Kat, "we can have your father come join us." Now her mother was legally eligible to apply to become the sponsor for her husband's entry into the States, just as Kat's uncle, who had lived here for close to thirty years, had done for the two of them.

Kat had been happy living with her American-born cousins in her uncle's house, a place full of life, where all the neighborhood kids would gather to watch TV or play video games or just hang out. But when her father arrived after two more years of her mother gathering the necessary paperwork and approvals, he was disgusted by what he found—a daughter with T-shirts so short they bared her ringed belly-button for all the world to see, nephews he'd never met hiding their faces under shaggy hair while displaying their underwear from the tops of their drooping jeans, and a wife with a job, a woman who would dare to talk with men other than her husband. The screaming matches between her parents were more than Kat could take, and she found herself avoiding her uncle's house as much as possible.

But it wasn't until after her father insisted they move out of "the infidel's" home that things truly became unbearable.

The three of them were now crammed into a tiny apartment, where the battles continued—her father's frustration at not being able to find a job without knowing English, his shame from having a wife who worked day and night to support the family, his unease in a world so unfamiliar to everything he knew—all of it driving him to twist his religion into a justification that vindicated, and heightened, his rage. He soon became so abusive to the two of them that Kat's mother knew the only way to protect her daughter would be to escape, with Kat, back to her brother's house, where she'd been promised their safety. From there she would figure out what to do next.

And that's where it all ended. Her mother had been found unconscious, her face and body unrecognizable beneath the charred layers of skin, the smell of gasoline unmistakable in the air. Nobody could say for sure exactly how it happened. There were no witnesses. Either a woman pushed to the limit, with suicide her only option, or a man committing a brutal crime in the name of honor. The only two people who knew the truth were now gone, one dead, the other disappearing into thin air, no doubt back to a country where murdering your wife was something you might get away with without punishment.

Now Kat wiped the backs of her wrists across her eyes and turned around to face Sunny. Maybe it had been a mistake to take this job—she should just tell Sunny she'd found something else, and couldn't come to the island anymore. Away from here she'd have more success blocking out all those reminders of a past she'd rather erase. It was her only choice, her only chance.

But Sunny was already gone, heading back to the barn, back to that junk that was so precious to her, all that crap from a place that Kat barely remembered, a place she simply could find no room for in her heart.

18

"*Khoda havez. Dostet daram.*" Goodbye. I love you. Yazmina blew three air kisses toward the computer screen and watched her little sister's image disappear with a click. As much as she worried about Layla, the girl seemed to be adjusting to her stay in America better than Yazmina had imagined. Maybe almost too well, she worried. When Yazmina had, just now, tried to ask Layla about a new friend she had mentioned, someone who had been trying to teach her some football, she thought she had seen the girl's cheeks redden a bit. Sky. Was that a girl's name, or a boy's? And football? What girl plays football? But even if she was playing football, Layla would know better than to have that kind of closeness with a boy, wouldn't she? It was difficult enough that she had been attending a school in Minnesota that mixed boys with girls, but this? At home, to have a boyfriend would be forbidden, at least according to traditions. Without the proper introductions, there was not to be any communication with a boy, other than brothers or fathers. And to play football with a boy? If this were to happen in Afghanistan, Layla would be called bad names by some, or even worse than name-calling. She must think of her reputation. Yazmina worried about what Ahmet would say.

Sometimes Yazmina wished she hadn't allowed Candace to talk her into letting Layla go, especially when Ahmet would point out the outrageous behavior of the children on those American television programs. Only Halajan would laugh at those shows, and at her son's wide-eyed reaction to them, telling Ahmet not to worry so much, it is only television. It didn't help matters that the men at the mosque were always sharing with Ahmet stories about how good children go bad once they go to the States, how they forget who they are, how the boys care nothing about the girls, how they use them and trick them. Maybe she should arrange for Layla to come home sooner, before the year was up. She'd have to look into that. She sighed out loud. At least she was with Sunny now, instead of in a stranger's home. And at least, *shokr-e-khuda*, thanks to God, the girl was still wearing her *hijab*.

Yazmina leaned back on her *toshak*. How tired she felt these past few days, like a fat goat being driven mercilessly up the mountains in the middle of the summer heat. But she was grateful she didn't have to keep this one hidden from those close to her, not like with Najama, who she had carried around like a secret treasure, relying on the heavy drape of her chador to keep her pregnancy from showing. Even Ahmet had not suspected until the baby was well on her way. She couldn't help but smile picturing the two of them together, playing chase in the courtyard, Najama squealing with delight as she scurried to outrun his exaggerated stride.

And now they were about to bring another precious life into the world, to join her and Ahmet and Najama as a family.

What would this little one be called? Najama had been named in honor of her father, Najam. Yazmina thought it was a beautiful name, with a beautiful meaning. *Star lighting up the night sky*. She could think of no equivalent to Ahmet's name, should she have another girl. There were no girls names she knew of that meant *highly praised*. Of course, it might be a boy, especially if the wish she suspected Ahmet was silently holding inside came true. He would not, like some Afghan men, be shamed by the birth of a daughter, but she assumed he still clung to the traditional preference for a boy. It was a boy's role, once he became a man, to continue the family legacy, to financially support the family, and to protect the family in case of any disputes.

There were many days, she had to admit, when she also prayed it would be so, that she would give birth to a son. The handful of times she'd run into Zara in the marketplace with her mother had been enough reminder of the difficulties a daughter might face; the girl had looked so forlorn. Yazmina had whispered her offer of friendship and support into the girl's ear as they kissed in greeting, so as not to arouse the mother's suspicions. And already Yazmina worried for her own daughter Najama, for her future in a world where it seemed as though for every step a woman took she was sent back two.

Even with the new law that made violence against women a crime, Yazmina was hearing more and more stories of young women being abused and beaten by their fathers and husbands, by their teachers and mullahs. She recalled being told of a young woman in the provinces who became ill, who was taken to the mullah by her family instead of to the doctor. The mullah's cure? He advised the family to beat the evil spirits out of the girl, blaming that for the cause of her illness. It was a fact that in Afghanistan, most men still believed that the Koran allowed the beating of a woman, but many of them had never even read the Koran. Many could not even read at all. They just listened to what the mullahs told them, which sometimes came in the kind of false words that only money could buy. She had heard Rashif talking about how the president was influenced by the religious leaders, and she worried that things could soon become even more difficult for women.

But then again, she thought as she pictured Najama's fierce green eyes, who will speak for us if we do not? This country needs strong daughters, girls who will grow into women with strong voices. Perhaps a girl would be best. And perhaps, *inshallah*, if we do have a girl, we will call her "Aarezo." *Hope*.

She slowly pushed herself up and onto her feet, dreading the morning chores that awaited downstairs in the empty coffeehouse. If only they were making enough money to hire someone to clean for her. Halajan was being of little help lately, the way she seemed to make herself scarce every time there was a job to be done. Of course she helped by watching Najama, but why couldn't she do that in the coffeehouse, instead of running around who knows where all the time? The two of them seemed to have so much fun together, in the courtyard laughing at that bossy peahen, who'd loudly and angrily cluck at anyone else, including Poppy, when they got too close. But the bird adored Najama, though the girl still didn't understand why it had no interest in chasing a ball. Well, at least things would remain quiet for a while this morning, she thought. But it was only minutes before her phone rang with the news of a visitor at the gate.

Yazmina hustled Zara into the empty coffeehouse and poured her some *chai*. It wasn't until the girl had removed the blue burqa she wore that Yazmina saw how bad she looked. Her sad eyes had turned fearful, her soft cheeks hollow and drawn, each sip of her hot tea coming from a trembling cup.

"What is it, *khwaar jan*? What has happened?" Yazmina placed her hand on the girl's bare arm.

Zara sat quiet for a moment, her eyes cast downward. "I am sorry to come to you like this. I have waited, and have searched for an answer to my problems. But there doesn't seem to be one."

"But you are taking this too harshly, little one. It is common for a girl your age to have fears about marriage. In time you will feel differently. You will forget about Omar, I promise."

"I will never forget about Omar," the girl snapped back, her face set with fierce determination.

Yazmina had thought a lot about this girl since her last visit. Puppy love, Halajan had called it. But still, this did not mean Zara's feelings were not real. Yes, in their world it was true that love had no place when it came to the business of marriage, that few had a right to choose in that way. Yet had not Halajan ended up eventually marrying Rashif, a love from her own youth? And had not Yazmina herself been granted the unlikely fortune of a marriage of love with Ahmet? Why must they think that this girl was wrong to feel the way she did?

Zara sat back in her chair and sighed. "But my troubles are worse than that."

Then, as Yazmina listened without saying a word, Zara poured out the story of Faheem and his threats, leaving no detail untold. By the time she had finished, Yazmina could feel her own anger pulsing from behind her eyes.

"My heart is with you, sister. But you cannot let this situation make you ill. You look as though you've been dragged through the forest by a hungry bear."

"I have not eaten or slept for many days now. I have barely left the house, not since the last day I went to the university."

"You are not going to school?"

Zara shook her head. "I was there, trying to talk to Omar after class, to tell him what had happened. But before I could say anything, I noticed a man I thought I recognized from my sister's school. I think he was watching me. I feel like there are people all around who are watching me. That's why I'm wearing this." She pointed to the bundle of blue cloth sitting in a heap on the chair beside her. "And these." She straightened one leg and wiggled a foot swimming inside a pair of red pumps that were about two sizes too big. "They are my mother's. Perhaps I might change them with yours, so that in case someone followed me here, I won't be recognized when I leave?"

Yazmina pitied the poor girl, with her imagination playing such cruel tricks on her worried mind. Of course, there were those types of men who followed pretty girls for no reason other than to make themselves known, to be noticed by the girl. She hoped this was simply one of them.

"Although I told my mother I was going to the university today, I came here instead," Zara continued. "I am too scared to go there. I am too scared even to talk to Omar."

"And have you spoken of this to your father?"

Zara shook her head. "He has already delayed his answer to Faheem. But I fear what this man might do should my father dare to back away from his proposal."

"But you must tell him!"

Zara shook her head. "You don't understand how powerful this man is, what he is capable of doing to me, to my family, to Omar. I have heard things. This is a man who uses his influence in a bad way, who trades in secrets and lies, who has the ear of powerful people and the obligation of others to do his bidding. I will never marry a man like this, as long as I live."

The look in Zara's eyes told Yazmina that the girl meant exactly what she said. Something had to be done. She knew all too well how quickly things could turn bad, and how sometimes it just takes one person to turn them right again. If Sunny had not taken the steps she had to return to the Women's Ministry the day after she had first seen Yazmina, to offer her a home at the coffeehouse, nothing would be as it was today. Little Najama might not have been allowed to live, and she herself could have been forced into prostitution.

She bent to pull the shoes off her swollen feet. "You must keep your head, my sister, and pray that things work out for the best. In the meantime," she said, placing the plastic flats on the ground and pushing them toward the girl, "when you feel despair you will come talk with me. It will be our secret. You must not worry."

Yazmina watched as the girl left through the courtyard toward the gate, her heart heavy with concern. She had no idea how to make things right for this girl, but she knew she must do something. She owed it to Sunny. She would speak to Ahmet. Perhaps he would know what to do.

19

"Aren't you hot in that thing?" Sky pulled the faded T-shirt over his head, baring his skin to the warm afternoon sun. Layla felt her cheeks turn the color of the pink scarf wrapped tightly around her head and shoulders. "Ow!" he yelled. "Jeez, Kat! Why'd ya kick me?"

"Just shut up." Kat shoved an apricot into his mouth.

"You just shut up," he laughed, sending the apricot flying across the picnic table and onto the sand, where a quick-thinking seagull swooped in for a snack. "Last one in is a loser!" Sky flung his tanned leg over the bench and ran toward the shoreline. Layla and Kat both sat watching as his body bowed into a perfect arc and disappeared beneath the deep blue surf.

"He's cute, right?"

Layla squirmed a little on the wooden seat and lowered her eyes.

"It's okay, you know. It's not a sin to agree with me. At least I don't think it is."

Kat pulled her two-toned hair into a knot at the back of her neck, unzipped her hoodie, and stepped out of her cutoff jeans. She might as well be naked, Layla thought when she saw the red bikini that was little more than three tiny triangles of fabric. She lowered her head, too uncomfortable to look Kat in the eyes.

"Be right back. Watch our stuff?" Kat skipped across the sand, leaping over piles of driftwood and dancing around the clusters of children building castles with their shovels and buckets. Layla pulled a beach towel from her bag and wiped away the dampness that was gathering under her long sleeves. The sea looked so refreshing, just like the cool waters of the rivers back in Nuristan, where she and Yazmina would hold hands and wade in deep enough to wet their dresses up to their thighs.

In the water, Kat was perched on top of Sky's shoulders, her glistening shins held firmly beneath his thick forearms. Layla could hear her laughter mixing with the squeals of an army of small boys doing battle with driftwood swords. She watched as Kat kicked her bare feet back and forth, sending foam splashing up into Sky's smiling face. Layla couldn't keep her eyes off of them, despite the alarming realization that she wasn't sure whether she wanted to shun the older girl, or be her.

"You should go in!" A few minutes later Sky stood before her, silhouetted by the golden sun. He shook his head back and forth, beads of water spraying from his long hair and onto Layla's lap. Kat wasn't far behind. She grabbed a striped towel and draped it over her shivering body, then sat down across the table from the two of them.

"Seriously, the water is awesome today, Layla. C'mon." Sky wrapped his damp, cool fingers around her wrist and pulled gently. Layla's arm jerked back a little, as if it had a mind of its own. Out of the corner of her eye she saw Kat send a quick shake of her head in Sky's direction. He shrugged his shoulders and let go. "Well then," he said with a smile, "let's eat."

Layla and Kat picked at the fruit as Sky dove eagerly into just about everything else Sunny had packed in the blue cooler. Layla laughed inside at how serious he became when he ate, how focused his eyes were, blind to the band of seagulls tiptoeing their way toward him.

"*Gom shoo!*" Layla kicked some sand toward the thieving birds. "Let us be." She watched as Sky bit into another sandwich, her growing desire to speak to him silenced by her traditions, and by her own shyness. How easy it seemed for Kat, who laughed and talked and joked with him as if he were not a boy.

"Does that not hurt?" she suddenly heard herself ask.

Sky looked at her with lifted eyebrows, his mouth full of food.

"That." She gestured to her mouth, surprised at her own boldness. "Does it not hurt to eat?"

Sky laughed. "You mean my smiley piercing?"

Layla nodded.

"Nah. I barely notice it now." Sky took another bite from his sandwich. "Do people do piercings where you're from?"

Layla shook her head. "No. Ears or nose is allowed—this from the time of the Prophet. But in other places, *muthlah*."

"Mutilation," Kat explained.

"Yes," Layla agreed, starting to feel as though she couldn't keep herself from this conversation she knew she should not be having. "Also it is seen as like *kuffar*, unbelievers. It is forbidden. But of course, I talk just of girls. Men who pierced would be copying women, a thing also not allowed. No man would do this."

"So you are a double badass!" Kat rumpled Sky's drying curls.

"Wow. That's harsh. Must be tough living over there."

"Really? You think so?" Kat responded in an exaggerated tone, her eyes like two round coins.

"I love my home," Layla protested, her voice rising.

"It's all good." Sky held out a cold bottle of water for Layla. "So which do you like better? Afghanistan or here?"

"That is a funny question. Of course I love my home more." Layla took a sip of her water. "But that does not mean there are not good things about here too," she quickly added.

"That's for sure," Kat said.

"Like what?" Sky asked. "What do you like about this place?"

"Well, I can turn the handle this way to get hot water." She pantomimed the gesture with one hand. "And that way to get cold."

"That's it?"

"The television! At home all we have is Afghan news, Bollywood movies."

"Hmm," Sky said.

"And the people," she added, not wanting to disappoint him with her answers. "People here are so nice. The cars stop when you cross. Everyone says have a nice day. You go in a store, they are frowning. They see you, they smile."

"Ha!" Kat laughed.

"Well, I hate to break it to you," Sky said, "but it's a law that you have to stop your car to let people cross, and those people in stores are probably being kind of fake."

"No, but also in school. Teachers sometimes beat us when we do not know answers. We are kids and girls, so they don't need to be nice to us. Here, they try to help you."

"Well that sucks." Sky wrinkled his sunburned nose.

Layla shook her head. "Sometimes I think people do not see the good that is here," she continued. "Like that show on television, about girls who are sixteen and pregnant. That you would have a child before even you have your wisdom teeth. To me that is shocking."

"Oh please," Kat said. "How can you say that when you come from a country where girls get married when they're barely out of diapers?"

"But that is different," Layla explained, suddenly anxious to continue. "That is forced. Here you have a choice. You are free to have the life you want. You have a government that makes your parents send you to school. You have laws that protect you from having to marry your uncle or your cousin when you are just twelve, rules that keep you from being a second wife, or a slave. When you have so many choices, I do not understand why anyone would make the choice to have a life that is so hard."

"So which do you prefer, Kat?" Sky rubbed his hand up and down her back to help warm her skin through the damp towel. She shrugged him off with a little jerk and didn't answer. "Do you even remember what it's like over there?" he continued.

"Of course I remember," she snapped. It was as if a dark cloud had suddenly appeared in the blue sky above. But the shadow passed over Kat's face as quickly as it had arrived. She picked a Frisbee out of the sand and placed it on his head. "But you, you could live like a king over there, just because you have a dick." Her hand flew to her mouth a little too late. "Oops, sorry," she said to Layla. "But really, it's true, right? They're all taught over there that men are totally superior to women. Men get to make all the choices, they control everything. They even buy their wives' and sisters' underwear for them. Seriously. I'd rather be a three-legged dog over here than a woman over there."

"Ouch," Sky said, glancing at Layla.

"It is true," Layla said. "Coming here, it is very strange for me to see how a woman can be the same as a man. That they do not need a man to take care of them. That they can even be the boss of men."

"Or just be super bossy." Sky jerked sideways to dodge Kat's playful slap.

Layla sat with her arms at her sides, biting her cheeks to keep from laughing at the funny faces Sky was making behind Kat's back. She could feel her entire body melt with the warmth from the sun and the smiles of the friends around her. It felt so strange, two girls acting this way around a boy. Yet it did not feel so wrong. But she knew it was wrong. And she knew that she must not let it happen again. So just today, she promised herself. She would let it be okay just for today. But, oh, how she wished this day could last forever.

20

Yazmina nodded toward the back corner of the coffeehouse where Omar sat at his usual spot, alone, waiting for the others to arrive and pass through on their way to the weekly meeting. The young man's gaze was turned downward, his concentration on a newspaper that lay open in front of him on the wooden table. Around him, the room was fairly busy. "Good to see you again," Ahmet called out as he passed a group of British embassy workers biting into Bashir Hadi's burgers. "I hope you are enjoying your coffee," he said to a pair of Canadian teachers whom he recognized from other visits. "*Salaam alaikum*," he nodded to a black-haired man with an expensive striped *chapan*, a jacket identical to the one worn by President Karzai, carefully draped over the back of his chair. The man acknowledged him with eyes so dark they seemed to have no end.

But today Ahmet had no time to wonder about the depth of a man's eyes. He removed his coat and went behind the counter to pour two cups of *chai* from the tall thermos he kept there for the family's use. He was expecting a good turnout next door at his mother's house, where this afternoon they would be debating how they might take action at the university. It had taken many discussions, some quite heated, to agree on what issue to focus on to best help their country move forward. In the end, the answer was very clear, and existed very close to home.

No one could argue that the corruption that ran like blood through the veins of Afghan society was one of the biggest stumbling blocks to the country's success. There was not one person he knew who did not have a story to tell of being solicited for money or a gift from someone with a service to offer, and plenty as well who would admit to making such an offer themselves—to a court official to avoid a fine, to a job recruiter to obtain a position, to a bank employee to secure favors, even to a doctor or nurse to ensure better treatment. *It is just the way things are done*, some would say. *It is simply a sign of my gratitude*, claimed others. And even if they considered the practice to be unjust, there were few who would lodge a formal complaint. Who could blame them, knowing that the police and the judges and the government workers were among those taking bribes most often? Not to mention the reprisals one might face from speaking out against a person of power.

Where the group was struggling was in deciding on the best way to combat the problem. They had discussed the importance of codes of conduct, and the need for impartial monitoring systems, but how could a small band of university students manage to force that to happen? It was Rashif who had suggested the answer.

"How can you right a wrong if nobody considers it a wrong?" his mother's husband had asked the group. "You need to convince people that even their meager offerings for a service or favor are causing big problems that affect us all. That corruption begets more corruption. When one gets what they want, everybody expects the same." And what better place to do that, he suggested, than at the university, where the content of an upcoming exam, or the changing of a grade, could be easily secured from a teacher or lecturer through money or gifts?

Now they had a plan, or at least the beginning of one. Though they knew where they were going to direct their efforts, it would take more conversation to decide how they would go about it. And today they would start that discussion. But first he had to make good on his promise to Yazmina and have a private talk with the solemn young man in the corner.

"*Salaam dost e man*. Hello, my friend. You are well? And your family is well?"

The boy responded and offered his own greetings in return.

Ahmet sat, and they both sipped their tea. On the other side of the room, over Omar's shoulder, he could see Yazmina watching, urging him on with her eyes. He paused for a moment before speaking, feeling a little unease at continuing to pry into the personal life of another man in such a way. But he had given his word to Yazmina that he would tell Omar of his Zara's predicament, and would discuss with him any way there might be to help the situation. So he squared his shoulders and went at it directly, as there was not much time before the meeting next door was to start.

"Do you know, *beraadar*, brother, that your friend the girl came again to the coffeehouse?"

The boy's head shot up.

"She did," Ahmet confirmed.

"What did she have to say? How did she seem?" Omar asked with an eagerness that washed away any attempt at propriety.

"I didn't see her. This time it was my wife who felt a reason to tell me about the visit. She seems to think that there is trouble with this girl."

"She was to be engaged," Omar said sadly. "I have not seen her or heard from her in weeks. I thought perhaps she had already been wed."

"Apparently she has not. She doesn't wish to marry." Ahmet thought he detected a slight smile pass over the boy's lips. "And apparently she seems to be making herself quite ill over it." He checked his watch and continued. The last thing he wanted to do was to waste the others' time by being late. "Do you know the girl's parents?"

Omar shook his head. "I have never met them. My family has no connections to them. But Zara tells me they are a good family."

"Well then, if they are a good family, we must trust that they will work things out for the best." Ahmet stood and pushed his chair back. "In the meantime, as I have said before, you must protect yourself. And if you do care for this girl, stay away from her. It is for the best."

Omar looked down at his cup. "I seem to have no choice in the matter."

Ahmet nodded to Yazmina in acknowledgment that he had fulfilled her request to talk with the boy. Yes, she had urged him to be gentle, to show some compassion for the young couple, but to Ahmet, protecting his own family's honor would always come first. If others thought they were advising the girl to disobey her parents' wishes, or worse, if they were suspected of turning a blind eye to coffeehouse meetings between the couple, the gossip and accusations would begin to fly like an angry swarm of bees throughout the whole neighborhood. Perhaps Yazmina might not have agreed with the tenor of his words, but he had handled the situation the way he felt was best for all those involved.

Omar stood to face him. "Do not worry," the young man assured him. "I will not do anything stupid. I will, as you say, trust that things will work out for the best, whatever that best may be."

"Yes," Ahmet replied, scanning the faces in the room one more time before turning his attention to the coming meeting next door. "Whatever that best may be."

21

"And the cups for the soda were bigger than the teapot for all my family! We could throw a party with that one cup of soda. A baby could fit in that cup."

They all laughed as Layla shook her head. She had been to the north side of the island with Sky and Joe that afternoon, and their stop at 7-Eleven was still on her mind. In general, she didn't seem to be getting along too well with the food over here—all the cheese and oil and sugar—but she was trying. She mostly seemed to go for Joe's cooking, which he had learned to tailor to her taste. But all in all, she appeared to be thriving. Sunny envied how quickly she'd managed to improve her English, even if there were still times Kat was forced to step in with a translation. And right before the five of them had settled down on the porch for dinner, Sunny had watched as Layla hopped and tripped across the lawn with a soccer ball, giggling at Sky's mock frustration with her unfamiliarity with the game and her inability to follow his instructions. Even now her cheeks were still flushed, her lips still turned up in a smile.

And why not? It was a beautiful evening, so warm that Sunny had asked Kat and Sky to move the kitchen table outdoors. Hummingbirds darted in and out of the blue columbine that now peppered the shady lawn, and the bleeding heart and shooting stars were in full bloom on the far side of the maple tree. Sunny loved those for their name alone. Now the low sun was turning everything to gold, and for once the snow-topped peaks across the water were as clear as day. They had picked the carcass of Joe's roast chicken clean, and now Bear, with all hopes of being offered a morsel dashed, sat eagerly by Sky's side with a ball in his mouth.

"Go ahead, you guys. I'll clean up." Sunny split the last of the wine between her glass and Joe's, while the three "kids", as he called them, excused themselves from the table and headed out to the lawn, the dog leading the way.

"Ah, youth," Joe sighed as he untucked the napkin from under his chin and folded it into a neat little square. "It is good to see that girl so happy."

"Guess it beats Minnesota."

"No, I don't mean Layla. The other one. Little Miss Toughie."

"Kat? She's not so tough."

Joe nodded his head up and down. "Hmm. How right you are, kiddo. But you know, sometimes a little bit of toughness can be a good thing, if it doesn't turn you so hard that you can't be cracked. And a toughness that comes from sorrow must be steeped with time before it can be turned into an advantage."

"Are you talking about yourself now?" Sunny assumed he was referring to losing Sylvia, and yet she still had a feeling there was more to Joe's story than he had chosen to share.

"Yes, I suppose I am talking about me. But also about Kat."

Across the lawn, Kat was squatted on the grass watching Sky and Layla toss the ball back and forth over Bear's head. "How do you know so much about her?" Sunny asked. Despite any details Joe might be withholding about his own past, he seemed to know everything about everyone else. He had a way of getting each person he met, including herself, to share their secrets with him, which, she thought, was an amazing feat considering he never seemed to keep his mouth shut long enough to let anyone else speak.

Joe shrugged his shoulders. "I don't know so much, really. It's just a sense I have about the girl. I imagine it must have been a difficult thing for her, coming so far so young, and still being looked at as an outsider no matter how American she becomes."

"She does seem to work awfully hard at that, right?"

"You know, kiddo, it's not easy to feel at odds with who you are, where you are from." Joe's gaze was fixed on the horizon, as if his thoughts were a million miles away. He swatted at a mosquito that had landed on his arm and turned back to Sunny. "It's a harsh world Kat comes from, am I right?"

Sunny paused before answering. "Well, yes," she agreed, "and no. It is true that there's a way of thinking that exists over there that none of us will ever be able to understand. You've got such an ancient culture, and tribal codes that still dictate how things are done. It's complicated. And yes, there is plenty of injustice and corruption and poverty and violence. But it's not all like that."

"So tell me something about the things that are not all like that. Tell me what it is about that country that makes you want to run back to it as if it were a long-lost lover."

"Oh Joe, where do I begin? It's not always easy to describe it to people who haven't experienced it themselves. Sort of like teaching someone to tie their shoelaces over the phone." Sunny pushed back her curls, her elbows coming to rest on the table before her. Just thinking about Afghanistan made her long to be back there. "You know, it truly is a spectacular country, not like what they choose to show us here on television. Mountains that seem to touch the sky, and lakes just as blue as that shirt Sky has on, so still and glassy you could use them as a mirror. Even in the city, you can find these incredibly lush rose gardens hidden behind dusty walls, and sunsets I'd hold up to the ones around here any day." She nodded toward the golden orb sinking slowly down to earth. "But honestly? To me the most beautiful thing about Afghanistan is its people. They've got to be the most generous people on earth. To a fault," she added, remembering the time she had casually admired a scarf that Bashir Hadi's wife, Sharifa, was wearing. It was deep purple to-die-for silk, so fine it felt like melting butter in her fingers.

"Well then it is yours," Sharifa had insisted, removing the scarf from her own shoulders and draping it over Sunny's. "May you wear it in happiness and good health."

Sunny, of course, had protested, knowing that the scarf must have cost Bashir Hadi a week's salary, if not more. But Sharifa would have none of it. Not even after Sunny had later neatly tucked it into Bashir Hadi's coat pocket while he was busy in the kitchen and nobody was watching. The very next day she found the scarf back on the hook by the coffeehouse door. Sunny quickly learned to keep her compliments to herself, at least around her Afghan friends.

"And kind? You don't know what true kindness is until you've been around Afghans," she told Joe. "You're arriving in town at 3 am? No problem. The entire household will get up as if it's noon and whip up a five-course meal to welcome you back.

Honest. It's happened to me plenty of times. And I tell you, those folks will have your back in an instant, keeping you out of harm's way and stopping you from saying or doing the wrong thing." She couldn't count how many times Bashir Hadi had saved her butt.

"I'm sure they loved you over there. How could they not?"

"Yeah, right," Sunny snorted. "But seriously, Joe. It's not just me, or other foreigners, who get that kind of treatment. It's just the way things are done in their culture. This is how most people treat others in their family, which, by the way, is a very loose term over there. Oh my God, you should see what happens when a couple gets married. A guy can walk into his own wedding and find over a thousand people in the banquet hall, half of whom he doesn't even recognize. But somehow, they are 'family', and he is obligated to welcome them, and feed them." Sunny paused to light the citronella candle in the middle of the table and watched as the dark smoke climbed into the twilight. "But what most people don't understand," she continued, "is how much these people truly love their country. They're proud of who they are and where they're from. We just assume that they're all dying to get out of there. Well, of course nobody wants to live in a war-torn place, but even with decades of battle after battle, Afghans never give up on their country. Their love goes deeper than that. Have you ever noticed the look on Layla's face when someone tells her how lucky she is to be here, or asks her *don't you want to stay*? Imagine how insulting their pity must feel to her."

"A love of a country can sometimes be a very complicated thing. I know."

Sunny now settled back with her glass in hand, knowing that whenever Joe ended a sentence with *I know*, a story was to follow. But for once he remained silent.

The last sliver of sun disappeared behind the distant peaks. Sunny shivered a little and stood from the table. Joe scraped his chair slowly back, and struggled to push himself up. Sunny held out a hand to stop him. "No, no, relax. You've been cooking all day. It's my turn."

"What, I'm going to just sit here like a bump on a log? I can help."

Together they scraped and stacked the plates, and brought everything inside. Joe stood leaning against the kitchen counter while Sunny rinsed, the warm water from the faucet running through her fingers like a soothing balm.

"So have you given any thought to my suggestion?" he asked, his voice coming in loud and clear over the clanging of dishes.

"Which one, Joe? You seem to have a lot of those," she shouted back.

"Come on, kiddo. You know what I'm talking about. You can't pretend that something doesn't need to be done. Sooner or later Rick is going to force your hand, one way or another. Better that the hand he tries to force knows which direction to push back."

"You know how I feel, Joe. And let's just say I did want this place, that I did want to do all that stuff you've dreamed up. I still don't have the money to do it. In fact, my savings are disappearing faster than a sneeze through a screen door, as my mom used to say."

Joe responded with a weak laugh. "My years ahead are few, you know."

Sunny quickly turned off the faucet. "What the hell does that mean, Joe? Are you okay?"

"Fit as a fiddle, and twice as squeaky," he said with a little cackle. "I'm just saying," he continued, clearing his throat, "what use does an old man like me have for money?"

"I don't want your money, Joe. I don't want any of this."

"So you keep saying. But we can do this. I don't have much, but perhaps with a loan or two we might just be able to make it work. I've already spoken to the folks down at the bank."

"But, Joe . . ."

"But nothing. Just come outside and sit for a minute, and listen to me."

Sunny wiped her hands on the dishtowel and followed the old man back out to the porch. In the purple dusk she could barely make out the silhouettes of the fishing boats returning from their last run of the day. Layla and Sky and Kat were seated on the grass, their backs to the house.

"Now, use your brain," Joe said as he pulled out a chair for Sunny. "What is Rick asking you for?"

Sunny repeated the last amount Rick had quoted for his half of the property.

Joe sat down next to her, Sangiovese the cat leaping out of nowhere and into his lap. "And this doesn't seem like a steal to you?"

"How would I know? All I know is that I don't trust the guy."

"Well you can trust me. I know. This is a bargain. Just the land itself is almost worth that."

"So why is he selling so cheap?"

"That, I couldn't tell you. But it seems as though he's certainly desperate for cash. Who knows what type of things he's messed up in? And who wants to know? Not me."

"Me neither." A vision of Rick's seedy smile popped into Sunny's head.

"So, anyway, like I say, this is a thing too good to pass up. Look at it this way," he said as he stroked Sangiovese's long fur with his gnarled hand. "We become partners, you and I. Sunny and Joe. We get the place, we fix it up, we get the business humming, and then you can do what you want. You can sell for a nice profit and pay me back and say goodbye, or . . ."

Joe left his last thought unsaid. Sunny slowly brushed the crumbs off her favorite Afghan tablecloth and onto the wooden porch. She knew a decision needed to be made. And she would make one. Eventually. Soon. She rose and stood behind Joe's chair, and bent down to circle his bony shoulders with her arms. "Thanks, Joe. I really mean it. I appreciate your ideas, but I really can't take your money. I'll figure things out. Promise."

Joe didn't answer. The two of them just stayed there, frozen together, their eyes turned toward a perfectly round beacon of a moon rising into the sky over the dark Sound.

22

The unmistakable smell of musky cologne crept through the crack of the door like a thief, stealing away any last shred of safeness Zara had been able to hold onto during the past few weeks. She had seen the big black car pull up to the house and, with legs that shook like reeds in a windstorm, had positioned herself on the other side of the wall from where her father now sat alone with Faheem. Her mother and sister were out, off to the Thursday market with the rest of the family. She half-prayed they would return early to disrupt this discussion that seemed to be turning ugly, fast. But their absence was what was allowing her to be alone in the kitchen to listen in on what was being said, and her fear of not knowing her fate was far greater than her fear of the spiteful words coming from Faheem's mouth.

The conversation had begun with the usual niceties— *welcome to our home, how is your health, how is your family's health, let me pour you some tea*—the politeness that one shows another regardless of how one feels inside. But it wasn't long before things took a sharp turn.

It was clear from their words that Zara's father had still not given Faheem an answer. For that, Zara was grateful. But just as she had feared, it was also clear that the arrogant man was not about to allow her father to refuse.

"You cannot seem to control your daughter." Zara could hear the sound of Faheem biting down on a mouthful of *nuqul*, the sugar-coated almonds he would have been offered, and could picture him leaning back on the pillows as if he were the head of this household instead of her father.

"My daughter is a good girl." Her father spoke with pride and assurance. "She would never dishonor her family." It took everything Zara had to keep herself from running out and hugging him tightly around the waist, as she had done as a child. Instead she just slid down the wall and sat quietly on the floor.

"Well, if you cannot control her, I can."

"I do not need your help."

Zara's heart leapt up into her throat. That her father would dare to speak in this manner to a man like Faheem was a shock. She feared what would come next. But Faheem simply laughed, a whiny laugh that made him sound like an injured cat.

"I mean no disrespect, *Haji* Faheem," her father said. "It is simply that my family is not prepared to make a commitment at this time."

Zara could not believe her ears. Surely her father knew of this man's power, and his unyielding will to get what he wanted. She had hesitated to speak up about her own confrontation with Faheem, as she would never have done anything to put her family in a bad situation. Yet now her father seemed to be doing that all by himself. She tried to imagine the look on Faheem's face.

"Is it that my bride price is not good enough? I have offered cash, a car for you, even furniture for your wife. You and I both know that I bring more wealth and status to this family than you could ever have imagined."

"It is not that. Your offer is a very generous one, *haji saib*. It is just that my daughter is very serious about her studies. That is the reason she is not eager to wed now."

Faheem let out a little snort, like a donkey. "She is so serious that she hasn't even been near the university for weeks?"

Zara could hear no response. She crawled on her knees to peer through the keyhole. Faheem sat like a king on a throne, his fancy green-and-white striped *chapan* draped over his thick arms. He slicked his black hair back and smiled smugly. "You see," he said to her father, "already I know what she does, where she goes, who she sees. Do you know she goes by herself to that American coffeehouse, in Qala-e-Fatullah? I see her going there. A place full of *khaareji*, foreigners, the same ones who are trying to ruin our country. I know what also happens there, what kind of place it really is. And if your daughter continues to go there, she will soon be no better than a whore, and then you will not even be able to pay me to take her."

Zara lurched back away from the keyhole, her face flushing with anger, her heart racing with dread.

"And did you know, my friend," she heard Faheem say, "that there is also a boy who goes there? It is no coincidence. My people have seen them together before, at the university."

"I'm sorry," her father said softly, "but I cannot believe that my daughter would do anything to shame our family, or herself."

"Then you are more of a fool than I thought."

Zara heard the click of a lighter, and could smell the smoke from Faheem's cigarette as it seeped into the kitchen. How she longed to rush out and beat her fists on the man's chest. Instead she remained hidden, a silent tear for her father's honor sliding down her warm cheek.

"All I ask for is some time," she heard her father say. "Perhaps once she finishes her studies my daughter will be ready to wed." Zara could detect the false civility in her father's voice.

"But you do not seem to understand, my friend," Faheem continued, his voice steady and low. "Your daughter is already mine. She was mine the first day I walked through this door. And now I apparently must be the one who is to keep her in line."

Again she did not hear her father give an answer. But there was no mistaking the fury that was rising in Faheem like a deadly volcano on the verge of eruption.

"I have had enough of this disrespect from your family," he hissed, "and I expect the entire matter to be resolved before the month is out. After all, you wouldn't want anything bad to happen to your other little one, would you? I would hate to be forced into teaching you all a lesson you would regret learning."

Zara could feel the bile rising from her stomach, and hurried to cover her mouth to keep the sound from her throat from giving her location away. She tilted her ear closer to the door.

"But for now," Faheem was saying, "I will take care of first things first. I know what I must do. Soon your daughter will have nowhere to run for her little encounters. She will learn to know better than to disgrace me. Trust me, my friend. With just one phone call, everything will be over. I will end it now. And you and your daughter will be forced to come to your senses."

Zara did not wait for her father's reply. She began to frantically pace the tiled floor, circling the small room with hushed steps, desperately trying to keep her head straight. Perhaps she should just go, vanish to a place where nobody could find her. She was the problem, and if she became invisible, the problem would disappear as well.

She paused in front of the shelf where bowls and cups sat among the spices and teas that were the signs of her family's daily life, where, from the corner in which the shelf met the wall, the faces of her sister and mother smiled at her from inside a gold frame. She thought back the day that photo was taken, at the henna party before her cousin's wedding last year. She remembered Mariam's delight at the intricate designs spreading across her small hands, and her mother's beaming pride as others complimented her on her two daughters in their finest dresses. Yes, she thought as a tear slipped down her quivering cheek, she was certain about what she must do. It was the only solution, the only way to protect her family and put an end to Faheem's ugly threats. There was no question about it. She had no choice but to leave.

But first she must warn Yazmina and the others. Who knows what Faheem meant by those words he'd spoken to her father? *With just one phone call, everything will be over.* She would tell them all to keep their eyes open for trouble. And, *inshallah*, she would find her Omar there, at the coffeehouse. If not, she would ask for their promise that word of her love would reach his ears. She tugged her scarf tightly around her head and ran out the door, past Faheem's sleeping driver and into the crowded city streets.

Down roads thick with mud and people she rushed, pushing and weaving until she had been swallowed by the crowds, too busy coming and going and buying and selling to pay her much mind. As she darted through an opening in the crush, a sharp shout and a clatter of metal crashed at her ears.

"Are you blind, you stupid girl? Do you want to get me killed?" The boy picked his bike out of the gutter and shook his small fist at her, but Zara just kept running, his cries trailing off behind her like echoes from the everyday world she was leaving behind.

23

"You missed a spot."

Sunny turned to see Joe on the lawn beside her, leaning heavily against the carved Afghan walking stick she had found for him inside the barn. "Very funny." She brushed away the curls that had escaped from under her purple bandana and stood back to admire her work. The six-foot technicolor peacock splashed across the south side of the barn was worrying her a little. "He looks like he's angry."

"Well, he is supposed to be screaming," Joe said.

"Screaming, yes. Angry, not so much." Sunny placed her brush into the bucket of soapy water with the others.

"Well you can't paint a smile on him and ask him to scream at the same time, can you?"

She cocked her head and squinted at her creation. "Maybe it's the eyes. They're too beady. He needs friendlier eyes."

"He's a bird. Birds have beady eyes."

"Well maybe his beak is open too wide."

"How else would we know he was screaming?"

"Have you ever actually seen a peacock scream, Joe?"

"Nope. Just heard them."

"Me too."

"Well then, we will just have to keep our eyes open, won't we?"

Sunny wiped her hands on her jeans. "No, Joe, *you* will just have to keep *your* eyes open. I hereby dub you the peacock spy. Me, I just want to paint." Painting had always been Sunny's favorite escape, and the bigger the canvas the better. She smiled to herself when she thought of how many times she'd painted and repainted the huge wall in front of the coffeehouse, trying so hard to get it just right, finally settling on an image that had haunted her from her last visit to Mazar-e Sharif, the thousands of white doves against the blue Afghan sky. She picked up the bucket of dirty brushes and circled the barn with Joe in tow. The rosebushes Sky had helped her plant needed watering, as it hadn't rained in weeks. The pale peach variety they'd found was perfect, exactly like the ones she remembered from Kabul.

"Can I be of assistance?" Joe asked eagerly.

"I've got it. Thanks."

"What?" Joe cupped his ear with his hand as a plane flew across the late morning sky.

"I said I've got it!" Sunny yelled. But the look on Joe's face made her regret her tone. "Be careful," she said, handing him the hose. "Don't trip. I'll be right back."

By the time she emerged from the house with a tray, Joe was already seated safely on the lawn at the picnic table, Bear at his feet. "*Chai?*" she offered, as she arranged the pieces of her favorite tea set from Afghanistan in front of him.

"Don't mind if I do." Joe picked up a blue saucer and turned it upside down and back again, as if he were considering a purchase. "You know, these would look very nice in a tasting room."

"Don't start, Joe. Although I have to say that I generally do like the idea of serving wine in teacups, like we had to do in Kabul. There's just something so wonderfully clandestine about it."

"You're nuts. Who is going to want to drink wine from a cup?" Joe shook his head in disgust.

Layla and Kat, both with one foot still in the land of dreams, wordlessly joined them at the table, their eyes heavy with sleep. Sunny poured four cups from the ceramic pot in her hand. The green lawn stretched before them like a soft carpet rolling down to the water's edge. In the distance a red tugboat coaxed a container ship in toward the harbor. It looked just like a postcard.

"But with a view like this, who knows?" Joe continued. "Our customers could be tasting their wine out of an old shoe and they wouldn't notice the difference."

"Stop already," Sunny pleaded. "But if I ever were going to have a tasting room, which I am not, thank you very much, I would want to do it just like they do it in Afghanistan."

"They have no tasting rooms in Afghanistan. They don't drink," Kat said, her first words of the morning coming out in a croak.

"That's not what I meant. I meant I would make it warm, inviting. I would make people feel more welcome there than they feel in their own homes."

"Ah, just like the Italians." Joe looked up at the sky. "*Se vuoi perdere un amico vino poco buono e legna di fico.* If you want to lose a friend give them not so good wine and a smoky fire. Or maybe

166

it's if you want to keep your friends don't skimp, and make sure the room you are serving in is nice and warm. Either way, it's how they do it over there."

"Well, you've never seen how the Afghans do it," Sunny said as she took a seat. "I've told you how hospitable they are, Joe. Am I right, Layla?"

"It is true." Layla sipped her tea. "We are taught even as young children the importance that comes from sharing a meal together. It is called 'aab u namak'."

"The right of salt," Kat explained.

Sunny nodded in agreement. "They view it as a religious obligation."

"Yes," Layla continued. "It is written that everybody must be ready to give daily bread to his neighbor. But also a guest must always be honest and faithful to his host." She paused for more tea. "There is a story, one that we are told as children, about some thieves who come into a man's home in the night, when everyone is sleeping. The leader tells them to start carrying out all the family's belongings that have worth, like the carpets and the cushions. Then the leader puts his arm into a cupboard and finds a hard, smooth object he believes must be a gem. His men are almost done when he puts this gem to his lips. He is disappointed to find that this gem is just a block of salt, but is worried that he has stolen property from a man whose salt he has shared. He quickly tells his men to put everything back into the house, and then sneaks away with nothing before the family wakes."

"So the moral of that story is always leave food out on your counters and you will never need an alarm, or a guard dog. Right, old Bear?" Joe reached down to scratch the dog's neck.

"But seriously, guys," Sunny said, "there are also some pretty funny rules they have over there about these things. Like you are never, ever supposed to offer to help in an Afghan's home. Just not done. It would be considered an insult. And whatever you do, you have to eat slowly. I learned that one the hard way. They just keep refilling your plate, again and again, and no matter how much you eat, they say, 'But you didn't eat a thing!' And if they invite you to dinner? Don't accept. At least not the first time, or even the second. If they really want you to come, they ask three times."

"Yeah, like they don't really mean it the first two times," Kat smirked.

"No, it is not that," Layla said. "It is like what you tell me here, when people ask how are you, and they are just being nice but do not really want to hear the answer."

"And over there," Sunny continued, "when someone asks you to stay for tea, you have to figure out if it's just a polite way to end a conversation, or if they're actually asking you to stay for tea."

"Still sounds pretty two-faced to me." Kat tugged her sleeves down over her wrists and cupped the tea in her hands.

Layla shook her head. "It is just being polite. By Islam, it is your duty to treat others as you want them to treat you."

"Ha!" Kat almost spit out her tea. "That's a laugh."

"What do you mean? Why is that funny?" Layla's brows furrowed with confusion.

"Maybe it's obligatory to treat strangers that way, but do you really think Afghan men would want to be treated the way they treat their wives and daughters?" Kat's eyes darted back and forth from Layla to Sunny.

Layla sat forward on the bench. "Not all men are like that. It is mostly just when shame is brought upon a family that men turn mean and violent."

"Yeah, exactly. Once again, it's all about what other people think. Shame isn't shame unless it's witnessed."

"But there are rules—"

Kat leaned in toward Layla. "Rules for what reason? Those kinds of rules don't keep people safe or protected. It's just the opposite! Those rules turn innocent people into walking targets for just trying to live their lives, for doing what other people do normally and naturally. And those are just the people who dare to live differently. The others are too oppressed to even *dream* of another life, so they're as much of a victim of those fucking rules as everyone else."

Sunny had never seen Kat so worked up. Nor had she ever seen Joe so quiet.

But Kat wasn't finished. "And what kind of place is it that makes a woman dress like a Halloween ghost just to go outside? How can you live in a place like that?"

Now it was Layla who was getting mad. "Freedom is not a miniskirt, or swimming with almost nothing on."

"So true!" Sunny chirped, trying her best to lighten the mood. "Me, I've always been a fan of the burqini. Honestly, I gotta say, sometimes being covered can feel kind of liberating. It's like you're anonymous, like a superhero in disguise."

"Oh please." Kat rolled her eyes. "I'm just saying a woman should be able to wear whatever the hell she wants."

"But it is our choice," Layla objected. "To me, I am proud to wear the *hijab*. I was taught that it's like the oyster protecting the pearl, or the wrapper around a sweet piece of candy."

Kat slammed down her cup. "Ugh. Don't you see how objectifying that is? It's like you're a thing, not a person." She covered her eyes with her hands and shook her head.

Sunny understood where Kat was coming from, to a point. And she also felt bad for the girl, always so full of anger. Yet at the same time, she sort of wanted to shake her.

But Layla wasn't done. "I don't think you really know what it is like there."

"I know enough. Trust me." Kat crossed her arms in front of her chest.

Layla shook her head. "Then I don't understand how you can feel that way about the country you are from. I cannot wait to get back there to taste the sweet *kharbuza*, to smell the fresh *naan*, to feel the soft air of spring after the long winter nights. You just do not know."

"Well, good luck to you the next time you get the hots for a guy."

Layla lowered her eyes to the table, her cheeks turning the color of the Autumn Fire Red Sunny had used for the peacock's tongue. She held herself back from comforting the girl, knowing that anything she did would embarrass Layla even further.

"At least I am not a *faahisha*," Layla muttered into her scarf, clearly not intending for any of them to hear.

"Whoa—" Sunny cautioned.

"Excuse me?" Kat interrupted. "Did you say *whore*? Speak English."

Layla whipped around to address Kat. "You are the one who is friends with him. The way you joke with him as if he is a brother or a husband. I have seen what you do. Are you going to marry him?"

Kat burst out laughing. "Me? Get married? No way."

"Well then it is you who shames our country."

"*Our* country? It's not my country, it's yours."

"How can you say that about the place you are from?"

"Because this, my country, is a free country. And thankfully I can say whatever I want." Kat swung her legs over the bench and stood. Layla did the same.

"What just happened?" Sunny asked as she watched them storm off in separate directions.

"*Amor, tosse, e fumo, malamente si nascondono.* In English? Love, smoke and coughs are hard to hide."

"Coughs, Joe? Really? And it started out as such a nice morning."

"It is still a nice morning. They'll get over it."

Sunny hoped he was right. Another complication in her life was all she needed now. Kat was clearly hurting, but who was she to offer advice? There were days when she still felt as though she was holding on by a thread, when the memory of Jack's touch or the mere mention of his name could turn her into a puddle of tears. How many mornings did she fight the urge to pull the covers up over her head and stay there all day, preferably with a gallon of mint chocolate chip ice cream? Sometimes she felt as though she was existing in limbo, perpetually wandering through a maze between a past so vivid that she could swear it had never ended, and a future as muddy and cloudy as Twimbly itself.

24

Yazmina leaned back on her *toshak*, struggling to lift her feet onto a pile of soft pillows, and rubbed her hands lightly over her growing belly as if it were a magic lantern from which she might make a genie appear. The time seemed to be moving so slowly with this one, not like with Najama, who had arrived long before any of them were prepared.

She yawned and allowed her eyelids to slide shut as she pictured the activity in the coffeehouse below. Along with the warm weather there would be more customers, she hoped, the front courtyard sprinkled with the afternoon regulars reading their newspapers, chatting over their espressos. Ahmet would be there by now, if he was already home from the university, which he would try to be on a Thursday, his meeting day. She felt good when he was in the coffeehouse to see all who entered—no one else had the gift he had of simply looking into a man's eyes to learn all that he needed to know. The Koran said that the eyes are the gateway to the mind. Ahmet could tell a man's evil intentions in a flash. Of course, Bashir Hadi had been urging them to purchase a metal detector, particularly after a recent suicide bombing of a bus full of policemen. But Ahmet felt confident with Daoud checking backpacks and purses at the gate, and with Khalid arriving in time to join him for the evening shift.

Once weapons had been checked and locked up for safekeeping in the shipping container at the gate, and after each and every person had been stopped for a final once-over at the door, greetings would be made, and only then would the customers make their way in to find their tables.

Rashif would not yet be back from his shop in the Mondai-e. Yazmina could picture him standing, stretching, carefully covering the still-warm sewing machine, unplugging the hot plate, and locking the door behind him. He would be anxious to return home to join Ahmet and the other men. Sometimes, after things quieted down in the coffeehouse, he and Ahmet would continue the discussions late into the night, long after she had headed up to bed. But to Yazmina, this was a good sign. Both she and Halajan were appreciative of Rashif's ability to draw out the good sense that had always lived inside of Ahmet, and for encouraging him to use his voice for the benefit of others.

She imagined Bashir Hadi downstairs, ruling the roost just as Sunny had done, with a firm hand and a smile that could charm *Shaytaan* himself. Bashir Hadi would be keeping one eye on the tables and the other on the kitchen, making sure that everything was being prepared exactly as his recipes dictated. Yazmina felt a rumbling from deep inside her rounded middle. She and her family owed Bashir Hadi the world for his dedication to the coffeehouse. There was no way they could have made it this far without the man's hard work.

Yazmina's stomach growled again. If she weren't so tired she'd head downstairs to help, and to help herself to one of his delicious burgers. Perhaps Halajan will bring her something after she returns from wherever it was she went today with Najama. How inseparable those two had become. Thick as thieves they were as they'd giggle together over something only they were privy to, or as they'd sit snuggled up in a quiet corner to look at books for hours on end. Her biggest wish for her daughter was that she'd grow up to become as strong and willful a woman as her nana.

Where were those two? she wondered as she checked the time. They should have been back by now. Maybe they were buying ice cream, or stopping at Shahr-e-Naw Park, so that Najama could run and play. The thought of that made her smile.

Yazmina's mind drifted into the world of the sleep, where loved ones long gone reappear as if they'd been among the living all along. In her dream, she and Layla were at their home in the mountains of Nuristan, where they had lived before their parents died. The small wooden house looked the same, but somehow different. Their mother, draped in bright, shiny beads, was at the stone hearth in the middle of the room in which all four of them had always eaten and slept, tending to the bread she had made from the wheat of her field. Her father, with his thick arms and proud eyes, was filling a tray with yogurt and cheese from his flocks. And, in the way that many dreams go, everyone else was present as well. Sunny, Jack, Halajan, Rashif, and Ahmet; all of them were gathered around the low, wide table, as Yazmina cradled a newborn in her arms. To welcome the child, a goat—or was it two?—had been sacrificed, the lifeless, blood-soaked pile of hide and bones still in plain view from the window facing the east, the one built to face the sunrise. If it were two goats, the bundle in Yazmina's arms would have been a boy. If only one, a girl.

In her dream, everyone was gathering closer as Yazmina held the baby to her breast. *Jalah . . . Sabir . . . Anwaar . . .* they began to chant, reciting from the list of her ancestors' names. Yazmina waited for the familiar tug at her nipple, knowing how tradition stated that the name being mentioned as the child first begins to feed would become the one he or she will carry throughout their life. *Rashad . . . Sulayman . . . Kawthar . . .*

Suddenly, the rhythm of her extended family's voices was interrupted by a racket so loud it could have wakened each and every dead relative on that list. Was this still a dream? She stirred and remained on the *toshak* with closed eyes, unsure of whether she wanted to wake or not. It wasn't long before her body made the decision for her, rousing slowly, limb by limb, as if she were a marionette being unpacked from a box. But as her consciousness rose, so did an awareness that the clamor hadn't stopped. Some unthinking person downstairs was not using their headset, again. Shouting, shooting, things breaking. A ridiculous Bollywood movie, no doubt. Do they not know they are disturbing those around them? And why hasn't Bashir Hadi told them to turn the volume down? It was not like him, to allow something like this to go on. She struggled to bring herself fully upright. She had better get downstairs fast or they'd have some very unhappy customers. The last time this had happened, a table of French contractors had stood and walked out without even paying.

She was halfway down the stairs when she saw the two women who came in every week from the Italian embassy peeking out from behind the closet door as if they were playing hide-and-seek. She smiled, but their faces remained frozen with an expression she couldn't read. The annoying racket had stopped, and now the coffeehouse seemed eerily silent. Then she noticed the overturned table. An Australian aid worker she recognized was standing behind it, facing toward her, but when she reached up to wave hello he suddenly dropped to his knees. As he did, another regular went flying across the room behind him, as if in slow motion, landing on his belly atop a pile of shattering dishes that came sliding from the tray he had tripped on. Then the vile smell of sulfur hit the inside of her nose, filling her with a queasiness that left her weak in the knees.

"Yazmina!"

At the sound of Bashir Hadi's voice, everything suddenly became horridly clear. Yazmina squeezed her eyes shut and ducked, one hand shielding her head, and the other her belly. The unmistakable clatter of gunfire bounced off the coffeehouse walls with a sickening echo. And then the only sound remaining was the ringing in her ears.

She jerked upright, her heart pounding its way right out of her chest, her eyes frantically searching the room for her family. But she did not see Ahmet or Najama or Halajan anywhere. What she did see was a man in black, lying crumpled on his side in front of the counter, an assault rifle cradled in his motionless arms. She remained frozen on the stairs, the shock of the brutal scene before her rendering her powerless.

"Yazmina! Over here!" It was the sound of Bashir Hadi's voice that unlocked her frozen limbs. He was behind the counter, dazed and pale on the floor, a red stain spreading rapidly across the bottom of his pants. Another gun lay abandoned at his side.

"You are hurt!" A driving pulse pounded in her ears as she stared down at the blood streaming from his leg. She called to the Italian women for help. "Please, you need to try to stop the bleeding." Yazmina ripped off her head scarf and handed it to them. "I must find my baby."

"You can't go out there!" one of them called to her as she turned to the door. "What if there are more of them?"

"I saw only the one," she heard Bashir Hadi's voice behind her.

"Call for help!" Yazmina cried out. "People are hurt!" An American journalist Yazmina recognized stood wide-eyed at the door, staring down at the dead gunman on the floor. Sounds of movement—plastic chairs scraping across the cement, people calling out for one another—were coming from outside. Yazmina ran back and pressed the phone from the counter into Bashir Hadi's hand, and rushed out the door.

"Najama! Halajan! Ahmet!" she screamed, their names echoing off the corners of the courtyard, blending with the soft whimpering and cries for help rising up from the pavement at her feet. "Najama!" she shouted. "Where are you, my child?" She desperately scanned the tables for her daughter's purple ribbons or her mother-in-law's big green chador, her husband's square shoulders and his slicked-back hair. Her family was nowhere in sight. They were safe, *inshallah*. Only then did she allow her eyes to open to the carnage around her, and what she saw made her heart break for all the world and everyone in it.

25

"No, not like that. Like this." Even through the thick gloves, the touch of Sky's fingers on top of her own made Kat tingle. It was as though a charge ran between them, like when you reach for a doorknob after walking across a carpet. He had to have noticed. But with his head so focused on the work to be done in the vineyard, it was hard to tell. She allowed his hands to guide hers down the thickening stems, sending the fresh leaves fluttering to a pile at their feet. "You got it?"

"I do," she said, struggling not to laugh at his seriousness. What she really wanted to do was grab his curls and plant a big one right on those juicy lips. But he was gone in a flash, off toward the spot three rows over where Layla was wrestling with her own vines.

It all seemed kind of stupid to her, throwing away perfectly healthy leaves. But Sky had carefully explained to both of them how important it was to make way for the sunlight to reach the grapes, to allow the fruit to ripen fully and evenly. Besides, watching the way he worked with the vines was something she could do all day. It was as if they were his babies, the way he cared for them so tenderly.

She had been up before dawn this morning, leaving him behind in the barn to sneak back under the covers on the living room couch before anyone could see her. They hadn't been caught, so far. It didn't seem as if anyone had really noticed, not yet, which was a good thing. Who knows what Sunny would think? She'd probably throw a fit about Layla being around that kind of thing. Besides, it really wasn't anybody's business, anyway.

Kat worked her way down her own row of vines, her strokes growing quicker and surer, her mind calmed by the repetitive nature of the task, her skin turning warm and brown under the rising sun. "You're a natural. You've got the touch." She felt Sky's breath on the back of her neck and smiled.

"You don't know that about me already?" she answered as she turned around to face him. Sky placed his hands on her hips and pulled her against him. "Wait." She held up a hand to his chest. Across the vines, Kat could see Layla unfurling her cotton shawl onto the dirt. The girl stood at an angle toward the eastern sky and set her feet squarely below her as she raised both hands to her shoulders. Then she placed her arms across her chest, her right wrist over the left, and stood with her eyes focused straight ahead, mouthing words only she could hear.

Kat rolled her eyes. "There she goes again. I swear, who needs a watch when Layla's around?"

Sky stepped back a little. "What's it to you?"

Kat shrugged. "She's in America. Why is she even bothering?"

"And America's a free country. If she chooses to take a break to speak to her God five times a day, that's her right. Who knows?" he shrugged. "Maybe she likes it."

"Yeah, right," Kat snorted. "Just like she must enjoy wearing that blanket around her head in the middle of summer."

Sky narrowed his eyes at her. "What's with you today, anyway?"

"Nothing's with me today. I just think it's kind of like brain-washing." She jerked her head in Layla's direction.

"So what if she's proud of who she is, and where she came from. It's more than I can say for some people."

"What's that supposed to mean?"

"It means just what I said."

They stood in silence for a minute watching Layla as she bowed down to touch her knees, her back as flat as the top of a table. She rose and then dropped down to a kneel, her forehead and nose coming to rest on the ground below.

"Ridiculous."

"Whatever, Kat. I think it's kind of cool."

"Whatever."

Sky turned his back on her and focused his attention on the vines. She continued to work in silence by his side. The sunlight hit the grapes in dappled patches as the sacrificed leaves sailed silently to the ground with the touch of their hands. What had happened to a perfectly good morning? She knew she probably shouldn't get so worked up about this stuff, but how could she help it, with Sunny and Layla throwing all that Afghanistan shit in her face every day? It wasn't good for her, being here, on this island. What she needed to do was to forget, and this wasn't exactly turning out to be the best place to do that.

But seriously? The house on Twimbly was beginning to feel more like home than any place had since her mother died. And how could she not see Sky every day?

"Did you used to pray?" It was Sky who spoke first.

Kat nodded.

"So why did you stop?"

"I stopped when my mother died."

"Me, I like to believe in a little bit of everything," Sky said after a beat. "Sort of like those bumper stickers you see around the island that spell out *coexist* with all the different symbols, like the crescent moon and Jewish star and cross?"

"Hmm. That must be nice for you." Kat couldn't stop the cynicism from creeping back into her voice.

"You don't believe in anything?"

"I believe that you're born, you live, then you die. And sometimes things suck a little in between, and sometimes they don't."

Sky's arms fell to his sides. "That's kind of random. And sad."

"It's just what I think." Kat pulled at the leaves with a new intensity.

"You've got some anger issues, girl."

"I'm not angry!" she insisted, knowing he was right.

"Okay." He held out his palms in a halting gesture. "You're not angry. Whatever you say."

"Don't act that way with me," she heard herself snap.

"Well then don't act that way with me, with us," he said, pointing to Layla across the vines.

"What way?"

"C'mon, Kat. You know what I mean. You can be all fine one minute, and then it's like a switch goes off, and you're another person."

"That's not true!" she protested.

"It is true, and you know it."

"You don't understand anything." She turned away from him.

"Whatever," he said to her back. "Maybe I don't understand. And maybe you don't either. But you need to at least try to deal with whatever is going on in your head, cause you're the only one who can fix what's broken in there." He knocked at the top of her head with a light rap of the knuckles, and moved on to the next row.

As if what was broken could ever be fixed. How she hated herself for arguing with Sky. But sometimes her mouth seemed to have a mind of its own, spitting out words she didn't really mean and things she didn't really feel. She ran to catch up with him, already five vines ahead and nearly finished with the row. He continued to pull at the stems, even as she ran her fingertips down the sides of his bare arms. "Sky-guy," she whispered into the back of his ear. "Sky-pie."

"Cut it out, Kat." He shrugged off her hands with a heave of his shoulders.

She plucked a greenish-purple grape from its stem, stuck it between her front teeth, and pushed her way between his body and the vines, smiling. Now Sky laughed, and bent to take the fruit from between her lips. His tongue had just begun a little dance with hers when Kat heard a gasp. Sky stiffened and stepped back, and from over his shoulder Kat saw Layla watching them, her hand covering her mouth and her eyes as round as pennies. "Stop looking at me like that!" Kat yelled over the vines. "You're giving me the creeps."

"Whoa. Chill, Kat." Sky brushed the hair out of his face, his eyes on Layla as she scooped up her shawl and began to run toward the house.

"I mean it," Kat continued, an unwelcome rage showing its teeth. "I'm so sick of feeling like I'm being judged all the time!"

"Well you're the one always trying to be careful, reminding me not to say or do the wrong thing around her, you know."

"Yeah? Well I'm sick of that too. Why are her stupid ways more important than our ways?" Her eyes struggled to hold back the tears she wanted no one to see.

"Jesus, Kat, get a grip, will you?" He threw his gloves down onto the dirt and took off after Layla.

Kat remained behind among the piles of rejected leaves, feeling confused, ashamed and angry all at the same time, holding fast to the one thing she knew to be true and good—the earthy taste of Sky's kiss as it disappeared into her own lips.

26

"And what did we do today, little one?"

"Magic city!"

"That's right. We went to the magic city. And the school with the cars. What is that?"

"Special secret."

"That's right. It is our special secret."

Halajan laughed to herself as they walked together toward Qala-e-Fatullah road. Such a clever girl. Just like her own daughter Aisha, now a big-shot professor at the German university. She had high hopes for this one as well.

"Poppy!" Najama held out her arms as the shaggy beast came tearing down the street toward them.

"Damn dog, on the loose again," Halajan muttered as she watched Poppy run right past them, her pointy ears pinned back flat against her head and her tail invisible between her legs. Strange, she thought as she turned back to continue toward home.

It wasn't until they made the last left onto their street that she noticed something was truly not right. Things were far too quiet for a Thursday afternoon. Where was everybody? A red bicycle lay on its side, abandoned in the hot dusty road, next to a lone goat rooting greedily through a pile of rotting garbage. She caught sight of two women in blue burqas huddled behind a parked car, and her eyes went straight to the skies in search of trouble. But she could hear no planes, see no flames, smell no smoke. Halajan tightened her grip on Najama's hand and quickened her pace. They had just hurried past the shuttered bread shop when she felt an urgent tug on the back of her chador.

"Please, you must not!" Halajan turned to find herself face to face with Fattanah. The baker's eyes flashed out a grim warning. "We have heard shooting." Fattanah placed her hand on Halajan's chest, as if that would be enough to keep her away from what she was now beginning to fear might be a situation that could change the lives of her family forever. The wailing of sirens rose in the distance. "Watch the baby," she said as she thrust the girl into Fattanah's arms and hurried toward home, her spindly legs carrying her with the speed of a horse.

The sirens seemed to be chasing her as she neared the coffee-house gate. A quick look into the guardhouse showed that it stood empty, Daoud's gun leaning idly against the back wall, the only motion coming from the small TV screen, where a man was trying to win a million dollars. The first real movement she saw was a customer stumbling out onto the street, dazed and dusty, his pants torn at the knees. "My family!" Halajan screamed at the man. "Where is my family?"

"You don't want to go in there," the man said in an eerily quiet voice as he fumbled for his phone.

Suddenly a parade of armed men in uniform was racing past them, through the gate and into the courtyard, disappearing through the coffeehouse door. Halajan hesitated only briefly, until it seemed clear there was to be no more shooting. Then she ran in behind them.

The sight before her eyes stopped her dead in her tracks. The patio was a bloody battle zone, the ground littered with bodies, some moving, others not. Daoud's motionless body was sprawled across the path as if he had been caught in midair. A man she didn't know lay facedown on the pebbles, his arms covering his head, a pool of urine seeping out from under one leg. One woman cradled the head of another in her lap, rocking back and forth as she offered a stream of quiet, comforting words. Like animals at the slaughter, Halajan thought as she heard the sound of wailing, deep and desperate. Never before had she seen such brutality. It was as if the coffeehouse itself were bleeding. And in the middle of it all stood a trembling witness—Najama's little peahen, her grey beak suspended in a silent scream.

"Halajan!" Yazmina screamed out from the coffeehouse door, her arms wrapped around her rounded body. "Where is my baby? Where is Najama?" The old woman picked her way across the wreckage, the broken glass and shards of pottery, the rose petals smashed like the skin of a peach, the spilled coffee pooling in warm little puddles, the chairs and tables lying abandoned on their sides.

"She is safe. But Ahmet? Where is Ahmet?" she cried, the name like a sharp stone in her narrowing throat as she whirled around in search of her son.

Yazmina shook her head. "I do not see him. Bashir Hadi is injured, but I think he will be all right."

Halajan ran her wrinkled hands slowly down over her face and breathed in deeply. "Then it is us who must help these people, Yazmina." She squared her shoulders and turned to assess the situation around them. Most seemed to be more stunned than injured, and to those Halajan pleaded for help with others in need, placing tablecloths over torsos shivering in the summer heat and tearing strips of napkins to be tied around torn limbs to hold back the bleeding. She sent Yazmina inside for water and towels. Around her the desperate symphony of pings and rings of those checking on their loved ones rang out as word of the attack spread rapidly throughout the city.

Then she turned her attention to the far end of the patio, where an overturned wooden bench lay on the pavement, two legs in jeans and a small pair of bloody sneakers sticking out from behind it. She knew who it was right away. Zara's eyes were open, searching Halajan's face for answers.

"It is all right, little one. Shhh, don't try to talk." She bent down next to the girl and took her cold hand in her own. A river of red flowed from beneath Zara's torso as the color drained from her face.

"*Khoda rahem kona*," Yazmina gasped at the sight of the girl. May God have mercy.

Halajan took the towels from her hands and placed them gently against Zara's side. "She needs help, fast. She is leaving us quickly."

"But what can we do? It will be forever until the ambulances arrive." Beads of sweat ran down Yazmina's face, which was looking as pale as that of the girl on the ground below.

Halajan ordered her back inside. "Go get me my scissors. And more towels." She lowered herself down onto her knees and brushed the hair out of Zara's eyes with her hand. The girl was awake, her eyes filled with pain. "It is all right, young one. Be strong. We must all be strong." She turned her face toward the sky. "Where is my son?" she cried out desperately, her voice ringing across the patio.

Two arms embraced her from behind. "Ahmet! You are here!"

"I've just arrived." Ahmet nodded toward the coffeehouse. His chest heaved with exhaustion, his face looking as if it had aged ten years in ten minutes. "*Shokr-e-khoda*, I thank God that my family has been spared. Bashir Hadi is injured, inside." Halajan gasped. "I think he will be all right, Mother. It is a wound on his leg. It was he who killed the gunman."

Halajan sat frozen, holding her son's shaking hands in hers. This madness, this evil, how men can use the veil of religion to wage such barbarity, was always beyond her understanding. And now they had dared to come to her door. *Her* home! *Her* family! And then they would proudly claim their responsibility for the attack, as if they had done something noble and righteous. It made an anger so fierce rise inside her that she could feel it pounding from head to toe. How can our people stand for this? Sometimes it seemed to her as if the whole world was mad, some joke made up by an insane puppet master for his own demented entertainment.

"We must help this poor child." The girl's body was limp, her blood smeared across Halajan's lap.

"She must go to the hospital!" Yazmina yelled as she made her way across the devastation.

"But I cannot leave the coffeehouse. We must tend to all these people, I must watch out for Bashir Hadi." Ahmet turned toward the carnage on the patio with tears in his eyes.

"Ahmet!" his mother suddenly barked. "Pick up the girl and bring her out back. To the alley."

"But why?"

"Don't ask. Just do!"

A dazed Ahmet looked at his mother, and then at his wife, then bent down to lift the moaning Zara into his arms and followed the two of them through the coffeehouse, out to the alley where the old Mercedes stood idle. Halajan opened the back door, and ordered Ahmet to lay the girl down across the seat.

"Mother, I told you I cannot leave now."

"Get in." She nodded at Yazmina and pointed to the back where Zara lay.

"But . . ."

"Get in!" Then Halajan opened the driver's side door and inserted herself firmly behind the wheel. With a flick of the wrist she turned the key sitting in the ignition, and the motor began to purr. Ahmet stepped back, his jaw dropping down to his chest. Halajan slammed the door. "We're going to the hospital."

"Yes, they are all fine. Ahmet and Rashif are at the coffeehouse now, doing all that must be done." Yazmina paced back and forth across the waiting-room floor, her phone glued to her ear. Halajan had left her there at the hospital to return, alone, in the car, to gather up Najama and carry her home. On the other end of the line Sunny's friend Candace was pressing for details. Candace had been the first to call, the news traveling straight to her Los Angeles hotel room from her people in Kabul within minutes of the massacre. At first Yazmina had no desire to talk, but now the words seemed to pour out like the tears she had yet to cry.

"I am at the hospital, waiting for a friend to get out of surgery," she told Candace. "She is a girl we have met. I'm trying to track down her family."

"Will she be all right?"

"I don't know. Oh, Candace, there was so much blood. I hope so. I hope she will be strong. The poor thing thinks she is the reason for the attack."

"What do you mean?"

Yazmina shared with Candace what had happened in the car. She had been in the back seat with Zara as Halajan jerked her way through the streets of the city, her bony hands gripping the wheel as if it were the reins to a wild horse. The girl cried out with every pothole they hit. Yazmina did her best to comfort her, keeping up a stream of talk that she hoped would mask her growing concern.

"Stay strong, little one. You will be fine. We are almost at the hospital."

Zara yelped as Halajan swerved sharply around a corner.

"Do not think of what you saw," Yazmina told her, as she tried, herself, to erase the horrifying picture of the blood-soaked courtyard from her mind.

"Omar?" Zara struggled to sit up, her eyes wide.

"No, I did not see Omar."

The girl slumped back onto the seat. "I should die. I hope I die." Zara closed her eyes and clenched her teeth.

"You mustn't say that! We are almost there."

"But it is my fault."

"Hush, young one. Calm yourself." Yazmina brushed the hair from Zara's forehead with her hand.

"He is punishing me for loving someone else."

Yazmina squeezed her hand, desperate for the girl to hold on to her senses.

"It is my fault. He did this because of me. I heard his threats. I saw his man."

"Whose man? What nonsense are you saying?"

"*Haji* Faheem. The man I am to marry."

"He is no *haji*, to do something like this," growled Halajan from the front seat.

Yazmina felt a sorrowful ache building inside. Had she not been careful enough before when listening to this girl's words? Had she and Ahmet not been forceful enough with their advice, and their warnings?

"I should die. And I would rather die than marry this man."

Now, telling the story to Candace, Yazmina felt even more anguish. "The poor girl," she said quietly into the phone.

There was a long silence on the other end. Yazmina was about to hang up, thinking they had been disconnected, when she heard Candace say, "Do you think it's true? That this man was the one responsible for all this?"

"It is possible. I know the girl was terribly frightened of him, and she tells me he has a very bad reputation. He has made some threats to her before."

"Well, I'm going to look into it. I need to make some calls. And in the meantime, *inshallah*, this girl lives, and if she does, the best way to help her is to make sure she stays in the hospital as long as possible. I know men like this. I've seen what they can do. The hospital is the safest place for her to be right now."

Yazmina poked her head out into the hallway, where a nurse was pushing an empty wheelchair piled high with sheets.

"Do you know this man's name?" she heard Candace ask through the phone.

"He is Faheem. The principal of the girls' school where her sister goes. A cousin of General Hakim."

"Shit. That's not good. I'll bet this guy's just an old *mujahid* with zero education, riding on his warlord cousin's coattails. But seriously, Yaz, be careful of this one. I'm sure he's the kind who thinks he can buy whatever he wants. You must keep this girl in the hospital, and whatever you do, keep Faheem out. I'm going to need a little time to figure this out."

"But what will you do?"

"I'm not sure, but you can bet I'll do something. Just hang tight, and don't let her out of there, no matter what."

Yazmina pictured Zara's face as she was wheeled away into the room for surgery. Her skin was so white, her breath so weak, that Yazmina was worried she might never see the girl again. She lowered herself down onto a lumpy, spring-less couch, closed her eyes, and offered a silent prayer for the girl's survival.

27

"But why didn't anyone tell me?" Sunny slammed her cup down angrily on the kitchen table.

"Whoa there, lady. Calm yourself. I told you, everyone is okay." Candace held out her own empty cup for a refill, as if this were a restaurant. She had been there less than an hour and already she was pissing Sunny off.

The knock on the door had taken Sunny by complete surprise. Layla and Kat were out, seeming—at least for the moment—to be getting along well enough to head into town together in search of donuts. And she supposed Sky was in the vineyard with Joe. There stood Candace with her flowing blond hair, now a shade less brassy than before, and her tight pre-distressed jeans. Sunny had been thrilled to see her old friend but could tell right away, just from the way she held their hug for a little too long, that something was wrong.

The news of the attack had stunned her. It felt as though her entire world had been turned upside down and shaken like a snow globe. Her legs seemed to melt beneath her, her head began to swirl, and Candace had to pull up a chair for fear she'd topple over. It couldn't be possible that something this horrific had happened at the coffeehouse. But, of course, it was. And now nothing would ever be the same.

Shortly after, over coffee, the shock had turned to anger, with the unfortunate Candace serving as her punching bag. "But still, why did they call you, and not me?" Sunny regretted the whiny words the minute they left her mouth.

"Please, Sunny. Your internet was probably out, as usual, and you know how bad your cell service is. And besides, they didn't call me. *I* called *them*, the minute I heard about the attack. I was lucky enough to reach Yaz at the hospital. And I busted my ass to get up here from LA as quickly as I did, thank you very much, before you and Layla had the chance to hear about it anywhere else."

"Wait, Yaz is in the hospital? I thought you said everyone was okay."

"They are okay. She's there with the girl that was injured. But she and the baby are fine."

"Thank God Najama wasn't hurt."

"Not Najama. I was talking about the other one. It can't be long now. Just a few months, right?"

Another thing Candace knew before she did. Sunny was all too aware, from the last time Yazmina was pregnant, how Afghan women hid their condition from the outside world as long as possible. But still, she wasn't exactly the outside world, at least not in her opinion. She wondered if Layla knew.

"Anyway, this girl?" Candace continued, glossing over Sunny's hurt and surprise. "She claims to know who was behind the attack. She seems to think she was the cause."

"Are you shitting me? All this was over a girl?"

"So she says. And from the sound of things, I do think it's possible. This girl is terrified, thinks her whole family is in danger. For now I've called in some favors. We've got people guarding her room day and night."

Sunny knew that, with Candace's connections, everything that could be done was being done. She wasn't the ex-wife of a US ambassador for nothing. But still. "Please tell me they're going to be okay."

"The family is fine, Sunny. Bashir Hadi's wounds are relatively minor. I don't know about the girl, though. She doesn't seem to have much of a will to live."

"This was really all about her? It just doesn't make any sense." Sunny rubbed her face with her hands.

"Yeah, I know. I also know how these things go down. Apparently the girl's family had agreed, sort of, to a marriage with him. But it turns out he's one of the bad guys, a real bully, and one with connections to a whole lot of power. Now the family feels terrible, with all that's happened. They know there's no way they can let their daughter marry him now, but they're also smart enough to know that the minute that girl comes out of that hospital, her life is over, one way or another. They're worried she'll jump off a bridge with rocks in her pockets or something equally as horrible. You've heard it all before."

Sunny's anger loomed even larger. The number of lives lost, the number of innocent people scarred and ruined by this way of thinking, was something she'd never understand as long as she lived. "So now what?"

"Not sure. All I know is that if she does make it, she's right about all of them being in danger. That is definite. Guys like him will never let a thing like this go. It won't be over until it's over."

Sunny knew Candace was right, and her worry for her friends made her insides start to churn like a boiling stew. "So why hasn't Yaz called me?"

"Give her a chance, Sunny. This all just happened. Besides, you remember how Afghans feel about sharing bad news. And I know she was worried about how Layla would take it. I suggested it might be better for me to tell her in person, so that you can blame me for. We'll talk to her together when she gets back, okay?"

Sunny let her head drop into her hands, and silently wished she could turn back the clock to yesterday.

"Remember, Sunny, their lives are going to be crazy for a while. Yaz says she'll be spending time at the hospital with the girl, and Ahmet will be dealing with the cleanup, the police investigation, helping Bashir Hadi and his family while he heals, a whole mess of things. Not to mention that they'll have to figure out what's next."

Sunny lifted her head and looked at her friend. "What do you mean figure out what's next?"

"The coffeehouse, Sunny. It's over."

"Oh, please. Don't be ridiculous, Candace. It can't be over. All they have to do is clean it up, slap on some paint, hire some new guards. I'll go help! I can make this happen."

Candace took Sunny's two hands in her own. "You just don't get it, do you? The game has changed over there. To run a business like that, one that's dependent on foreigners, it's just too risky. Everyone is a target, Sunny. It may have been a lone wolf attack this time, but it won't be the next. And really, if you were Yaz or Ahmet or Halajan, would you want to spend your days haunted by the memories of that day? Imagine."

"But, my coffeehouse . . ."

"It's over, Sunny. The coffeehouse is over. And it wasn't even yours anymore."

Sunny winced at the sting of Candace's words. "But Layla's going to want to go home. I know it. I'll have to take her. I'll check for flights—"

"Just stop, Sunny. Layla will be fine. She's stronger than you think. You know what that girl has been through already in her life. The best place for Layla right now is here with you."

And me, Sunny thought. Where is the best place for me?

Candace decided to remain with them on the island for the rest of the week. As she had predicted, Layla reacted to the news of the attack with remarkable strength. There were tears all around, but as soon as she was assured that her family was safe and that Bashir Hadi was going to be fine, and that a Skype session with her sister was scheduled for later that evening, internet gods permitting, she seemed to calm down a little.

Sunny worried that perhaps the girl hadn't fully processed what she'd been told—which had not included all the horrifying details Sunny had heard—but Candace disagreed. "You remember what it's like over there. Things happen, and life goes on. These people are strong." And Sunny did remember. But personally, she didn't think she could find it in herself to feel that way. At least not yet.

Candace kept her busy during the rest of her visit. There were long walks on the beach and even longer lunches in town, visits to galleries and farmers' markets, and, Candace being Candace, lots of shopping. Sunny tried her best to enjoy their time together—she had almost forgotten what it felt like to have a girlfriend to hang out with. And Candace had changed, seeming to have lost that feeling of entitlement she used to carry around with her like a treasured Chanel bag. But just when Sunny would start to lose herself in gossip and conversation, visions of the devastation in the coffeehouse courtyard would come flooding into her brain, filling her head with feelings of guilt and uselessness that derailed any attempt at diversion. And it didn't help that Candace was constantly on her phone, pulling all those distant strings that were needed to put a plan in place to help the injured girl in Kabul.

"Trust me, you're doing a lot of good yourself, Sunny," Candace assured her early one morning as they strolled barefoot along the deserted shoreline. "Knowing that Layla is safe and happy over here must be a huge relief for Yazmina right now."

Sunny tossed a piece of driftwood across the water for Bear. "I guess. She does seem to be feeling more and more at home, right?"

"Uh-huh," Candace answered, her latent southern accent drawing out the two syllables into one long note.

"And what's that supposed to mean?" Sunny stopped and watched as the dog paddled back with the stick clenched in his jaws.

"Please, don't tell me you haven't noticed how she looks at that boy."

"You mean Sky? No way!"

"Jeez, Sunny. Has it been so long for you that you don't even recognize a crush when you see one?"

"Ouch."

"Seriously, she's like a colt itching to escape the barn."

"Are you sure? Maybe you're just reading your own cougar desires into this."

Candace swatted at Sunny with the jeweled sandal in her hand. "Not my type, anymore. Just mark my words. There's some heartbreak ahead for that one."

Sunny wanted to kick herself. She threw the stick again, this time with all her might. How could she have not seen this happening? Poor thing. She'd have to find a way to nip this in the bud, or Yaz, and most definitely Ahmet, would never speak to her again.

"It'll work out somehow. And she does seem happy here." Candace reached for the stick Bear had dropped at her feet and threw it back in the water. "And you know?" Sunny followed her friend's gaze across the piney strip of land that jutted out from behind them and sloped gracefully into the Sound. "Why shouldn't she be? I've gotta say, it really doesn't seem like such a bad place to live."

"That's because you don't live here." Sunny bent to pick a pebble from between her toes.

"So tell me, what's so wrong with the island, anyway?"

Sunny hesitated for a moment. "Well, for one thing, it's so hard to get off of."

"So don't." Candace shrugged. "Civilization is overrated."

"Easy for you to say. I haven't seen you sit still this long for like, well, ever."

Candace tilted her head skyward as a seaplane buzzed overhead. "I don't know, it's kind of growing on me. You'd better watch out, or the next thing you know I'll be settling in as your roomie." She jogged ahead a little to try to get Bear to run. "We'll wear flowy clothes and no bras, and make jam, and let our hair get long and grey!" she called back to Sunny. "You could paint, and on Saturdays I'll go hang out with those witches down in Chittleham."

"In a pig's eye!" Sunny struggled to catch up with her.

Candace stopped and turned around. "What, you don't think this island is big enough for the both of us?"

Sunny just laughed. She was panting as she reached her friend's side, stopping with her hands on her hips and her eyes turned toward the blue horizon as the water lapped gently at her toes. Not so deep inside, she kind of wished Candace wouldn't leave. "Do you think I should put him out there?"

Candace raised her eyebrows at the question that seemed to come out of nowhere. "What? Who?"

"Jack. His ashes. Either here, or in the vineyard. Or maybe both. I really should let him loose from that box in the linen closet. I just haven't been able to bring myself to do it. Is that weird?"

Candace shrugged her shoulders. "Not so weird. I still have my cocker spaniel's ashes, and he died when I was eighteen. You'll know when it's time to let him go." She hooked her arm through Sunny's and together they walked slowly along the shore, their feet becoming entombed by pebbles with each ebbing of the tide. "Well look at that." Candace stopped and pointed toward the water. Just above the surface of the Sound, tiny shimmers of silver were slicing through the air, popping up from below as if shot from a cannon, then returning with a swan dive back into the deep. As they watched, the air became thick with the shiny creatures, as if a frenzied mirrored curtain was being dropped from the sky.

"Wow. Beautiful." Sunny shaded her eyes with one hand. "I've never seen anything like that." To Sunny, it looked like magic—an optical illusion created just for her. It was a vision she wanted to remember forever. "Candace," she asked after a moment, "why do you think fish jump?"

Out of the corner of her eye she could see Candace shrug her shoulders. "Because they can?"

Sunny took in a deep breath of the lavender and anise that was heavy in the air. As simple as a fish, she thought. That's how life should be. Jumping cause you can. If only.

28

Ahmet sat with his forearms resting on the counter, his hands folded together, his eyes pointed straight ahead yet not focused on a thing. The ticking of the clock seemed as loud as a pounding hammer, making it even harder to think than it already was. Outside, where the courtyard should have been filled with the sounds of the vendors shouting out their morning greetings to one another as they set up for the Friday market, all was quiet. There would be no more Friday market at the coffeehouse, not now. And there would be no more coffeehouse, not ever. His own stupidity had taken care of that.

If only he had been more forceful with his opinion about the foolishness of those two. If only he had been stronger with Omar, and had shown more firmness in his warnings to Yazmina about her dealings with that silly girl. He had allowed himself to become distracted by his meetings and the thoughts that came from all that talk, and now they were paying the price.

Today he would make a special prayer to Allah, a promise of renewed dedication to his faith and to the traditions of his people.

Ahmet could feel his nostrils burn from the smell of ammonia that cloaked the room, left behind from the endless hours of scrubbing it had taken to wipe away the physical signs of the attack. How he missed the aromas of Bashir Hadi's burgers, and the strong scent of the dark coffee that would come from the copper machine, whose shiny surface, he could now see, was beginning to cloud from neglect.

As he ran his fingers lightly over a small nick left in the counter by one of the gunman's bullets, the fear that had been stabbing at him ever since the attack suddenly rushed back in full force. His heart began to pummel furiously at his chest. It could have been his wife now lying there in that hospital bed, or even worse. He pictured Yazmina upstairs, where he had left her to sleep. Had Bashir Hadi not been able to put a stop to the madness, Ahmet might have never had the chance to hold her in his arms again, or to welcome their unborn son into the world. How close he had come to losing everything he loved, everything that mattered in his world. I told him to leave her alone, he thought as he replayed the conversations with Omar in his head. I told him that this is not the way our country works, that this is not the way things are done in our culture. If they had simply obeyed the rules, if they had honored the traditions, none of this would have ever happened. Of course, perhaps, as the authorities suggested, it wasn't because of Omar and the girl that the coffeehouse had been targeted. The Taliban had claimed responsibility for the attack and the two who had died, just as they claimed responsibility for practically every incident involving foreigners in Kabul. But it could very well be true. Either way, Ahmet had failed to prevent it. He blamed himself.

The stack of empty coffee cups rattled as he banged his fist down onto the counter. Behind him came the sound of a throat being cleared. He turned to see Yazmina standing at the bottom of the staircase, one hand on the banister, the other resting on her bulging belly, now clearly visible beneath the big lightweight chador she wore over her clothes.

"Good morning, my husband."

"Good morning to you as well." He turned back around on the stool, the clock's relentless pulse marking the silence between them.

"What are you doing?" she asked in a gentle voice.

"Thinking."

Yazmina came and sat on the stool beside him and took his hand in hers. "Well, while you are thinking, perhaps you can think about driving me to the hospital on your way to the mosque today?"

Ahmet shook his head. "You were just at the hospital yesterday. I do not think it is necessary for you to go there again today."

"But it is! Zara needs me." She gave his hand a little squeeze, as if that would be enough to get him on her side. But Ahmet would have none of it.

"Isn't her family there to watch over her?" he asked, his eyes fixed on the counter below.

"Yes, but she is still in a very bad condition. And she remains in grave danger."

"What," he responded in a voice full of scorn, "and it is you who will protect her from Faheem? I thought it was your friend Candace who was in charge, who had snapped her manicured fingers for a private room and a guard to appear at the hospital door."

Yazmina withdrew her hand from his. "Yes, there is a guard there. But I still have a desire, a responsibility to help."

"You must stay out of their business!" Ahmet turned to face his wife. "Being there is what brought us this trouble in the first place. We have no room for more trouble."

Yazmina leaned away from him and straightened her back. "There is no need to shout. I am right here beside you."

"And that is where you will stay." Ahmet nodded firmly and crossed his arms in front of his chest. "There will be no more going back and forth to the hospital. You must stay home to tend to your duties as a good Islamic wife and mother."

Yazmina's green eyes narrowed into two angry dashes. "I *am* a good wife and mother," she hissed, the indignation from his words causing the color to rise in her cheeks, "and also a good follower of Islam, one who cares about the fate of others, who believes in doing service for humanity. And I thought you were as well." She turned her face to the ceiling and shook her head.

Ahmet slammed his two hands down on the counter. "I care about my family, not about some ridiculous girl who refuses to obey the rules."

"You and your rules," Yazmina shot back. "I ask you, where is it written that a man or woman cannot marry the one they love? We are here together, are we not?" she asked, her voice now soft and beseeching.

Ahmet turned away from her pleading eyes. "She should just run away. The family should take her and go back to where they are from."

"But it is not her fault!" Yazmina grabbed his forearm with her hand, forcing his attention back upon her. "It's Faheem who is responsible for all this." She swept an arm across the empty room. "And you and I both know that running away will never work. He will find her no matter where she goes." Yazmina let him go and began to yank at the scarf around her neck. "Now please, stop with all this nonsense, and let's get going."

Ahmet didn't budge. "I told you that you are not to go to the hospital anymore."

"Then I will take the bus," she said, struggling to lift herself off of the stool.

"Or perhaps you should ask my mother to drive you," he said with a snort.

"Well perhaps I should. At least she has the decency to act on her beliefs."

Ahmet was tempted to run after his wife as she stormed out the coffeehouse door. But an unseen force kept him frozen in place, his body and mind both stuck in a pit of confusion. How was it that he had lost control of his family, his wife ignoring his demands, his mother bringing them such shame with her flouting of convention? And with the flash of a rifle, it seemed as though he had been robbed of control over their futures as well. How would he provide for them, and keep them safe from whatever dangers might come from a world so unsettled and unsure? He crossed his arms on the top of the wooden counter and lowered his head down to rest, exhausted by his own thoughts, and by the string of sleepless nights he'd endured ever since the attack. He quickly drifted off into a world no more easeful than the one he left, and it wasn't until he heard the muezzin's call that he woke.

29

Bear groaned as Sunny flopped over onto her back and gave him a shove toward his side of the mattress. The room was dark and chilly. She pulled the covers up to her chin and stared at the ceiling. She didn't even want to know what time it was, how many hours she'd been lying awake. She was still a bit reluctant to shut her eyes, worried that the images of the devastation on the coffeehouse patio that had plagued her all week would return. For nights, all she had dreamed about were the blood-spattered pebbles, the broken furniture, the nicks from the bullets freckling the walls and doors, the customers injured and scared. Not one of them would ever pass through those gates again. And, if Candace was right, neither might she.

On top of it all, Candace would be leaving in the morning. Sunny was so tempted to go as well, to just hop on that ferry as it chugged away from the shore and kiss this place goodbye. So what was stopping her? What, really, did this island hold for her? She took a silent inventory: a half of a house she didn't really want. A half of a crumbling barn, a half of an old shed, a half of a ton of grapes that would turn into a barrel of wine that, in all probability, nobody in their right mind would want to drink. And, of course, let's not forget the whole dog and whole cat.

But there was even more she'd been left with. There was Layla, for one. It was true that she needed a home, for now. And what about Kat? She had been spending so many nights on Sunny's couch lately that it felt as though she had practically moved in. And how could she bring herself to abandon the girl without a job, especially after convincing her to leave the one she had to come to the island? And while she was at it, what about Joe and Sky, and those grapes on the hill growing fatter and riper by the day? Was she going to be the one to jeopardize their dreams of having their very own harvest, as iffy as it might be?

She squeezed her eyes shut and tried to concentrate on something soothing, a pleasant scene or a comforting memory. Jack's strong arms around her body, his cool skin against her bare back, the feel of his calm, even breath whispering across the base of her neck. How many nights had she spent in this bed summoning up that dream? But now, thinking about Jack made her think about the house, which made her think about Joe and Sky and Layla and Kat, which made her think about Rick and the dilemma she was in, which made her bolt upright and curse Jack out loud for getting her into this mess in the first place.

Now Sunny was wide awake. Getting up and out of bed appeared to be the only option, so she padded into the kitchen to make herself a cup of tea. As she flipped on the light, Sangiovese appeared at her side, rubbing up against the plaid flannel pajama bottoms she'd swiped from Jack. Maybe Joe had the right idea, she thought as she waited for the kettle to boil. Maybe she didn't need to commit to staying on Twimbly Island forever. What she really needed was to buy herself some time, to buy them all a little time. And Candace might have had a point. It wasn't all that bad here, as long as you knew you'd be leaving someday. She'd stick it out through the harvest. She'd find a way to convince Rick to either buy or sell, and in the meantime she'd shut him up with that "good faith" money the asshole was asking for. But she wasn't about to take Joe's money. She'd figure out a way to do it on her own. She was Sunny Tedder, and she was going to make this happen. Somehow. And then she would decide where to go.

"Shit!" Out in the hallway Candace was pale and makeup-less in her yellow silk pajamas, hopping up and down on one bare foot while rubbing the other with her two hands. "I needed a blanket. You call this summer? It's colder than my poor lonely hoo-ha in here." The door of the linen closet was open, and a grey metal box lay on its side on the floor next to Candace. "Damn thing fell off the shelf and onto my foot."

Sunny bent down to retrieve the offending object, a strong-box, just like the ones they'd make change from at a carnival or a street fair. As she lifted it from the floor the top swung back on its hinges, causing everything inside to scatter across the hallway. Typical Jack, she thought as she tried to brush the cat away from the mess. So trusting, he never even bothered to buy a damn lock for his lockbox. She and Candace knelt down together without a word to clean it all up. There didn't seem to be much of value—a few afghani bills and coins, a checkbook in a leather case, an expired driver's license, a yellowed ID card, some old bank records. But when Sunny glanced at a wrinkled piece of paper she'd managed to wrestle from under Sangiovese's paw she had to stop for a second. She scooted back on her rear and leaned up against the wall, smoothed out the creases and read the words to herself again.

"What?" Candace asked, pulling a blue blanket down from the shelf and wrapping herself up tightly in it. "What's that?"

"Listen to this." Sunny read out loud, "*I, Rick Stark, hereby acknowledge the receipt of $325,000 from Jack Scott for the purchase of my existing share of Screaming Peacock Vineyards, and all property included. Jack Scott is to be the sole owner of said property. The official transfer of deed will occur at Twimbly Bank at the earliest convenience of the two parties involved.*" Sunny let the paper fall to her lap. "Huh."

"That's all you have to say? *Huh?*" Candace asked, plopping down beside her friend. "Rick's signature is right here, in black and white." She grabbed the agreement from Sunny's lap and shook it in her face. "This was signed and dated last year, before Jack died. It was all going to be made official when Jack got back to the island. And he didn't."

"And?"

"Don't you see, Sunny? The place is all Jack's!"

"You mean it's all mine?"

"Well duh, of course that's what I mean." She rolled up the paper and swatted Sunny on the head.

Sunny snatched it back from her friend and crammed it into the pocket of her pajamas. "The guy's been playing me, Candace. What a dirtbag! Lying through those big old shiny teeth." Sunny could feel her nails dig into the flesh of her own palms. "He just sat there, with a straight face, telling me Jack would have wanted this, Jack would have done that, you should do this, blah blah blah. Why did I ever even listen to that guy?"

"Uh-huh."

"I knew something was wrong. I should have trusted my gut."

"Yep."

"Taking advantage of a good man's good will, after he is dead and buried." Sunny kicked the hardwood floor with the back of her bare heel.

"Well," Candace added after a beat, "maybe not quite so buried." She reached for the small, square cardboard box that sat on the floor of the closet. "Is this what I think it is?"

Sunny nodded absent-mindedly.

Candace cradled the box in her lap and gave it three little pats. Now Sunny was paying attention, her eyes moving back and forth between Candace's face and the box, the box and Candace's face.

Candace lowered her own gaze to her lap. "He tried to screw us, Jack. What are you going to do about it, huh?" She jiggled her thighs a little. "You just gonna sit there?"

Sunny's mouth dropped open.

"Big help you are, Jack-in-the-box," Candace continued. Sunny reached for the box but Candace wasn't through. "Whatever happened to Jack-be-nimble, Jack-be-quick, huh?"

Now Sunny couldn't help but laugh. "Yeah, you're doing jack squat just sitting there in that box," she added. "Can't you see we need a little assistance around here?"

Now the two of them were giggling like schoolgirls, and it wasn't long before Sunny felt a tear slipping from her eye. But for once, it was the good kind, the kind that comes from the relief of letting go.

"Well now, we don't need Jack to help us, Sunny. We're not going to let old Rick get away with this," said Candace, her southern attitude and the accent that went along with it taking over. "That man doesn't seem to know who he's messing with, does he? I'll just bet he's never tangled with a couple of down-home girls before, cause I'm sure they don't make them up here like they do over in Arkansas or in ole Missouri." She folded her arms across her chest and gave a sharp little nod.

Seeing Candace like this made Sunny crack up even more, and it felt good. It was as if being with her friend had opened a pressure valve that had been sealed shut for months. Above all she loved to hear her laugh, the same laugh that had let Sunny know, back in Kabul, that deep down, behind the bluster and glitz of Candace's la-di-da exterior, there was another Candace, one who was a lot more like Sunny and the girls she knew growing up back home than anyone would ever guess.

They laughed so long it got to the point where she didn't even know what they were laughing at anymore. "Shhh, shhh, we're gonna wake the girls." Sunny managed between giggles. "They need their sleep."

Finally they wore themselves out. Candace yawned. But to Sunny, sitting there on the cold wood floor with her best friend, in their pajamas as the early morning light began to peek through the living room shutters, sleep was the last thing in the world she wanted. For the first time in ages, she was excited for it to be tomorrow.

30

The white sack was lifted with care from the back of the battered SUV and hoisted onto the shoulders of the six bearded men, each one wearing a mask of sorrow beneath the *pakol* on his head. Zara's father led the way, his heavy eyes cast downward toward the scrubby soil below. The group snaked through the field of graves, stepping gingerly around each jagged slab of rock that stood as the only sign of a body below, until they reached the hole that had been prepared for their grievous load.

They came to a halt and, without a word spoken, the two men in the back began to lower their end of the shrouded figure into the ground, as if the act were a dance they had done many times before. The pair in front followed, until the motionless form was completely prone, at rest atop a bed of gravel and dirt. *Bismillah*, they softly chanted. In the name of Allah and in the faith of the Messenger of Allah.

Halajan stood in silence well behind the rest of the small circle of mourners, trying to remain confident that she was in no danger of being recognized beneath the white *shalwaar kameez* and turban she wore to pass as a man. She had been determined to attend the burial, to witness it for herself and to report back to Yazmina the details of the ritual in which only men were allowed to take part. From her location, she watched through a thick-framed pair of Rashif's old eyeglasses as two of the men positioned the covered shape onto its right side, against the wall of the grave, to face the *qiblah* in Mecca. Then Zara's father reached down to undo the ties at the head and the foot of the shroud, which he did as if he were performing a delicate surgery. As he stood to allow the others to place a thin piece of wood on top of the lifeless figure—to prohibit dirt from falling directly on the body when the grave was filled with earth—Halajan noticed a heave of his shoulders. Yet still the man remained silent, as did everyone else around her. There would be no crying, none of the wailing she had seen in some of the western movies Sunny had rented to show at the coffeehouse. Here in the Kabul cemetery, the only sounds to be heard were the birds in the sky, and the occasional airplane heading south to India. Death was a serious matter.

She closed her eyes for just one moment, to accept the comfort of the early afternoon sun on her wrinkled face, and by the time she opened them the men in Zara's family were already scooping up dirt from the ground and tossing it into the grave. Three handfuls each, according to the tradition. Within minutes, the rest of the hole had been filled with sand, and the burial complete. For it was important to put a body to rest quickly, to allow the soul to lie in peace.

The mourners stood by the grave to make *dua* to the deceased. Halajan imagined that *namaaz jenaaza* had been performed earlier, as normally the funeral prayer would take place in the women's section of the mosque, after the midday prayer.

O Allah, Halajan mouthed silently along with the men, *forgive her, have mercy on her, give her peace and pardon her. Receive her with honor and make her entrance spacious. Wash her with water, snow, and ice, and cleanse her of her faults like a white garment is cleansed of stains. Requite her with an abode better than her abode, with a family better than her family and a spouse better than her spouse. Admit her into Paradise and protect her from the torment of the grave and the torment of the Fire.*

As they continued with their supplication, Halajan's eyes wandered to the brown hills rising from the edges of the cemetery, and the houses that seemed to grow from the craggy rock, their windows offering a daily dose of mortality to the inhabitants within. At the far edges of the burial grounds, she could see little clusters of blue moving in packs—burqa'd women visiting their deceased. Still there was no sound; no talking, no weeping among the graves that stretched out as far as the eye could see. Suddenly all the sorrow she'd been holding inside came rushing out in a sob. She quickly turned her face away and coughed into her hands to cover her blunder. When will it ever end? she wondered as the anguish pumped through her veins, this madness that has taken so many from those they loved, and who loved them, this insanity that rips families apart and turns devout men into instruments of evil? And for what? If there was a larger purpose for this, it was a purpose that Halajan failed to see.

It wasn't until she calmed herself a bit and brought her focus back to the scene that she saw him, standing there to her left, with his crisp green-and-white *chapan* and blacker-than-black beard. She'd seen those dark eyes with no end before, in the coffeehouse. And now, just as they had then, those eyes caused a chill to climb from the base of Halajan's spine right up to the top of her head. Her knees suddenly buckled, and she fought the temptation to sit, for she could not afford to draw the slightest bit of attention to herself. There was no mistaking who he was. Zara's father must have noticed Faheem as well, as Halajan could have sworn that for one split second her eyes connected with his in a shared solace, before they both quickly turned away.

Halajan placed a rock of her own to mark Zara's grave. Then the girl's father and the others left as swiftly as they had arrived. Halajan remained behind, until the last mourner was gone from sight. It was then that she finally allowed herself to fold into a pile on the hard ground, the strain of the day and all that had led up to it rushing in with the rallying cry of a tribal drum.

31

"Hey, Skyrider, don't forget the ones we put way over in the corner." Joe stepped back into the middle of the barn as more plastic bins came tumbling down from the hayloft above. They'd started early today, and for good reason. Joe had almost forgotten how much work there was to be done to prepare for harvest, it had been so long. Today's plan was to hose down the bins that would be used to hold the grapes after picking, and maybe even clean the fermenters, too, where the grapes would sit and bubble until they were ready to be put to sleep in their barrels. Hopefully he'd succeed in convincing the girls to take on the chore of washing, so he and Sky could start concentrating on testing the crushers to make sure they still worked after sitting idle in the barn for so long. "Is that all of them? Are you taking a nap up there or what?" he yelled up to the loft.

"Jesus, Joe. You'll be waking them up in Seattle." Sunny stood just inside the barn's doorway, coffee in hand, her messy brown hair streaked with yellow from the morning sun sneaking in through the gaps in the worn wooden roof.

"Well, aren't you a beautiful sight," he said, taking in her new denim work shirt, the crisp cargo shorts and the spotless work boots fresh from their maiden voyage across the lawn.

"It's the latest in barnyard chic. You like?" she asked, pirouetting and ending with a bow.

"You've never looked lovelier." In fact, Sunny did look lovely. There was a glow in her cheeks and a sparkle in her eyes that Joe had never witnessed before, and a pep in her step that made him feel as though she was ready to take on the world.

As if she had read his thoughts, Sunny put down her cup and rolled up her sleeves. "What's next?" she asked, looking around the barn for something to do.

"When Sky is done we will go say hello to the grapes."

"Okey-dokey." Sunny joined him at his side and squatted down onto her haunches, a move that Joe marveled at as he lowered himself with a groan onto an overturned barrel. "You know, Joe," Sunny said as she picked at a loose strand of straw by her foot, "never in a million years did I expect to be this happy about being saddled with this heap." She pointed her chin toward the house. "Who would've thought?"

"*Ogni cosa ha cagione.* Everything has a reason."

"Not that I'm saying I'm staying, mind you."

"Whatever," he laughed, using that marvelous response he had learned from the kids. It came in so handy so much of the time.

"I'm just relieved about the harvest and all. That I'll be here, that we'll all be here, that it will happen no matter what. You know."

"Fair enough." What he really wanted to ask was exactly where she'd thought she was going to be rushing off to so quickly, before she'd made up her mind to at least stay through harvest. And after the harvest? What then? But he knew better than to push. Whatever Sunny decided to do or not do, she was going to have to believe it was her own idea. That was one thing he'd learned from his fifty-six years with Sylvia.

Sky jumped down from the loft and brushed the dust from his jeans. "Where's Kat?"

"I just woke the two of them up," Sunny answered. "They'll be out soon." She tipped the remaining coffee into her mouth as Joe hauled himself up from the barrel.

"Well, as they say, *chi tardi arriva, male alloggia*." He pivoted on his walking stick to face the barn door. "The early bird catches the worm. Time's a wasting!"

The morning dew clung to the grass and weeds carpeting the paths between the vines, which hung heavy and low to the ground. Joe took the lead, his snowy head swiveling from side to side as they marched up and down the aisles.

"What are we looking for?" Sunny called out from the rear.

"Company, halt!" Joe held his walking stick high in the air. "Okay, here is your first lesson. The most important thing a winemaker needs to know is when to pick. Too early? The wine will taste sour. You must use patience," he said, looking directly at Sunny, who rolled her eyes at him. "But if you pick too late? Too sweet. You've tempted the fates, and they will not give you a second chance. It's like all else in life. Timing is everything."

"Now a lot of it, it comes from in here," he said, patting his gut. "But there are also other tricks you can use to know when the time is right. First of all, do you remember the color and size of these babies when you first arrived, back in April?"

"I don't even remember there being any grapes when I got here."

"Exactly my point! They start out tiny and green, like pale little peas. You can barely see them." He plucked a dark purple grape from its stem. "And now? A thing of beauty. But appearances aren't everything." He punched through the thick skin with his thumbnail. "You see this?" he asked Sunny. "Not ready. What we want is for it to be plump and juicy."

"Who you calling plump and juicy?" she asked with her hand on her hip.

"Very funny. Now pay attention."

"And, may I ask, why are the insides of that grape white and not pink? I thought you said we were making a rosé."

"Tell her, Sky," he said with mock exasperation, and turned to continue to walk.

"Well, actually, all grape juice starts out white. It's the contact with the skin once it's crushed that gives a wine its color." He turned to follow Joe.

"Hmm, what do you know," Sunny said, joining them both.

Two rows down, Joe stopped again. "And then there are the seeds. We can learn a lot from even the tiniest of them. Here we have," he said as he squeezed some pulp from its casing, "some little green seeds. Now is that a good thing, or a bad thing?"

"Jeez, Joe, you would have made a rotten teacher. How the hell am I supposed to know?"

"Logic," he said, tapping her head with the stick. "Green is still good. Now if the seeds were to be brown, they'd be cooked, and so would we. You have to get them when they're just right. And now we taste." He popped a whole grape into his mouth and chewed, gesturing for Sunny to do the same.

She closed her eyes and scrunched her nose, as if expecting the worst, and took one dainty bite. And then another, and another, until the first grape was gone and she was reaching for more.

"Don't eat up the profits!" admonished Joe.

"Oh my God, they're just so sweet and yummy."

"Well they'll be even better in a bottle."

Sunny shook her head. "I think they're too sweet for wine, Joe. Maybe we should be making jelly."

"Already an expert. No, not too sweet. We need them to have some sugar for it to turn into alcohol. *Capisce?*"

"I get it, I get it."

When they returned from the vines, Layla and Kat were up by the barn parked on two kitchen chairs they'd dragged out from the house, their feet resting on an upside-down bucket and their faces angled toward the sun. Kat's black-and-white ponytail sprouted from the top of her head like a fountain, and Layla wore her head scarf like a shawl, loosely draped over her head and shoulders, providing a shady little tent for the sleeping cat across her lap. Both girls had their eyes closed against the morning brightness.

"Rise and shine, you slugs." Sky kicked the bucket out from underneath their feet with his leather boot. "There's work to be done, women!"

"Don't you 'woman' me, you jerk." Sky leapt back as Kat swatted in the air. Sunny laughed, but couldn't help but think of Jack and how they used to tease each other just like that.

The girls followed Sky into the barn to help carry the bins outside. Sunny helped herself to one of their chairs and patted the other for Joe to settle. They sat in silence, watching as a cruise ship crossed the horizon.

"A penny for your thoughts," Joe said, his eyes still trained on the water.

"Just a penny? They gotta be worth a lot more than that."

"I will be the judge of that."

"Well I'll give you a dollar's worth, for free." She bent to loosen the laces on her boots. "Here's the thing," she said, straightening back up in the chair. "I was just thinking about Candace, and how she ends up being right about so many things, and how that kind of pisses me off, but not really."

Joe laughed. "And what was she so right about this time, that makes you so angry, or not?"

"Oh, I don't know. Everything. Like with Layla, from the beginning she seemed to know how good it would be for her to stay here with me. Who knew? I know nothing about kids, especially teenagers. But she seems to be doing okay, right?"

"Better than okay, if you ask me, which I suppose you are. Although I do think we might have a little problem on our hands sooner or later, with that crush she has on Sky."

Sunny raised her arms to the sky. "Why do I seem to be the only one who didn't know about this?"

Joe shrugged his shoulders. "I'm just saying."

"And I'm just asking. But back to Candace. The way she orchestrated that maneuver in Kabul? Brilliant." And it was brilliant. Sunny marveled at the way Candace had, from afar, staged the mock funeral, the burial of the rice-filled shroud and all. Everything had gone exactly as planned, with Faheem there to bear witness to the end of his story with Zara. Last she heard the girl was still in Kabul, in hiding, and that her family had gone west, back to Herat, to the home they had left when the Taliban took control of that city eighteen years earlier. As an added layer of protection, great pains had been taken to make it seem obvious to Faheem that the grief they felt from their daughter's death was what was now driving them away from Kabul. In fact, he was told they were leaving Afghanistan altogether, to go east through Pakistan, with hopes of eventually joining other family members living in Ireland.

"You know, Joe? Sometimes I wish I could be more like Candace."

"What, with that yellow hair and those boots up to here?" Joe brought his hand up to his waist.

"No, not that." Although she couldn't deny her envy of Candace's looks, even though she, herself, had dropped a few pounds since her friend left, which she wished was something Candace could be here to see. "It's more about the way she sees herself, the way she sees us, as a couple of tough girls who know what they want, who can waltz right into a situation and make things happen, who can fix things and make them right. I know that's who she is, but I'm not sure it's who I am. I just wish I could live up to her expectations."

"Are you talking about any particular situation?"

"Well, yes, and no, I guess. The big thing is really more the part about knowing what you want, and committing to it. I know I used to be like that, but I don't seem to have it in me anymore, maybe since Jack died, or maybe even since we left Kabul. Candace never seems to question where she is, or what she is doing. And to top it off, she's helping a boatload of people. What the hell is wrong with me?"

"There is nothing wrong with you, kiddo. How are you feeling right now, right here, today?" He opened his arms wide, as if to hold up the entire place for her consideration.

"You mean besides confused?" She paused to take in a whiff of the lemongrass that had popped up around the south side of the barn. "Pretty good."

"You are happy here, right this second?"

"I guess so."

"So, be honest with me, and with yourself. This isn't such a bad place, is it?"

Sunny found herself unable to disagree. Yet another thing Candace had been right about.

"Then what is the problem?"

"I don't know, Joe. It's just that sometimes, when I think about staying here forever, I can't breathe."

"Who said anything about forever? Haven't we talked about this before? You think it's like a horror movie, where the island won't ever allow you to leave?"

"Well, kind of."

Joe ignored her answer. "And if it's breath you want, you'll need to stop all that running around for enough time to catch it. Get those ants out of your pants and sit still for a while."

"But here? Even you didn't want to be here when you first came back. And now look."

"I had my reasons. But like the Buddhists say, if our mind is peaceful, we shall be happy all the time, regardless of external conditions. And, by the way, you don't think you've been helping people as much as Candace has? Just look around you."

Sunny turned toward the squealing coming from behind her, where Layla was brandishing a flowing garden hose, a smile as wide as the Sound itself plastered across her face. Sky laughed as Bear leaped and bit at the stream of water as it squirted skyward before showering down on Kat's head.

Joe chuckled. "You said that is the big thing. And what is the little thing?"

"Well, maybe I'm being childish, but it's the whole thing with Rick. I feel like it's unfinished business, though I know the place is mine and all that. But really, he shouldn't be allowed to get away with what he tried to do, am I right? Candace and I talked about it while she was here."

"Well, you know what they say. *I fatti sono maschi, e le parole femmine.* Deeds are fruits, words are but leaves."

"Meaning?"

"Meaning just what it says. Don't just talk about how you want to be more like your friend Candace, about how you don't want to have unfinished business. Finish the business. Jump in there and do something to make things right."

"But it's not like I'm saving the world or anything. I just want this guy to feel a little pain for the way he tried to use everything good about Jack for his own greedy schemes. He just sat there and lied straight to my face! More than once! I can't tell you how badly I want him to pay for what he did. Is that wrong?"

"So let's do that."

"What? You're not going to quote me some stupid saying about revenge? Don't tell me you don't know any."

"Oh, I know plenty. But revenge quotes? They're really not so good."

By the end of the day, after a long lunch outside under the trees, a plan had been hatched. Sunny walked down toward the water to make her call. Rick answered after the first ring.

"Sunny! How's everything?" he asked in a syrupy voice.

"Fantastic, and you?"

"All good. All good. Any news for me?"

"Well, Rick, as a matter of fact, there is. I've thought a lot about what you've said, and I've realized you're right. I'm going to keep the house." Sunny bit her lip to keep from laughing at the silence on the other end of the line. "You there?"

"Yeah, yeah, I'm here." Rick cleared his throat. "So at the price we talked about?"

"Sounds more than fair to me. Still good with you?"

"Well," he sputtered a bit, "even though I'd be practically giving my half away, I'll go with it. For Jack."

Sunny suddenly had to fight the urge to throw the phone down and stomp on it. Instead she put on her sweetest air. "That is so kind of you, Rick. Really."

"So how soon can we make this happen?"

She could hear the hunger in his voice. "Well, here's what I'm thinking. I'll need a little time to come up with the whole amount, but if you're open to it, I could give you, say, ten thousand as sort of a deposit, or whatever?"

Rick hesitated for a moment on the other end. "All cash?"

"Yep, all cash."

"This week?"

"If you say so. How about I meet you at The Dirty Monkey around six o'clock on Wednesday?"

"Sounds good."

She pumped her fist in the air.

"And Sunny?"

"Yes, Rick?"

"You're doing the right thing."

Sunny covered the mouthpiece as a pair of adolescent peacocks came screeching across the lawn. "Oh, I know I am, Rick," she said with a smile. "I know I am."

32

Zara stood looking out the window, her uncovered silky-straight hair framed by the soft afternoon light. Her shoulders lifted and sank with a sigh that said a thousand words, words that need not be spoken out loud. Yazmina's heart ached for the girl. Though her wounds were healing on the outside, inside there remained a suffering too deep for even the most tender hand to reach. It didn't help that she was locked up like a prisoner here in Halajan's house, cut off from the pulse of the city around her, unable to feel the late summer warmth on her face. But the plan they had agreed on with Candace was to keep her hidden, dead and buried in the eyes of Faheem and his men, until they could find a safe way for her to join her family back in Herat.

Yazmina patted the *toshak* beside her. "Come. Sit and help me." She flipped her long black braid over her shoulder and handed Zara a tiny pink sweater from the pile of clothes Najama had long outgrown. "This one needs just a little fixing, right here on the seam."

"Your boy will be the prettiest dressed in Kabul, should you have one." Halajan laughed as she struggled over control of a hairbrush with a fidgety Najama.

Yazmina sat back and used one swollen foot to pry the plastic shoe off the other. "But I know she is a girl. I am sure of it."

"How do you know?" Zara asked.

"I dream of it, in the night. A mother can just know. You will see for yourself, when you marry." Yazmina regretted her words as soon as they left her mouth. The girl's eyes turned downward, her mouth becoming a thin, straight line.

"*The moon stays bright when it doesn't avoid the night.* You must stay positive, my child." Halajan must have noticed as well. "And if it is your Omar you are worrying about, relax. He is in good hands with Rashif. My husband knows people who will help see him safely to Herat, far away from Faheem and his men. Perhaps you will be able to see him again before too long." She pushed the sleeves of her cotton tunic up over her bony elbows, feeling a twinge of guilt at the lie she'd used with Ahmet; that Rashif had gone to Mazar-i-Sharif to visit his cousin.

Yazmina quickly agreed with her mother-in-law, assuring Zara of Rashif's fine character and firm principles. If only Ahmet had been the one to step up to help. But instead of igniting a fire beneath his growing concerns for justice, the attack on the coffeehouse seemed to have blown him straight back toward the old ways.

"I forbid you from bringing that stupid girl into my family's home!" was how their last argument had begun, right before the pretend funeral, when she had told him Zara had been taken from the hospital to Halajan's house, hidden under a blanket on the floor of a van. Ahmet's dark eyes flashed with anger, but the girl was already safe behind Halajan's strong oak door. "It is her parents who are responsible for her. They are the ones who made her this way, who were not able to control her. They are the ones who sent her to the university, to fill her head with useless thoughts."

"This girl should not study, should not be allowed to learn?"

"For what?" he asked, jerking his head toward her. "To make her husband's meals, to keep his house, to bear his sons?"

Yazmina wrapped her belly in her arms, the sting of his words piercing deep into her core. She narrowed her eyes at him and replied with a hiss, "My girls will do more than that. And they will have the chance to go to school if they want. Not like me, who is lucky to even read."

"Your girls," he answered with a smirk. "Well it will be my son who runs this household someday, who will be the one to say what 'your girls' can and cannot do."

Yazmina could not believe her ears. Who was this man her husband was becoming—or had he really been like this all along? Had she been wrong to believe that he would welcome a baby girl into the world? Now he was acting just as those in villages far from the city did, those who celebrate the birth of a son with elaborate celebrations where guns are fired, drums are beaten, and food is given to the poor. Even the ritual for driving away evil spirits would be forgotten when a girl was born, as if her future didn't matter. For it was only a boy who could truly establish the virility of his father, the fertility of his mother, only a boy who would bring an heir to the family property and honor to its name.

On the far wall of Halajan's sitting room, atop of the high chest where the old woman used to hide the secret letters from

Rashif, sat the mosaic box Yazmina knew Ahmet's father had presented to Halajan as an offering of thanks for bearing him a son. "Your husband, did he only want a boy?" she asked her mother-in-law.

Halajan handed Najama and the hairbrush over to Zara and went to the window. She unlatched the handle and pushed it open just far enough to allow some air to enter. The shiny draperies ballooned like sails into the room. Halajan pulled a loose cigarette from her pocket. "They all want a boy," she said as the flame from her plastic lighter shot into the air. "Of course, we already had our Aisha, and Sunil was a very good father to her. I cannot complain. But when I finally gave birth to Ahmet, many years later, my husband was overjoyed, as if he had won the Afghan Cup championship." She took a drag from the cigarette and slowly exhaled through the slit in the window, the smoke curling out toward the empty courtyard.

"But I do not blame him for that," she added, to Yazmina's surprise, knowing how modern her mother-in-law's views always were. "Since forever it has been with a son that the parents will live out their lives, and a son on whom they will rely on for their needs, and for the growing of their family. And it is the stronger child that a farmer must have after his daughters are married off, for when he can no longer do the work that must be done. And unless things change, it's still a son who is needed to accompany the women of the family in public to protect their honor."

"So basically, women have no value." Zara slid onto the rug with Najama, and began to turn a pile of small wooden blocks into a teetering tower.

"Well, it is not that simple." The old woman took another puff from the cigarette she held out the window. "It is true, that in some ways our value is considered half that of a man, like when someone dies and we inherit half of what a man gets, and in some courts, where a woman's testimony is worth half that of a man."

"That is true," Yazmina agreed. "Or when blood money is paid to a family who has lost somebody to murder, the amount if the victim was a man is twice that it would be had the victim been a woman."

Zara sat up on her knees. "Yes, and what about a woman whose husband has four wives? He is allowed four, and she is allowed just one husband? In that marriage, is she worth just one quarter of a man?"

"Ach, who would want more than one?" Halajan laughed. She carefully extinguished her cigarette on the windowsill, to be finished later. "But it is also true," she said, "that without us, these men who are so valuable would have no sons. *Heaven is under the Mother's feet, so treat her kindly.* Have you not heard that said? Our tradition tells us that women should be given kindness, love, and respect if a man truly wants to be righteous."

"Well then there are some very impure men around." Zara turned her attention back to Najama and the blocks.

Yazmina was a little taken aback by her mother-in-law's words. Usually she was as quick and unbending with her opinions as a donkey eager for the trough. Yazmina always thought her wise, but today her tongue seemed to have softened. "Are you feeling all right, *maadar*?"

Halajan laughed. "Why? Because I am telling two sides of a story? I am an old woman. I have seen things change, and change again. Some beliefs that are there for such old reasons will take many years to erase. And some ideas that are falsely spread in the name of religion will take even longer."

"But how can you know they will be erased?" Yazmina thought back on her conversation with Ahmet, whose words she had not shared with her mother-in-law.

"I have seen a very different Afghanistan than any of you," she said, passing her eyes over the three girls in her sitting room. "When I was born, women could already vote. I was a child when *pardah*, the separation of men and women, was ended. We wore miniskirts and went to the cinema."

"Yes, and look at us now." Zara flung her discarded head scarf into the air.

"But at least you can go to school," Halajan said. "There were many years when that was not possible."

"Still, the boys taunt us and say what is the point for us to be studying, when after all the foreigners leave we will have to go inside the home again."

Halajan leaned out the window and re-lit her cigarette. "It is true that we live in uncertainty."

"It is such a difficult time. Sometimes I think I should not be bringing another innocent child into this world, especially a girl," Yazmina said in a quiet voice.

Halajan hastily brought an index finger to her mouth and bit down hard, in an old gesture meant to ward off a jinx. "Eat your words," she snapped back, sounding like her old self again. "It was not such an easy time when I gave birth to Ahmet, either. The Russians were sitting on us like a cat with a mouse, the mujahideen were firing missiles though the skies night and day, half the countryside had left their homes for Iran or Pakistan, with the rest of them flooding the streets of Kabul, turning it into a place where there was not even room for an apple to fall." She paused for another puff of the cigarette. "We had no idea what would be coming next, and we worried for our children.

But still we happily welcomed them into the world. Because if not for them, who will it be who decides the future of our country?"

Again Ahmet's words echoed in Yazmina's mind. How disappointed his mother would be to know of the things her son had been saying.

Halajan took one last taste of her cigarette, and exhaled slowly into the afternoon air. "And I will tell you one thing I know," she continued. "It is with our girls that change will happen. Girls who will grow up like Zara, and like Layla, who have the blessing of an education. It is the power of a girl with a book that is the best weapon for progress."

"So that is why the extremists try to keep girls from going to school? That is the reason we are poisoned and beaten, and our teachers threatened and killed?" Zara joined Halajan at the window, her eyes searching the skies for an answer. "How are we to be the ones to make anything happen?"

"Because with educated women comes prosperity. And with our voices comes mercy. And with our strength comes change. Like Rumi says, *when a bird gets free, it does not go back for remnants left on the bottom of the cage*."

Yazmina looked at her mother-in-law, with her lined lips and permanently furrowed brows. "Since when did you become so positive, *maadar*?"

Halajan laughed. "I have gained and lost hope so many times in my long life, *dokhtar*. Today, I just choose to be hopeful."

Yazmina shifted on her *toshak* as she felt the baby stir inside her. How she envied her mother-in-law's strength, and the courage she showed with her actions. She reached out and pulled Najama close, placing her daughter's little hand on top of the rippling surface of her belly. And was it not her duty to pass on those virtues to her own daughters? She sighed at the weight of it all. Sometimes she wished she were still back in the mountains, hidden away from all the difficult thoughts that had been poured into her head since she had arrived in Kabul. But yet, she was grateful to be here, and thankful for the opportunities she had been given. Maybe helping Zara was a start, but there had to be more she could do to help, perhaps with others. She would teach her daughters not with words, but with action. But first, it was her troubles with Ahmet that needed her attention.

33

Inside The Dirty Monkey it was as dark as midnight. The cyclists and joggers she'd passed on the drive over might as well have been living in another world, one where the summer twilight hours were a gift, a bonus for the daily grind, as opposed to a time to drown their sorrows and forget the day ever happened. The lineup at the bar came into view as her eyes slowly adjusted to the lack of light in the windowless room. Regulars, she thought, as she took in the stooped spines bent over thick, sweaty glasses of brown liquid. Above the corner of the bar, the Mariners were silently playing to a near-empty stadium. The only one watching the muted set, from behind the counter, was Sky.

"Hey." Sunny pulled up a stool.

"Hey yourself," he answered, pouring her a glass of red wine without her even asking.

"You seen him yet?" She scanned the faces in the darkness around her for Rick's pearly whites.

"Nope. You're a little early."

Sunny took a deep breath and planted her leather knapsack firmly between her two feet. "Good. I could use this." She took a nice long sip from her glass.

"It's all good, Sunny. You'll be fine." Sky turned to pour a refill for the beefy-faced man two stools to her right.

How sad it must make Sky to work here, she thought. It was no wonder he spent every spare minute outside. A fleeting sliver of light slid across the bar as the door behind her opened and shut. The look on Sky's face told her who it was.

"It's showtime," she mouthed to him before swiveling around to greet Rick.

"Good evening, Sunshine." Rick tossed his car keys on the bar, lifted her hand from her lap and planted a warm, wet kiss on its back. She wondered how long she'd have to wait before heading to the ladies room to wash it off.

"Hello, Rick. You're certainly in a good mood."

"And why not?"

"Why not indeed?" She scooted over a little as he pulled out the stool beside her and sat. "I don't know about you, but I think a celebration is called for. Sky?"

Sky reached across the bar to shake Rick's hand. "How's it going?"

"Couldn't be better," Rick answered, his knees jiggling up and down as if he had just consumed a quadruple espresso.

"Surprise us with something special, would you, Sky?" Sunny flashed him a huge smile.

"You're on." He scooped up some ice into a silver cocktail shaker with one hand and grabbed a bottle of gin with the other, and began to pour. Sunny watched as his tanned arms danced around the shelves—a dash of this, a squirt of that—and then he shook with a beat worthy of a Latin jazz band. He slid the two dewy glasses across the bar to Sunny and Rick.

"I'd like to propose a toast." Rick lifted his glass toward Sunny. "To Jack. A real stand-up guy, and one helluva friend. I owe more to you than you'll ever know."

Sunny covered her laugh with a cough and tightened her feet around the knapsack below. Then she raised her own glass to the ceiling. "To Jack. May you be enjoying all this from up there somewhere." She turned to Rick. "Bottoms up!"

"Chin-chin!"

Sunny watched with glass in hand as he consumed half the drink in one shot. Sky deftly topped it off with what remained in the shaker.

"You know, Jack sure was a lucky man."

"Yes he was," Sunny answered, thinking about all that time he'd spent in the remotest parts of Pakistan and Afghanistan and Iraq, all those near misses and narrow escapes. And that day he'd headed up into the rugged mountains of Nuristan to search for Layla, well aware of the dangers that lay ahead in the isolated, lawless villages run by drug lords and warlords, the chances of locating her like finding a needle in a highly combustible haystack. The fact that they both came back alive was a miracle. Thank God he had luck on his side for as long as he did, with that fearless attitude of his. If she had to, she'd make a bet that the biggest risk a guy like Rick ever took was to leave the house in November without an umbrella.

"I mean it, Sunny. He was lucky to have a woman like you."

"Thank you, Rick. That's a very nice thing for you to say."

"No, really. What you're doing, keeping the house and all, it's what would have made him happy. You made the right decision."

"Well, sometimes a girl's just gotta do what a girl's gotta do."

"Amen to that."

"Did you know we're making some wine this year?" she said as she briefly looked down to check her phone.

"No shit? Well, more power to you. Better men than you have tried and failed around here. It's not easy."

Sunny nodded and took a tiny sip from her still-full glass.

"It's kind of a fool's errand, if you ask me. But hey, it's what Jack wanted, right? So here's to Jack."

"To Jack," she repeated as she watched him drain his glass. Sky was there with a fresh shaker-full before she could even blink an eye. Rick sat motionless with his elbows resting on the bar as Sky poured, his legs having finally ended their relentless jig. Sunny stared at her phone, willing the call to come.

"C'mon, Sunny, drink up!"

"I'm good. Just savoring what I have." She bent to take another sip just as her phone buzzed. "Hey, Joe. What's up?"

"Everything going A-Okay there, kiddo? Are you reeling him in like a fish on a line?" he yelled from the other end.

She jammed her thumb into the volume down button and held the phone tighter to her ear. "Holy shit. It is? How bad?"

"Ha!" Joe said from his end of the line. "You're too good at this, Sunny Tedder. I'll have to remember to watch my back around you."

"You mean the whole thing is busted? I'll be there in twenty. Call the plumber." She stuffed the phone into her pocket and reached down for her bag. "I've gotta go, Rick. I'm so sorry to run out like this, but it's an emergency. Here you go." She pulled out a half-inch thick envelope and transferred it to him under the bar. "You can count it if you'd like."

Rick laughed. "I trust you, Sunny." He waved her away as she reached back into the knapsack for her wallet. "I've got this one. It's on me."

"Really?" Sunny's smile could have melted an iceberg. "That is so sweet of you, Rick. And thank you again for being so understanding about all of this. I promise I'll get the rest of it to you as soon as I can."

"That," he took another slug of his drink, "would be excellent."

"Well, bye. I'll be seeing you." She stood and flung her bag over her shoulder, giving Sky a little wink before turning to go. She headed out the door, stepping aside to allow a familiar figure in a short, tight, low-cut green dress and a tousled black-and-white updo to pass.

The stool was still warm from Sunny when Kat slid in beside Rick at the bar. She tugged at the hem of her dress and let the six-inch patent leather heels that had been borrowed from her cousin for the evening dangle off her feet. She'd pretended not to notice Sky's double take when she came through the door. Now he looked as though he was trying hard not to laugh. She'd laughed herself when she first saw her reflection in Sunny's mirror, after all the makeup and hairspray had been plastered on. The look was either hooker or prom queen, she wasn't sure which. Even Layla had giggled at the sight. And the perfume! Sunny had sprayed it on so thick it had made her eyes water. She couldn't wait to get home and shower.

"Well, hello there, little lady," came a voice from her left.

She looked across the bar at Sky, who gave her a quick nod. "Well hello to you too," she answered, turning her big brown eyes toward Rick.

"You new around here?" His gaze made a slow journey down the length of her body and back up again.

Kat crossed one long leg over the other and swung her half-shod foot back and forth a little. "Sort of."

"I thought so. I would have noticed a girl like you before."

Kat smiled.

"That black-and-white hair thing you've got going on is kind of sexy. Sort of Halloween-y, but in a good way."

She bit her lip and tried not to laugh. "I like to experiment a lot." Now Rick smiled. His teeth reminded Kat of those little shiny pieces of gum that crunch when you bite them.

"Might I buy you a drink?" he asked.

Kat placed her hand on his forearm. "That is so nice of you. I'd love one."

"Name your poison."

"Poison?"

"What do you drink? How about a martini? Me, I like them dirty," he said with a wink.

"Well then," she winked back, "dirty works for me."

"You've got it." He snapped his fingers in the air.

Behind the bar Sky got busy, his hands moving around in a blur. "Enjoy," he said with a lopsided smile as he slid the drink across to her.

The watered-down gin tasted like shit. "Mmm, delicious," she said to Sky. "You must have the magic touch."

"So I've been told." Sky's eyes sparkled even in the dark.

"Yeah, by whom?" she teased back.

"So," Rick leaned into the bar between them, "now that I've bought you a drink, what do you say you tell me your name?" He propped his chin on his hands, his elbows resting heavily on the sticky wood.

Kat hesitated for a moment. "Bella. Bella Swan," she answered, the name of her favorite fictional character the first thing that came to mind.

"Bella Swan," Rick repeated slowly. Sky silently replaced his half-empty glass with a fresh one. Rick, his glassy eyes locked on Kat, didn't seem to even notice. "And where are you from, Bella Swan?"

"Guess," Kat answered with a toss of her head.

"All right. Now let's see." Rick leaned back, cocked his head, and squinted at Kat. "You talk like an American, you act like an American, but you look kind of like, hmm, let's see, a Mexican?"

Kat smiled and shook her head. "Guess again."

"Peru?" He sipped at his drink.

"Nope."

Rick leaned in toward her. "Guatemala?"

"Wrong again, *mon amour*."

"Wait, I think I've got this. France!"

Kat laughed. "Fooled you! One more guess. What'll it be?"

Rick shrugged his shoulders. "I don't know. You're Jewish?"

"That's not even a place. Give up?"

"That's no fun. Gimme one more chance." Again he drained his glass. "How about Spain?"

"Nope. I'm from LA," she laughed, and took another sip of her watery drink. "So where are *you* from?" She scooted in a little toward him. Sky pretended to be busy with a customer two stools down.

"Right here, bornanraised," Rick said, the three words slurring into one.

"Really?" She batted her mascara-coated lashes at him. "I don't believe you. I didn't think anyone nearly as good-looking as you lived on this island." Sky shot her a look from behind Rick's head.

"Well, I do."

"Prove it. Show me your driver's license." She could see Sky's look turning into one of awe. "C'mon, I want to see." She reached her hand out toward Rick's back pocket.

"It's in here." Rick pulled a worn leather wallet from the inside pocket of his jacket. Kat took it from his hand and flipped it open. "Told ya," he said as he slid off the stool and onto his wobbly legs. "Gotta pee."

Kat watched as he weaved his way through the men's-room door. "Yes!" She tossed the wallet to Sky and flashed him two thumbs up.

"Bingo," he said, as he slid it to the back of a shelf under the bar.

"Can you believe this?" she whispered loudly. "It's just way too easy, right?"

"So far so good."

"Give me a real drink, please? My hands are shaking like crazy, not that he'd notice. God, I hope we don't end up going to jail for this."

"You're doing great, babe. We're almost there." Sky scooped Rick's discarded keys off the counter and into his own pocket.

"Shhh, here he comes."

Rick returned, looking as though he might puke. "Ready to settle up, buddy?" Sky picked up the empty glasses and wiped the bar top with a towel.

"I'm not your buddy," Rick answered, his mood having turned quickly sour.

"Whoa! It's all good, pal. No offense meant."

"S'all right," Rick answered with a wave of his hand. "Want another?" He plopped his clammy hand on Kat's knee.

"I'm good."

"You are good. You're real good. Wanna show me how good you are, baby?" Rick's hands slid down her thighs.

Sky looked as if he were about to leap over the bar. Kat stopped Rick's hands with her own and forced a laugh. "And I'll just bet you're real good too, aren't you?" She stood and smoothed her tight dress over her hips, and leaned in to whisper in Rick's ear. "Now how about we go somewhere else and get to know each other a little better?"

Sky rolled his eyes.

"Sounds like fun to me." Kat watched as Rick fumbled around inside his jacket. Then he stood and steadied himself with one hand on the bar while the other made the journey from pocket to pocket, searching for his missing wallet.

"Wallet's not here. Dunno what I did with it." He bent down to look under the stool. Kat steadied him with both her hands as he swayed forward. "Not there either."

"Well then, you're just going to have to let me look." She ran her hands playfully over his ass and over his hips to the front pockets of his dark denim jeans. Then she patted the bulge in the front of his jacket. "You sure it's not in there?"

"Ha!" he said, his eyes widening. "No problem. I got this." He pulled out the envelope Sunny had given him, and a pair of stiff hundred-dollar bills were delivered across the bar to Sky. "Keep the change, my man." Rick tucked the envelope back into his jacket and started for the door.

Kat and Sky exchanged a quick glance. "Hey, Rick, very funny," Sky called after him.

"Huh?" Rick returned to the bar, his face a rubbery question mark.

"What, did you print these up yourself?" Sky pulled out a thick-tipped marker and ran it across one of the bills. "See?" He held it up for Kat. "Fake as they come. If it were real, this black mark would come out as yellow."

"Why, Rick, you're quite the bad boy, aren't you?" Kat laughed.

"What are talking about? C'mon, Bella, let's get outta here."
Kat pulled back as Rick reached for her arm. "I said let's go," he
repeated, louder this time.

Sky appeared from behind the bar in a flash. "She's not going
anywhere with you, jerk. And if you don't leave her alone and
get out of here right now I'm gonna call the cops and tell them
you've been trying to pass off fake bills. That's a federal offense,
just in case you didn't know."

"What the . . . ?" Rick's features appeared to harden as the
realization of what had happened began to sink in through
the gin. He stood frozen for a moment, his gaze moving from
Sky to Kat to the handful of regulars remaining on their stools,
their eyes now all on him. It wasn't until Sky pulled a phone
from his pocket that Rick began to back slowly toward the door.

Kat could tell that Sky was trying hard not to laugh, the
corners of his mouth held firm and tight. She scooted around
to the back of the bar as she tried to control her own laughter.
"And don't forget this!" she cried, tossing Rick's wallet across the
worn wooden floor to his feet. "You might want to buy a girl a
drink someday."

And then the door of The Dirty Monkey slammed shut, as
Rick disappeared into the silent Twimbly evening.

34

Najama sat cross-legged on the pebbled ground, tirelessly bouncing the red ball up and down in front of Poppy's flaring nose. The dog, flopped on her side in the afternoon heat, looked back at the girl through half-closed eyes, her tail rising and slapping back on to the ground every so often in a lazy wag.

Ahmet and his mother watched them in silence, lost in the haunting echoes that remained within the courtyard's walls. Neither of them had spent any time out here since the attack, save to walk back and forth from the front gate, its guardhouse now standing empty and still. But today's balmy weather had drawn them both from the house, with Najama as an excuse to take in some fresh air. Now Ahmet noticed that the hyacinth and fuchsia vines that had once helped to provide shade for their customers had turned brittle and bare from lack of care. Even the silly peahen was gone, nowhere to be seen since the day of the attack. Some *Shangri-La*, he thought, remembering what Sunny used to call this spot.

Upstairs, above the dark coffeehouse, Yazmina was resting, exhausted from the nine long months of carrying another life within her. Ahmet felt a twinge of regret as he pictured her up there struggling to find a comfortable position for her swollen body. They had had yet another argument yesterday, this one lasting so long into the night that he had trouble rousing himself for morning prayers. Again they fought about that ridiculous girl. That Yazmina and his mother insisted on allowing her to hide in their home was unacceptable to him. And that he did not seem to have the power to stop them made him feel as though he were as weak as a newborn calf.

"What is wrong with you that you need to be so involved in this family's problems?" he had lashed out at his wife after yet another refusal to make the girl leave. "All the unnecessary drama, with that funeral that wasn't a funeral. You are just being lured into things that will bring more trouble to our family. And I refuse to allow it."

"I know you might not believe that Zara was the cause of the attack. But I have seen the look in this girl's eyes, I have heard the fear in her words. I have been this girl in the past, trembling at the sound of a footstep, freezing at the touch of a hand." Yazmina shifted clumsily on her *toshak*. "I had no voice of my own to protect me, yet I did have the good fortune to find women like Sunny and Halajan who spoke up for me and helped me make my way. Helping this girl is important to me, and I would hope that with something so important you would grant me your support."

"Support? Why should I support something that brings such a risk to our home?"

Yazmina straightened her back against the wall, the anger growing like a freshly lit flame in her green eyes, the same pair of eyes that had once warmed him and weakened him and confused him. "And you don't think it was difficult for me to support you and your endless meetings?" she continued. "That I didn't worry about the rumors I heard being shared by those who pictured gambling and prostitutes and the drinking of alcohol going on behind those closed doors? Did I ever ask you to stop? No. I was willing to take the risk because I trusted in your belief that you were doing something good."

"And what good is it doing to hide this girl?" Ahmet stood and crossed his arms defiantly in front of his body

"I know it is doing good for her. And that must mean something," she said with her face turned up toward him. "Whether it is just one girl or many is not the measure of how important it is to me. This way of treating girls cannot be right, and it cannot continue. It is a problem in our country that must be fixed. And maybe this is my way of trying to fix it," she continued, her cheeks now moist with tears.

"You are just feeling this way because of your condition," he said, pointing to her belly.

"How dare you use our daughter to doubt the strength of my feelings!" she hissed.

"It will be a welcome day when this is over and my son arrives to help me keep my sanity in this house of crazy women!" he spat back.

And so it had gone throughout the night, without either of them backing down. He had seen his wife angry before, especially during the weeks since the attack on the coffeehouse, but never had he felt such fire coming from within her. And he did have to wonder, to himself, if perhaps he was witnessing the beginning of a new Yazmina, one who might manage to match her courage with her heart in ways he feared he never could.

Now, sitting in the courtyard with Halajan and Najama, he felt irritable and tired. He scowled at his mother as she pulled the scarf from her head.

"What? It is only us out here." She ran her fingers through her short grey hair.

"Well someone might come in."

"Then let them. Do you think an old lady's bare head will cause the world to end?" She reached into her pocket for a cigarette.

"And what kind of example are you for the child?" he snapped.

"What kind of example are *you* for the child?" she snapped back in a harsh whisper. "You sit around here all day as if you were a brooding hen. I do not even see you going to classes."

Ahmet lifted his eyebrows. "What is the point of me going to school when I need to be working to support my family?"

"Is that what you are doing here in this courtyard? Working to support your family? Because I don't see much work happening in front of my eyes."

"So just what do you expect me to do?" he shouted, throwing his arms into the air.

"Lower your voice!" she warned, pointing toward Najama with her chin.

Ahmet continued in a quieter, clipped manner. "The only thing I know is being a *chokidor*, and there is not much use for guards these days. Just look around you, at the half-built houses and deserted construction sites. Everyone with any money to pay another man is leaving. There is no more work for translators or drivers, or uneducated *chokidors* like me."

"Well, then you are just going to have to try a little harder. Do not wait for someone else to hand you the answers." She

248

flicked her lighter and held the flame to the tip of the cigarette. "You have wings. Learn to use them and fly."

"And what do you mean by that? Is that your beloved Rumi speaking once again?"

Halajan simply shrugged her shoulders.

"No, I mean it," Ahmet insisted. "What are you saying?"

She inhaled and exhaled slowly toward the sun, the smoke rising above their heads like a genie escaping from a bottle. "You are still acting like a little boy, my son," she began, "taking what others give, yet not able to give to yourself."

Ahmet placed both palms on the table as if preparing to rise.

"No, you sit right here and hear me out," his mother demanded in a tone he hadn't heard since he was a child. Ahmet remained frozen as she continued. "You had your job in the guardhouse thanks to Sunny, and then it was the money from the coffeehouse that allowed you to go to the university. And it was Rashif who provided you with the ideas that freed your mind from its rusty chains. And what have you done with all those gifts? You have become a big man with a big mouth. You think I don't hear the things you say to your wife? And the way you treat me, as if you are now my Taliban."

Ahmet leaned in toward her. "What I say to my wife is not your business. And you, sometimes I think you are the way you are just to annoy me." He sat back up and fixed his gaze straight ahead, away from her.

"Do not flatter yourself," Halajan snorted. "I am the way I am because it pleases me. And because there are things I believe in that I, unlike some people, must take a stand for."

"How can you dare to say that to me? What about my meetings?"

"A bunch of boys sitting in a room talking. All that babble about changing the world, what good has it done?"

"These things take time," Ahmet protested. "Do you think we can simply demand the end to ways that have existed for so many years?"

"Yes." Halajan closed her eyes and rubbed them with her palms. "You are right that big changes take time, but there are also things we can do every day that can make a difference to the future of our people."

"I am not willing to wear my inner thoughts on my sleeve for all the world to see. I am not like you, Mother." Or like Yazmina, he thought, remembering with a little envy her spirit from the night before.

"Ah, but you are smart like your father, and clever like me, my son." Halajan touched her cropped head with one bony finger. "And you also have the blessing of being surrounded with good fortune."

"What good fortune? A business that can have no more business? A wife who cares about a strange girl more than she cares about her own husband? A mother who thinks nothing of doing things that bring shame to her family? What good fortune is that?"

"Ach. Listen to yourself. It's all the way you look at it." Halajan crushed the remainder of her cigarette under her foot. "Now me," she continued, "what I see is a door open for you to do something of your own. And a wife with the desire and strength to travel down that road with you. And a mother who has hopefully given you a brain to someday use for yourself. Do you not know the story of the man who wanted to change his luck?"

Ahmet slumped back in his chair, knowing that whatever his answer was, it wouldn't make any difference.

"The man asks his lucky brother," his mother began, "'Where can I find good luck?' 'In the forest,' his brother tells him.

So the unlucky man sets out for the forest. On the way he meets a sick lion, who asks where he is going. 'To find good luck,' the man says. The lion then asks the man to find him some luck as well, to make him feel better. Then he meets a horse who is lying on his side, too weak to stand. The horse asks him to also find some luck to help him find strength. Next he sees a tree with no leaves. 'Please ask for me why I am leafless,' the tree begs. When the man reaches the place where he finds his good luck he seizes it. Then he asks the questions he carried for the lion, the horse, and the tree. His fortune replies, 'Tell the lion that he should devour a fool and he will recover his health. Tell the horse that he should take a master who will ride him and he will grow strong. And tell the tree that under its roots lies the treasure of seven kings. If the treasure is dug up, the tree's roots will flourish.' On his way home the man stops first at the tree, who begs him to dig the treasure from his roots. 'What good are riches, since I have my fortune?' the man replies. Next he comes upon the horse. 'Please sir, become my master,' the animal begs. 'I have my fortune now, so look for somebody else to be your master,' the man says as he continues on his way. When he reaches the lion he repeats the advice his fortune had given, that the lion should devour a fool. Then he tells the lion all about the tree and the horse. The lion licks his chops, and swallows the man in one big gulp."

Ahmet sighed. "That is a very nice story, Mother, but I am not going to allow myself to be eaten by a lion."

"Exactly. You must use the brains and the wit we have given you to take advantage of all the good fortune around you."

It was then that Ahmet saw Halajan's eyes light up at the sight of something over his shoulder, and he knew that Rashif had returned. He stood to greet the man. "*As-salaamu alaikum, padar.* It is good to have you home safe, Father. We have missed you here. How was your visit to your cousin?"

"*Wa-alaikum-salaam,* my son." Rashif turned to Halajan with a look of sorrow in his eyes, and took her two hands in his. "I am sorry, my sweet wife. I did what I could."

Halajan's hands flew to her mouth.

Rashif turned to face Ahmet. "And to you, *bachai ma,* my son, I am sorry as well. It was your friend Omar I was with in Mazar, not my cousin."

"So you lied to me? This is why you are sorry?"

Rashif shook his head. "I was helping Omar find his way to Herat. I was there to use my eyes and my friends to keep him safe, but I failed."

"What do you mean you failed?"

"He is gone, killed by a bullet from one of Faheem's men right after I left him in Mazar. I do not know how they found him. I'm out of my mind with sadness that I could not protect him from that madman."

Ahmet sat in silence for a moment, stunned by this news he wished was instead the lie Rashif had told him. "Omar? Omar is dead?"

Halajan turned a sharp eye on him. "Now do you see for yourself why we must act and not talk? Now do you believe the idiotic reason for what happened here?" She waved her arm around the courtyard. "Now do you understand the lengths to which a man will go to hold on to a pride that is based on a twisted belief?"

Ahmet's cheeks burned with anger and shame. But before he could respond to his mother's reproach, a small voice could be heard coming from the door of the coffeehouse.

"Please, will someone drive me to the hospital?" Yazmina asked. "It is time."

35

"Well, if it isn't Bella Swan." Kat was emerging from the house, her hair pulled up into a messy bun and her eyes still sleepy. "Good afternoon. Where's Layla? Don't tell me she's still in bed. You're such a bad influence on her."

"Ha! *I'm* the bad influence? I just watched her down some Frosted Flakes and Mountain Dew for breakfast. I wonder where she learned to do that?" Kat took a seat on the other side of the picnic table, facing the water, her back to Sunny and Joe.

"Bella Swan? Why do you call her that?" Joe scratched his snowy head.

"It's the fake name she used when we played the trick on Rick. Now Kat will forever be Bella Swan to me."

Joe laughed. He seemed to have gotten more of a kick out of the whole Rick escapade than any of them, making them recount how it had all gone down over and over and over again. He was particularly proud of his own role in the scheme, the fake phone call to Sunny about her busted pipes. None of them had heard a peep from Rick since that night, save for a call from the bank to say that the deed had been signed and the paperwork readied for transfer.

Sunny gathered her own hair up on top of her head and covered it with a floppy red hat. "So where is Layla, now that she's had a hearty breakfast with all that recommended daily nutrition?"

"Trying to Skype with her sister, I think," Kat answered without turning around.

Sunny was tempted to go inside and join Layla—to hear how everyone was doing, to see for herself how Yaz was coming along—but she wanted to give the girl her privacy. If there was any news, Layla would pass it on. Candace had been checking up on everyone, and last they spoke she'd assured Sunny that Bashir Hadi had healed, and had told her that Yazmina looked as though she were about to give birth to a pair of elephants. Right now everything over there seemed to be at a standstill, on hold until they figured out what to do with the coffeehouse, a matter that still pained Sunny terribly if she let herself dwell on it. But it wasn't long before Layla joined them outside, ready for work under the baseball cap that sat on top of her head scarf.

"Everything okay?" Sunny asked.

"I could not get it to work. Maybe they are not there," Layla answered in a quiet voice.

"It won't be long now before you see them."

"I know."

"I miss them too."

"I know."

Sunny felt for the girl, but at the same time envied her, heading back to Kabul in less than a month. But perhaps it was just Sunny who felt homesick for the place, and it was instead the whole crush thing with Sky that was getting to Layla. She had taken it upon herself to warn Sky, who had laughed a little at the young girl's infatuation, and promised to be extra careful not to encourage her. She hadn't yet come up with a way to talk to Layla without causing the inevitable embarrassment the topic would bring, but with some luck maybe the flame would burn out by itself in due time.

"Let's go, people! Those grapes aren't going to pick themselves, you know." As if on cue, Sky came bounding out of the barn, his bare chest already damp with sweat, his khaki shorts caked with dirt. "Everyone have a hat?" he asked as he plopped a straw fedora on top of his long curls. "It's gonna get hot out there." He raised a plastic bucket above his head. "Come choose your weapons!"

Sunny obediently accepted a pair of work gloves and a set of clippers, and hitched up her shorts. If only Jack could see me now, she thought with a snicker. They formed a motley parade down to the vines, Sky in the lead and Joe close behind, steadying himself with a thick walking stick Sky had ingeniously fashioned, which doubled as a portable stool. The two girls brought up the rear, both still seeming a bit out of sorts.

"So we're going to be working in pairs today," Sky explained when they reached the vineyard. "One will work one side of the vines, the other the opposite side. That way you won't have to reach around. Understand?" He scanned their faces for a response. "Now listen up," he said, sounding way too much like the gym instructor whose Gatorade Sunny had once spiked with cayenne pepper. "The most important thing is to concentrate on what you're doing. You don't want to miss anything. No waste. We don't have a lot of grapes here, so we can't afford to leave anything behind. Now, that doesn't mean that we want to use every single grape on the vine. If you see a bunch that looks like raisins already, you snip them off and let them drop to the ground. The others, the good-looking ones, you toss into the bins." He pointed to the lineup of plastic yellow boxes he'd scattered throughout the vineyard earlier that morning. "And just leave them there. I'll bring the truck around later to pick them up for de-stemming. And now, we cut." Sky paused, and turned to Joe. "Would you care to demonstrate for the ladies?"

"With pleasure," Joe smiled.

Sunny fanned herself with her hat as she waited for Joe to set up his cane-stool in front of a vine dripping with heavy grapes. He groaned a little as he sat, then held out his gloved hand to Sky as if he were a surgeon preparing to operate. Sky delicately placed the shiny clippers into his palm. Then Joe leaned forward and reached his arms between the leaves, and with one snip a bunch of dark purple grapes were flying from his hand into the bin, where they landed with a soft thud.

"Easy-peasy." Sunny turned to get to work.

"Not so fast there, missy." Joe shook his clippers at her. "It might look easy, but take your time. These are our babies you're dealing with."

The first few vines went quickly. She was paired with Kat, who worked quietly and efficiently, filling the bin on her side of the vine at the same rate as Sunny filled hers. Layla and Joe were teamed up on the next row over, with Joe attacking the lower parts of the vines from his seat on the stool, and Layla using her height to take care of the grapes on top. Sky acted as a one-man reaper, his clippers slashing and flashing in the mid-morning sun. Really, Sunny thought, what was the big deal?

But it didn't take long for her to realize it was harder work than she thought. Her hands were becoming cramped like a crab's claw, and her T-shirt was beginning to feel as though she had worn it into the shower. She wiped the sweat from her face and stepped back from the vines, removed her gloves and stood with one hand on her lower back. "Water?" she asked Kat, offering the bottle she'd hooked to her belt loop. Kat shook her head and continued to snip. Sunny checked the time on her phone. "Twenty minutes?" she said out loud. "You've gotta be shitting me!" It felt like an hour. And still so many grapes to cut, she thought, her eyes scanning the green canopies that now seemed to go on for miles. She capped the water, pulled on her gloves, and went back to work. Pull-clip-toss. Pull-clip-toss. Pull-clip-toss. The bins were filled behind them as they edged toward the end of one row and started up the next. Pull-clip-toss. If the heat didn't kill her, the tedium surely would. What they needed was some music, or at least a little conversation to pass the time.

"So," Sunny said as she and Kat made the U-turn into the next row of vines, "nice day, right?"

Kat peered at her through the leaves.

"I mean, if you like the heat and all." Sunny swatted at a bee circling her head. "Personally, it makes me feel like a billy goat in a pepper patch."

Kat didn't laugh. They finished another row together in silence. Halfway through the next one, Sunny tried again. "How are things in Seattle? Your uncle, your cousins, everybody good?" she asked, going for the Afghan way of small talk.

But Kat just shrugged her shoulders and kept on working. Pull-clip-toss. Pull-clip-toss.

"You know, once, when I was in Morocco, it was so hot that we literally put our sheets in the freezer before we went to bed, and filled our hats with ice cubes. And did you know that eating spicy foods is actually supposed to be good on hot days? It raises body temperature, which makes you sweat, which cools you off."

The hand holding Kat's clippers dropped to her side. "Would you mind if we just didn't talk? I really need to focus."

Sunny closed her mouth and watched Joe head up toward the house. Lunch soon, thank God. She bent over and resumed cutting. She could hear Sky and Layla's laughter coming from the far end of the vineyard. Kat moved on to the next vine. Sunny squinted at the grapes through eyes burning from sweat and sunscreen, trying her best to follow Sky's good grape–bad grape instructions, but it was getting difficult to see. She hurried to keep up with Kat.

"Come and get it!" Joe finally called from the top of the hill, his voice booming through the silence. Sunny was the first at the picnic table, where she unlaced her boots and pried them off her sweaty feet. "So," Joe said, "what do you think?"

"Me?" Sunny asked, squeezing her aching arches with her cramped fingers.

"Yes, you. How do you like the harvest?"

"Well," she said after a pause for a desperate gulp of cold water, "I've gotta say, it's not exactly how I pictured it. You know, holding up my peasant skirt, stomping on grapes, everyone all happy . . . drinking . . . singing, maybe a little hanky-panky in the vines. At least you got the checkered tablecloth part right." She flicked an ant onto the grass.

"Poor Sunny," Joe laughed. "Maybe we can make the rest of it happen for you later in the week. Wine is hard work."

"Doesn't have to be. You know they even sell it with screw tops. Barely need to lift a finger."

"Ha! But you know what they say. *Non ha il dolce a caro, chi provato non ha l'amaro.* To taste the sweet, you must taste the bitter."

"Okay, Joe." She poured the rest of the water down her parched throat. "Whatever you say."

The others soon followed, their faces streaked with dirt and their hair plastered to their heads. Everyone seemed too tired to talk. "*Mangia!*" Joe passed around the plate of sandwiches as they all settled in, and a feeding frenzy worthy of Sea World began. Sunny could have sworn that nothing in her life had ever tasted anywhere as good as Joe's prosciutto and mozzarella on ciabatta did that day. They were already on seconds before anyone uttered a word. And, of course, it was Joe who spoke first.

"I'd like to propose a toast." He tapped a spoon on the edge of his water glass, as if he needed it even quieter than it already was. "Harvest," he cleared his throat, "is a special time of year. It is the end of something, and the beginning of another. The cycle of life." He paused to allow for a seaplane to pass overhead. "It is a bittersweet time of year, but also an exciting one. And with that," he held his glass into the air, "I offer a special blessing to our friends Sky and Layla." Sunny wiped the tomato from her chin and picked up her glass, and elbowed Kat to do the same. "To Sky, off to school and new adventures. May you come back and teach me a thing or two someday." Sky nodded, his grin stretching from ear to ear. "And our dear Layla, heading home to your family as an even lovelier young lady than the one who first crossed our doorstep. We will miss you. To both of you, *Cent'anni.* May you live a hundred years—although, personally, there are some mornings when I wake up feeling that it is way too long."

Sky clinked his glass against Layla's and downed the rest of his water.

"Wait, I'm not finished." Joe pulled a bottle of wine from under the table and poured two glasses, one of which he handed to Sunny. "To the man who made this all possible. Without him, we would never have had the good fortune to find ourselves in each other's company. To Jack." Joe looked Sunny squarely in the eye as they drank to his toast.

"To Jack," she echoed, her heart suddenly feeling as weary as the rest of her.

Sky stood and stretched his browned arms high above his head, then turned to Layla. "Back to work?" She nodded and followed him down to the vines. Sunny watched them go, their shadows peeking out from behind them in the early afternoon light. Beside her Kat was watching as well, her silence weighing heavily in the air.

"So what's next for you?" Sunny asked, picking a stray piece of cheese from the table and popping it into her mouth.

"What do you mean?" Kat asked.

"Do you have any plans?"

"Plans? Like what?"

"You know, for the fall. After Layla leaves."

Kat shrugged her shoulders.

"Nothing?" It dawned on Sunny that she'd been peppering the girl with the very same questions she should be answering herself. It was harvest day, after all, and much to her disappointment, she had not awoken to a light bulb flashing over her head heralding the solution to her own dilemma. "Well you're welcome to stay here, you know, for at least as long as I'm here, though it might not be for that long," she offered. From the corner of her eye, she thought she saw Joe chuckle a little to himself. "But it could get kind of boring, without Layla and Sky."

"Thanks," Kat answered in a quiet voice.

"I suppose you could always find work back on the mainland, especially around the holidays."

Kat lowered her head.

"But if you did want to stay on the island, maybe Joe could help. He seems to know just about everyone around here, right, Joe?" She looked at the old man, who gestured toward Kat with his chin. Sunny turned to see a tear escaping down Kat's dusty face. Sunny reached out to touch her arm, but Kat jerked away. "I know it's hard."

Kat shook her head as she tried to mask her tears. "You don't know."

"He'll be back next summer. And there are weekends, too."

"I know. It's not just that."

"Layla?"

Kat shrugged her shoulders.

"I thought you'd be sort of happy to have your freedom back, and your privacy."

Kat didn't answer.

"Well I get where you're coming from. Me, I've spent all these months sticking around for Layla, waiting for Joe's grapes, and now what?"

"At least you have a house."

"You're right. There is that. And like I said, the door is open for you as long as I'm here."

"I don't belong here," Kat said, shaking her head.

"Don't be silly. Of course—"

"I don't belong anywhere," the girl interrupted with a sudden sob.

A lump formed in Sunny's throat. "I know how you feel."

"Really?" Kat asked as she wiped the tears from her face with the back of her arm. "You think you do? I doubt that."

Sunny cocked her head at the girl. "Yes, I do." Sunny felt a little stung by the girl's accusation. "You don't really know much about me, do you?"

Kat didn't answer.

"No, you don't. You're just too busy being all critical and angry all the time to learn much about anybody."

"I know more than you think I know," Kat shot back. "And you're so busy telling everyone about how it's so much better in Afghanistan than it is over here that you don't even know what you're talking about."

"That doesn't even make sense." Sunny felt the crack in her voice.

"You don't even make sense!"

"Whoa there, ladies, whoa," Joe interrupted, waving a white napkin in the air. "Listen to the two of you. A couple of top-notch goldbrickers I've got here. Enough already. Are we going to make those two pick the rest of the grapes by themselves?" He reached across the table for the empty plates, stacking them one on top of another with exaggerated care.

Sunny knelt down to lace up her boots, her own tears invisible to the others. No, this was not at all how she had pictured this day. And she was pissed.

"You know," she said to Kat as she straightened up on the bench, "I'm sorry that you're feeling so bad. I truly am. And I'm sorry you lost your parents. But you do realize you're not the only one around here to lose somebody they loved, don't you?"

Kat lowered her eyes toward the table.

"And I know it hurts, believe me. And it will always hurt. But your anger isn't going to fix that, not at all."

"I wouldn't go there if I were you," Kat muttered, as if talking to herself.

"You have your parents with you forever, you know," Sunny said, her voice softening a bit. "They're who you are. You're a lucky girl, having the blood of those people, and all those who came before them, inside you. You're the daughter of thousands of years of incredible history, of a resilient and noble spirit that's lived forever. You should be proud of who you are."

Kat brushed off Sunny's words with a snort. "Yeah, well I also have the blood of a monster in me."

"Oh come on, Kat. What are you talking about?"

Kat sat up and looked Sunny straight in the eye, as if sizing her up for a difficult task. "You really want to know? Then I'll tell you. My father isn't dead, at least I don't think he is. He's back in Afghanistan, that wonderful country you love so much, where nobody gives a shit that he murdered my mother."

Sunny felt as though she'd been kicked hard in the stomach. Across the table, Joe was nodding with a faraway look in his eye, as if he were trying to recall something he'd forgotten. It was he who spoke first. "Your mother, she died in a fire, am I right?" Kat nodded. "I remember now, from the newspaper. A terrible story."

"I'm so, so sorry." Sunny placed her hand on Kat's arm. This time the girl didn't pull away. Sunny didn't need to hear the details. She'd heard all too many of these types of stories in Afghanistan. Honor killings. There was certainly no honor to be had for those left behind, she thought.

They sat for a long while in silence, under the bright midday sun. Kat suddenly looked to Sunny like a little girl, her eyes soft and round, her lips relaxed and full. Joe, on the other hand, seemed stirred up. She could practically feel the wheels turning inside his head as she bent over to finish lacing her boots. Sunny felt as depleted as a flat tire on a desert highway. She'd give anything and everything for an afternoon alone with a long shower and a cool pillow. But there was work to be done, so instead she heaved a sigh as deep as the blue Sound itself, and started back down toward the waiting vines.

36

Halajan had wanted to do things properly this time, unlike with Najama, who had come into this world so suddenly, and under such difficult circumstances, that they'd never even considered a celebration. She had been picturing a big party for months, one where every woman she knew would gather in their finest glittery party dresses under her roof. She had hoped her daughter Aisha would fly in from her home in Germany; it had been so long since they had seen her. She would invite Bita and Tamra from her driving class, along with their teacher, Anisa, of course. Fattanah from down the street would arrive, perhaps with some bread still warm from her ovens. And maybe even crazy Candace would pop in on her way to who-knows-where, with her bright yellow hair and sparkly jewels that would make the other women stare with wonder. Together they'd all dance to the beat of the harmonium and *tabla*—the reed organ and goat-skinned drums played by Bashir Hadi's wife's brother and cousin—until they were dizzy with laughter, collapsing onto the *toshaks* in Halajan's sitting room with exhaustion, eager for the *hawasaana*, special treats she would have asked Bashir Hadi to prepare for them. They would feast on lamb and *sheer-brinj*, the sweet rice pudding with almonds and rosewater that was Halajan's favorite, *aashak* dumplings filled with chives, and sweet *baklava*, all washed down with Coca-Cola and green tea. The women would present gifts for the baby; little clothes and soft blankets and gracious offerings of money. And they would all be fussing around Halajan, offering their congratulations to the proud grandmother for the new addition to her family.

But, of course, none of this would be happening now. Not with all that had occurred at the coffeehouse, and with the news of Omar's death arriving just seven days earlier. Now Zara was back in Herat with her family, driven there by a Canadian couple, NGO workers Candace knew, who had arrived two days after the baby was born. Halajan could still hear the girl's brokenhearted sobs as the woman helped her gently into the SUV. But Zara was young, and had a good family who would do whatever they could to help ease the pain of losing Omar, and make her whole again.

Ahmet seemed to be taking Omar's death hard as well. It was as though he had been walking around in a daze since that day of the baby's birth, as if he were the one up all night offering his breast, as opposed to Yazmina. She couldn't help but wonder if part of it was disappointment at having a girl. But perhaps it was just panic at the new responsibility that comes with a child, especially for a man so uncertain of his own future. Whatever it was, he had hardly looked at the baby since Yazmina had returned from the hospital. Lately it had become nearly impossible to tell what was going on behind her son's wooden eyes.

So today's *shaw-e-shash* celebration would be a quiet one. Just their little family, with Layla and Sunny attending from across two continents, thanks to the computer they'd set up in the middle of the carved wooden table.

Rashif turned the screen and tilted it back to allow them all to see. "Hey, everyone!" Sunny's voice boomed across the miles. Rashif rushed to turn down the volume, so as not to wake the child.

"Hello, Sunny. Do you see our new daughter?" Yazmina tugged at the long yellow scarf she wore across her body, revealing a tiny pink face with kohl-smudged eyes peeking out from a tight cocoon of blankets tied up with a ribbon, like a gift-wrapped peanut in a shell. Sunny's hands flew to her mouth.

"Hello, my little niece! *Khosh aamadi.* Welcome!" Halajan could see Layla craning her neck to get a better look. Then she disappeared from view. "Kat!" they heard her call. "*Bya tefla bebi!* Come and see the baby!" Then there were three people crowded into the screen, their faces stretched and warped, as if they were made of rubber. Halajan was puzzled by this Kat's hair, part white and part black. And Layla speaking to her in Dari? Was this the one who was teaching her English? But it was the look on this girl's face that unsettled her the most. She clearly seemed as though she wanted to be anywhere but here, a part of this little gathering in Halajan's home. Yazmina held the baby closer to the screen. Then Halajan noticed the girl's hard eyes softening.

"She's beautiful," Kat said. "So beautiful."

"*Nazar nasha!*" they all shouted out at once. "*Nazar nasha!*"

Kat, and Sunny, looked confused. Halajan had to laugh. "It is not good to let someone compliment too much, or bad luck may fall upon the child. *Nazar nasha* is what we say to keep the baby from becoming jinxed."

"Sorry," the girl said as she slipped out of view.

Yazmina settled back onto her *toshak* and tucked the baby back in her sling. Rashif sat leaning against the wall with a sleepy Najama in his lap, Ahmet silent and solemn beside him, picking at a dish of *bolaani*, the spinach-filled flatbread Halajan had put out at the last minute.

"Well then," Halajan spoke, suddenly aware of the stillness of the room. She wished they had at least thought to play some music on the radio, something, anything to liven things up a little.

It was Sunny who broke the silence. "Now what do we do?" she asked eagerly.

Yazmina shifted the bundle in her arms and leaned in a bit toward the screen. "Today," she explained, "we are mixing some of the things we normally do right away when the baby is born with some of the things that we do on the sixth night. It is better this way, given the sad news we received on that day she was born. And I am happy that my sister, and of course you, can now be a part of our celebration."

Sunny nodded. "Me too. You have no idea." She moved in closer to the screen. "So what happens first?"

Yazmina picked up a date from the dish on the table. "A baby's first taste must be of something sweet," she said as she popped the date into her own mouth and chewed. Then she withdrew the sticky morsel with her fingers and gently pried open the baby's tiny beak, and rubbed the softened fruit onto her gums. "This is called *tahneek*," she explained. "It is also supposed to strengthen the jaws and the muscles of the baby."

"She likes it!" Sunny laughed. "Better keep that one away from Bashir Hadi's cookies."

Halajan could see Sunny and Layla, with the shadow of the black-and-white-haired girl behind them, smiling and gushing over the baby's every move. She also noticed Ahmet's eyes darting back and forth from the screen to the bundle in his wife's arms as he straightened on his pillow. "Please, get me the bowl and razor," she said to him. He stood and crossed into the other room, and returned obediently with the two objects in his hands. "Now we will shave the baby's head," Halajan explained.

"What?" Sunny gasped. "And ruin her little 'do? The poor thing will be bald as a cue ball."

"She seems to have enough to spare." Layla laughed at the mop of black hair that sprang from the knit cap pulled from the infant's head.

"Well then maybe we should just shave a part of it, because according to the traditions, we must make an offering of silver equal to the weight of her hair to the needy," Halajan said.

"Mother!" Ahmet scolded in a harsh whisper.

"It's just a joke. Of course we will give to the poor. And don't worry, Sunny. It is said that shaving will make the hair grow back even thicker."

"So is that why you shave it? To make it thicker?"

Halajan shrugged her shoulders. "That is what some people say. They also say that the shaving of the head provides the child with strength, and opens up the pores of their skin, and that it is good for their hearing and eyesight—just like the kohl—and improves their sense of smell as well."

"Wow. I might just go shave my own head. What do you think?" Halajan and Yazmina laughed as Sunny pulled back the mop of curls on her head into a smooth flat cap.

Halajan pushed up her sleeves and dipped her knobby fingers into the warm, soapy water, then ran them gently over the baby's head, feeling the soft spot where the bones of the skull had not yet joined. She breathed in the sweet, familiar scent of a newborn's scalp, then picked up the razor and dipped it in the water as well.

"Be careful, Mother!" Ahmet leaned in, as if to grab the sharp tool from his mother's hands.

Halajan paused and smiled a little, then began to stroke the razor lightly across the baby's head. "It is important that I get it all, and not leave one strand on the head," she continued with her explanation to Sunny. "That is called *qaz*, and is disallowed. It is not fair to the head to make some of it bare and keep the rest hidden. Like wearing a shoe on one foot, and none on the other, which is also forbidden. It would be as though a part of the body receives sunlight, and the rest of it shade."

"Just like the grapes!" Layla exclaimed. Halajan stopped for a second and tilted her head to the screen. "We pulled off the leaves to give sun to all the grapes," the girl explained.

"Okay," Halajan said as she returned to her task. "So we are pulling off her leaves to give sun to all her grapes." With the baby's eyes seeming to stare straight into hers, she finished the job without even the tiniest of nicks, and extended the bowl and razor toward Ahmet. "Done." Her son took them from her hands and released a breath he seemed to have been holding inside the entire time.

Yazmina dried the baby's scalp with the edge of the scarf. "And now," she addressed the laptop screen, as if she were instructing a class, "it is time to recite the *aazaan*. The call to prayer is normally supposed to be the first words a newborn hears, to invite the child to embrace Allah, and to keep away the temptation of *Shaytaan*." Yazmina held out her arm to Rashif, who stood and helped her up onto her feet. She lifted the bundle from the sling and held it out for him to do the honors.

He solemnly took the child from her with a ceremonious nod, and cleared his throat.

"No," came a voice from behind them. "I will be the one to do it."

Halajan could barely contain the grin that was fighting to take over her face. She bit down hard on the insides of her cheeks and looked over at her daughter-in-law, who appeared to be frozen on the spot. Finally Halajan noticed her breast rise as she took in a deep breath, one that seemed to make her grow three inches taller in front of their eyes. Then Yazmina lifted the baby from Rashif's arms and placed her gently in her husband's embrace, their two pairs of eyes meeting with a bolt of passion that could be felt throughout the room. With Yazmina's help, Ahmet carefully lowered himself down to sit on the pillow, where she perched on her knees behind his left shoulder. He then bent his head toward the baby's right ear, and a soft sweet tune began to flow from his lips. "*Allaahu Akbar, Allaahu Akbar,*" he sang. "*Allaahu Akbar, Allaahu Akbar.*" Halajan and Yazmina's eyes connected through a blur of tears that were fighting to spill from their eyes. "*Hayya' alas Salaah,*" Ahmet continued. The baby cooed in his arms, as if the sound of her father's cracking voice were a lullaby meant just for her.

"*Laa ilaaha illa-Lah.*" Ahmet had barely been able to finish the *aazaan*. Yazmina reached out for the child but Ahmet held her tight, against his heart, as a rosy glow filled his face. Halajan had not seen him look this way for months. It was as if he had awoken from a stupor. "Do you see my girl?" he asked as he leaned in toward the screen with the baby, a tear sliding down his face onto hers. "Sunny, do you see my daughter?" he wept.

Halajan willed the lump in her throat back to wherever it came from, with no success. She took the hem of her chador and dabbed at her own tears that came bursting out like water from a shattered dam.

Ahmet gently bounced the tiny bundle as he crooked his neck to wipe his cheek on the back of a sleeve. "My precious Aarezo," he whispered. "My daughter of hope." A soft coo escaped from between the blankets. "I have so much to say to you too!" he answered with a smile. "But first, my little one," he paused to kiss the top of her head, "I want to make you a promise, today on the day of your naming. It is a special promise for you, and also for your big sister Najama." He tilted the swaddled baby up toward the girl now asleep on Rashif's lap. "It is for you two, but also for your Aunt Layla, that I say this now. Actually," he leaned in close to the baby's ear and whispered loudly enough for the others to hear, "it is also said for all the bossy women in my life, the ones who have made me as crazy as I am." He paused and looked at his mother and Yazmina, and then at Sunny, who chuckled a little as she wiped her own eyes. Ahmet turned back to the child and then went on. "For it is thanks to your mother and your nana and also your auntie Sunny that I have eyes that see what they see, and a heart that feels what it feels." He spoke softly, his face almost touching hers, as if there were no one else in the room. "We are lucky, are we not?" Again the baby cooed. "But today, my precious daughter, it is you who I am grateful to, you who has made me discover a love that feels oceans bigger than what can possibly fit inside of me."

Across the room, Halajan reached for Rashif's hand.

"How, my tiny girl," Ahmet continued in a voice breaking with emotion, "how can I not wish a life full of promise for you, a future where anything you dream of can be possible? You are my sun and my moon and my reason for being, and there will be no man who will keep away the happiness I crave for you."

Behind him, Yazmina tightened her grip on her husband's trembling shoulders. Ahmet's eyes remained fixed on the baby. "But I cannot just wish this life for you," he said, shaking his head slowly back and forth. "No. I must *make* it so." He inhaled deeply, as if attempting to force the tears that were now falling like rain back inside. "Here is my promise to you, my beautiful Aarezo," he continued, pulling himself up straighter on the cushion. "From this day forward, I will devote myself to fixing what is wrong for the girls and women in this country. It is my duty. Because without you, we would have no country. And when we silence you, we are cheating ourselves of half the power that is needed to make this place whole again."

"Your words come from the mouth of a strong man, my son," Rashif said quietly, one arm firmly sheltering the sleeping Najama.

Ahmet raised his head at the sound of Rashif's voice, as if surprised to find all eyes in the room upon him. "And no more talk," he added, looking at his mother. "Just doing. My wife has said to me that helping one girl is like helping a hundred. So maybe together we can help a hundred, which will be like helping a thousand. And if we can help a thousand? Well, as my mother's friend Rumi would say, *the garden of the world has no limits, except in your mind.*"

Ahmet relaxed back on the pillow, his face a mixture of pride and determination. Halajan could barely control herself from jumping up and grabbing his cheeks, just as she had done when he was a little boy. Instead she remained seated, basking in the echoes of her son's words, which had suddenly filled the room with a distinct warmth, and with the melodious tune from a drum and organ only she could hear.

37

"Scones!" Sky nearly trampled over a family pushing a double stroller in his haste to reach the vendor sitting right inside the fair's entrance gate. It had been all the young man talked about during the entire trek over on the ferry. "You guys will love them, I swear. Am I right, Joe?" Joe just nodded. The truth was, he hadn't set foot on the fairgrounds in a little over seventy years, and last time he had been there, the sight of a scone would have been rare indeed.

"Have a bite," Sky urged Sunny, butter and jam dripping down his chin.

Sunny put up her hand. "I'm good. Looks way too much like the biscuits and gravy I grew up—and out—on," she said, patting her thighs.

"Well, you don't know what you're missing. Hey, look! Krusty Pups. C'mon!" Sky grabbed Kat's hand and loped toward the crowded red and white clapboard stand. Layla turned to Sunny, eyebrows raised.

"Corn dogs," Sunny explained, spying the giant cutout on the roof. "It's like a hot dog, but dipped in batter." Layla still looked confused. "Just go try it." She waved the girl off toward the others. "Make sure it's beef!" Sunny turned to Joe, taking his arm in hers. "She'll probably hate it." Together they made their way to a bench, where they sat to wait.

On the edge of the midway, a train of metal cars rattled and chugged up to the first peak of the old wooden roller coaster, then came whipping down and around its twisty curves with a symphony of screaming kids giddy with fear. Joe could remember the first time he rode that roller coaster, promising himself that no matter what he would not cry in front of his older brother. He had kept his eyes clamped shut as they flew high above the fairgrounds at breakneck speed, but once they had stopped, all he wanted to do was ride it again. And again. Which they did, until George dragged him off to try out the giant Ferris wheel, the Octopus, and the Fly-O-Plane, all equally thrilling to a ten-year-old boy. Why was it that kids these days seemed to need to feel so much more of a sense of danger in order to have fun? he thought, watching from a distance as the cars of the new coaster zoomed upside down and sideways and back again as if desperately trying to shake their cargo out from inside.

"You okay, Joe?" Sunny asked, making him realize that the sigh he thought was only in his head had escaped out loud.

"I'm fine. Just thinking."

"Nice idea, bringing us here today. We could all use a break."

"I know."

"Though me, I'm not one much for the cows and pigs, or the quilts and jams and pickles you find at these things. But it's nice for Layla and those guys."

"Uh-huh."

"We had a fair back home, in Arkansas. There were beauty pageants, for girls and women, even women older than me, if you can imagine that. They had the same guys who judged the livestock judging the pageants. Seriously."

"Hmmm."

"I won once, you know. *Tubbiest Toddler*."

"That's nice."

"That was a joke, Joe. You aren't even listening to me. Are you sure you're all right?"

Just then Sky, Kat, and Layla joined up with them, their hands full of food—elephant ears, turkey legs, caramel apples— it seemed as though the only thing they weren't sampling was the deep-fried butter that filled the air with a sickening aroma. Whoever invented that cockamamie concoction should be tied to the last car of the roller coaster and forced to eat the stuff until they begged for mercy, in Joe's opinion. "Shall we go look around?" he asked, struggling to rise from the bench. The younger ones ran ahead, while Sunny stuck by his side as they wound their way through the growing crowd, making a left around the attraction where people were actually paying money to be dropped from a twenty-story tower like the stuffed mouse on the end of a rubber band that was Sangiovese's favorite cat toy.

"Oooh, can we go in there?" Sunny pointed to a series of low buildings where old-fashioned carnival barkers with microphone headsets were wooing the crowd with miracle cures for modern woes. She pulled Joe through the double glass doors.

Inside it was brighter than the daylight they'd come from, and jammed with people with money to burn. They might as well burn it, Joe thought, as he eyed the pans that promised perfect pancakes, the glue guaranteed to hold up a car, the lipstick that would turn the perfect shade once it touched your lips. What a bunch of hooey.

Up and down the carpeted aisles they went, Sunny's eyes as round as pennies at each new useless device that came into view. "Hold out your arms," a guy in a black cowboy hat commanded as they passed a booth lined with boxes of vacuum cleaners. "No, really. You'll be amazed," he persisted. Joe tried to keep walking, eyes straight ahead. But with Sunny's arm hooked around his own, he had no choice than to stop. "Two hands, lady. You won't be sorry." Sunny groaned a little as he placed a blue bowling ball on top of her open palms. He continued with his spiel as a crowd began to form. "That's right, folks. The one and only piece of cleaning equipment you'll ever need. Guaranteed for a lifetime. No strings attached. Step right up and take a look." Sunny's arms began to throb. She was about to suggest to Joe that he step back out of the way when the ball flew upward out of her hands and onto the nozzle of a purring machine.

"Did you see that, Joe? He sucked it right out of my hands!" Sunny said with awe.

"Must not have been that heavy," Joe snorted, dragging her away by the arm.

"Come on, Joe. Don't you just love this stuff?" They passed a guy selling knives that could cut through a penny, whose fingers, Joe noticed, were covered in Band-Aids.

"Hello, pretty bird!" Sunny yelled at a mechanical parrot on a perch across the aisle.

"Hello, pretty bird!" it yelled back.

"Just what we need," she whispered loudly in Joe's ear. "God forbid I'd have to listen to everything you say twice."

Joe forced a little laugh, his wandering mind keeping his thoughts elsewhere.

Sunny stopped in the middle of the aisle as the crowd continued to flow around them. "Are you sure you're all right, Joe? I've never seen you so quiet."

"Of course I'm all right." He patted her arm. "Why wouldn't I be? Look over there!" He nodded toward a booth where a thick-waisted man had just poured a whole can of soda onto the tiled floor. As if he were a magician on a stage, he whipped out a mop from behind his back and sopped the entire puddle up in one pass, then held the mop head over his own head to demonstrate its dripless powers. His final trick was to wring it out over a glass. "Ready to drink all over again!" he bellowed as he licked his lips.

"Gross," Sunny said, turning her attention to a ropeless jump-rope—simply two weighted handles you held as you jumped—that would supposedly melt off unwanted pounds. "Now there's something for you, Joe." She pointed at a small desk chair. *Take The Work Out Of Your Workout*, the sign read. She urged Joe to sit, which he gladly did. But suddenly the little round seat beneath him began to swivel, pivoting around like a gyrating top, faster and faster, forcing his hips into a frenzied belly dance.

"Get me outta this thing!" he yelled.

She turned the switch to off and helped him up. "What, you don't want six-pack abs, Joe?" she laughed.

"Six-pack my ass. The only thing that piece of crap did was make my behind hot."

Next Sunny was drawn to a small crowd that was building around a buxom woman in a black negligee, who was curling up on a full-sized bed. They watched as the woman snuggled in next to a pillow shaped like half a torso connected to a single arm, which she gently cradled around the back of her shoulders, leaving its stuffed and stitched hand resting on her hip. "The Boyfriend Pillow!" barked a man with a mic. "Feel safe and warm in his embrace!"

"I think I might need one of those, Joe," Sunny sighed.

"Like they say," Joe said as he lured her away with the tug of an arm, "there is a sucker born every minute."

"What, you're not going to tell me that in Italian?"

Once he finally pried her out of there, Sunny was ready to explore the old Hobby Hall, where Joe remembered seeing woodcarvers and quilters competing for the prized blue ribbon many years ago. He told her to go on ahead, and take her time. They'd meet back out here.

Left alone, he remained in front of the building, leaning against its aluminum siding. With his eyes closed against the afternoon sun, he could almost hear the sounds of another time: the rain falling on a tarpaper roof, the coughing, snoring, whispering, arguing, and lovemaking ricocheting in the dark through open spaces between walls and ceilings. Other memories—the taste of canned meat and the stench of over-crowded latrines—were as sharp on his tongue and the inside of his nose as if it were yesterday. And that feeling of being trapped like a bird in a cage, or a rat in a hole—that was something that had never quite left him. Suddenly he felt as though he couldn't breathe.

"Seriously, Joe, we can go home if you want." He opened his eyes to find Sunny at his side.

"No, no. I'm really fine," he assured her, standing up tall. "Stop worrying so much."

"There you are!" Sky was trotting toward them with a burger in one hand and a Coke in the other, followed by Kat sipping a snow cone and Layla holding a sticky pink cloud of cotton candy as far away from herself as her arm could reach, as if it were a muddy shoe or a wriggling snake. "This place is awesome, right?" Sky offered his Coke to Joe.

"Well it certainly looks like you three are enjoying yourselves." Sunny pinched a swab from Layla's sugary blob and popped it into her mouth. "Delish."

"How about we check out the Pig Palace?" Sky suggested.

"I wanted to see the hypnotist." Kat pouted, pointing to the sign on the building next to where they were standing.

"Show's not till three," Sky said. "Let's get in line for the Rainier Rush, okay? It's only going to get longer later." He cocked his head toward the towering tracks up on their right.

Kat shook her head. "Not me. I don't do roller coasters."

Sky turned to Layla, who shrugged her shoulders.

"Why don't you two go ahead?" Joe suggested, looping one arm through Sunny's and the other through Kat's. "I'm sure these two lovely ladies wouldn't mind keeping me company while I rest for a bit."

Layla frowned. "I don't know—"

"C'mon," Sky urged. "When are you ever going to get a chance to do something like this again, right? Man up, girl!"

Layla giggled and handed her cotton candy to Sunny, and followed Sky through the crowd.

"Sit." Joe led the way to an empty bench. Sunny picked at the sweet pink nest and Kat sipped loudly through her straw as he allowed his eyes to take in the scene around them. "You know," he paused to clear his throat, "I lived here once."

Sunny turned to him with a furrowed brow. "We all know you were born in Seattle, Joe. Are you sure you're okay?"

"No, I mean I lived here. Right here." He swung his arm around the fairground.

"What, did you hide out one night until the gates were closed or something?" Sunny laughed.

"I'm being serious, kiddo. Our room was over there, under the grandstands. That's where they built the barracks."

"What are you talking about? Was this a military base or something?"

Joe shook his head. "Not a military base. It was more like a prison. A camp. Camp Harmony. Yet it beats me why they would call it that. Harmony my ass."

"You mean like a summer camp?" Kat asked.

"No. An internment camp, during the war. Where they locked up all the Japanese people. Although most of us were about as American as they come."

Sunny choked a little on the pink fluff. "Are you kidding me, Joe?" she asked, catching her breath. "You were in an internment camp? Here? How old were you?"

"I was just out of high school. We had a farm, over in the valley. After Pearl Harbor, it was decided that the Japanese were too much of a threat to the nation's security, so President Roosevelt issued an order to evict us all from the West Coast. They threw up the entire encampment in less than two weeks, to hold us here until they could figure out what to do with us."

Joe could picture the day his parents had been told the family had one week to report to the camps. They had scrambled to get the house in order, storing their entire belongings, along with those of their friends and neighbors, in the old barn for safekeeping until their return. One suitcase per person was all they were allowed to bring.

"They brought us here on buses, and once inside, we weren't allowed to leave. We were penned in by barbed wire, separated from the rest of the world like cattle with hoof-and-mouth disease, patrolled by armed guards in watchtowers." Joe paused and took a deep breath before continuing. "Each family was assigned to one small room, with one tiny window, one electrical socket, a bare bulb hanging from the ceiling, and a wood-burning stove. Some were over in the parking lot or out in the middle of the old racetrack, and others were made to live in the stalls that had been used for the cows and pigs. We had no toilets or running water. You had to go to the communal showers to bathe—out under the Ferris wheel. And the mud! Everywhere there was mud."

"How could you stand it?" Kat asked, her eyes wide, her neglected snow cone melting into a puddle of slush. "That just sucks."

"Well, I'll tell you." Joe settled back into the bench. "It wasn't easy. But we tried to make the best of it, and being the young man that I was, I took particular advantage of being surrounded by so many teenage girls. I'd never seen so many Japanese girls in one place ever! We had dances sometimes on the weekends, in the recreation hall. Glenn Miller, Jimmy Dorsey, The Andrews Sisters, we would swing to them all." Joe smiled at the memory of those long-legged girls with their soapy smell, their silky hair, the touch of their soft hands against his own. "But honestly," he continued, "the whole thing was so hard for us to understand. Being called enemy aliens? Most of us were born here, had never been to Japan, and couldn't even speak Japanese. Were they locking up German Americans, or Italian Americans? No they were not."

"So how did you get out?" Sunny asked.

"Well, after a couple of months we were transferred to a relocation camp in Idaho. I guess they figured the farther away from Japan they got us, the better. Then, in 1943, my brother and I got the option to either remain in the camp or join the army to go fight in Europe. There was a unit, the 442nd Regimental Combat Team, made up of all Americans with Japanese ancestry, and they were getting a reputation for being tough as nails. My father encouraged us to go, to get out of the camps any way we could. And we wanted to fight, because we knew our record on the battlefield would be proof of our honor and the loyalty Japanese Americans felt to our country. So we left our parents and our uncles and aunts and cousins behind, and joined the army."

"Ah. And then came Italy, and Sylvia, right?" Sunny placed a hand on Joe's knee.

"Exactly."

"Well now I understand why you stayed away for so long. How could you have ever wanted to come back, Joe?"

"Of course Sylvia and I talked about moving back here, to the States, after the war. But we had both heard so many stories of men from my regiment who had returned with European brides, only to be treated at home with scorn and prejudice for being an interracial couple. A white man could return with an Asian war bride, but the other way around? That was asking for a lifetime of trouble. And yes, there was also this." He nodded at the view before him. "My feelings for my old country, this country, had changed. I was proud of what I did in the war, and I know it was for the right causes. But the way my family was treated was something I felt I could never forget."

"So what finally made you change your mind?" Sunny asked.

"After Sylvia was gone, the last thing I wanted to do was to leave Italy. No way no how, I thought. So many memories, it was as if she were part of the land I walked on day after day, part of the air I breathed. How could I ever leave her?" Joe shook his head. "But then my brother became ill. He needed me. So here I came."

"And you stayed."

"You know, at first it was very difficult. This wasn't home for me anymore. There was nothing about it I liked. Nothing. But you know what its biggest problem was? It wasn't Italy." Joe paused and shifted his eyes in Sunny's direction.

"Oh, so now we're talking about me?"

"I'm just saying." He shrugged. "You know, sometimes a place becomes more than just a place in our minds. We let it become who we are, instead of knowing that who we are stays with us wherever we go. And sometimes we also let a place become about who we love. It's complicated. You know, my whole life with Sylvia was somewhere else. I had made no memories with her here. I missed her so much that it hurt, and I kept thinking that maybe it wouldn't hurt so much if I stayed where we had been together, where I could be reminded of those memories every day, and never forget. Perhaps if I had gone back to Italy earlier, I would have had the chance to find out if that was true or not. But I couldn't leave my brother. And then, without me even knowing, something changed inside of me. When my brother died, I didn't really want to leave. I realized that I hadn't forgotten one of those memories I had of my life with Sylvia, because they were all inside me, and would never leave no matter where I lived.

"And there was something else important that I also realized." Now he turned toward Kat. "I had begun to come to terms with the things that had happened earlier in my life, here. I learned that although we cannot deny that wrong was done, that people commit terrible injustices upon others in the name of protecting what they hold most precious, we cannot put blame on an entire country and all of its people. This country is a part of who I am, and I'm proud of that. But not until I faced the demons of my past, and stared them straight in their ugly eyes, did I feel truly comfortable in my own skin. And so here we are."

"I get it. You brought us here to teach us something, didn't you?" Kat stood up from the bench.

"Smart girl, but wait and let me finish." He reached into the inside pocket of his jacket and pulled out an envelope that he slowly opened as she and Sunny waited in silence. "Airplane tickets," he said, handing a fluttering piece of paper to each of them. "Round trip. To Kabul and back."

"But—" they both responded in unison.

"You will accompany Layla back home. No objections, no excuses, no arguments. You are both going, whether you like it or not. After all, you wouldn't want to disappoint an old man, would you?" He smiled, feeling very pleased with himself.

38

Despite the incessant banging coming from two flights below, Sunny could taste the calm with every sip of warm tea that passed through her lips. That first whiff of cardamom drifting up from the cup had been enough to erase the years she'd been away. Even with everything that had gone on between then and now, the coffeehouse rooftop remained her favorite place on earth. Up here, under the golden blush of the slowly setting sun, she could breathe.

Downstairs, behind the heavy curtains that had been hung in every window, it was a hive of activity. On one side of the wall that Ahmet and Rashif were erecting, Yazmina and Halajan were busy placing thick carpets across the marble floor, and arranging the *toshaks* and pillows that would serve as beds at night. Sunny had left Bashir Hadi behind the counter in the kitchen— not before nabbing one of his chocolate chip cookies—where he was taking an inventory of the dishes and utensils, to make sure there would be enough to accommodate everyone should they reach full capacity. On the other side of the new wall, in a smaller area, Layla and Kat were working side by side, with some dubious help from little Najama, unpacking the boxes of toys and games and crayons and paper Yaz had asked Sunny to bring from the States, without explaining why.

They had waited until they were face to face with Sunny to break the news. At first she thought they were kidding, but it wasn't long before she saw how it all made perfect sense. Of course it had been Candace who was the mastermind behind turning the former coffeehouse into a safe house for endangered women and girls, a place for them to remain hidden from vengeful families seeking to rid themselves of shame by beating, maiming, or even killing their own daughters and sisters and nieces. There, the women—some with their children—would be protected until they were secreted away to another, more distant destination in the underground network of shelters that dotted the country. It would be the only hope for many of those unjustly accused of committing so-called moral crimes: adultery, sex out of wedlock, running away to escape the fate of an unwanted arranged marriage—basically the crimes of falling in love with the wrong man or being a victim of an abusive or violent one. And now, with support from the international community drying up, and with so many foreign aid workers leaving the country, their commitment to this cause was needed more than ever. Forming an Afghan-run NGO had been Ahmet's idea. Candace was teaching him all she knew about how to set up, and grow, the organization, and had raised enough funding from her connections to get them started. He was already deep into the business end of things, and had changed his major at the university to Enterprise Management. But right now they were all hurrying to have everything ready for their first two girls, who would be arriving with Candace in the morning. One, they'd been told, had been punished for running away after being raped by an uncle and was now carrying his child. The other had been charged with intent to commit adultery after fleeing her drug-addict husband.

But the news about the shelter wasn't Sunny's first surprise. It was Halajan, standing there next to the old brown Mercedes all by herself, welcoming them to Kabul with open arms after the three of them had completed their journey from the plane, through the brand-new international terminal, through passport control and registration, to baggage claim and X-ray scans, and finally out onto the hilly sidewalk. There they'd pushed their carts up and down and through a barrage of security check-points for the half-mile it took to reach the parking lot, the closest distance to the terminal a car was allowed. The whole family had wanted to come, Halajan explained as they loaded their luggage into the car, but there clearly wouldn't have been enough room. Sunny was left momentarily speechless as she watched her old friend slide in behind the wheel without a blink of an eye.

"Well, get in!" Halajan ordered. "We don't have all day."

"Since when—"

"I am a good driver, right?" Halajan grinned at the girls' reflection in the rearview mirror as she merged confidently onto the road leading into the city. "I am even thinking of starting my own taxi company," she said with pride. "But do not tell Ahmet," she quickly added.

Sunny rolled up her window against the dust and diesel that hung in the air, and twisted around to check on the girls. Layla sat back against the seat with her eyes closed, clearly exhausted from the long journey, but with a tiny smile on her lips. Kat, on the other hand, was wide awake, the silk scarf she had reluctantly accepted from Sunny—after a woman in the terminal had berated them for being bare-headed—slipping off the back of her head and onto her neck. "What do you think?" Sunny asked. "Does it feel at all familiar?"

"Not really," Kat answered with a shrug of her shoulders, but Sunny couldn't help but notice that it wasn't quite the usual Kat *I'm blowing you off* shrug. Sunny was relieved. Kat had at first reacted like a bull on the end of a leash to Joe's plan, until Sky somehow convinced her how good it would be for her to connect with her roots, to have a chance to come to terms with her past, and probably how good that would all be for their relationship, no doubt. Now the girl seemed actually a little bit curious, staring out the window through the mass of cars choking the roads to get a glimpse of the passing scenery.

It was funny, Sunny thought. In some ways the city didn't seem so familiar to her, either. Sure, the buildings that had survived decades of war were still surviving, and the hilltops continued to push their way through the same blanket of smog that was right there where Sunny left it, and the streets seemed as crowded and lively as ever—only with fewer donkeys and more people—but as they approached the city on roads that were surprisingly smoother than the crater-pocked menaces she remembered so well, there was an undeniable change in the air.

"*Padar naalat!*" Halajan cursed as a mini-convoy of bullet-proofed Toyotas cut in front of her like a pack of wild boars, the foreigners inside crowded together under helmets and body armor. These were not the huge armored trucks Sunny was used to seeing everywhere. In fact, she realized, so far she hadn't felt at all as if she were in a city under foreign military occupation.

They drove past the embassies in the Wazir Akbar Khan neighborhood, where the sidewalks, once sprinkled with *chokidors* lined up like toy soldiers in front of their guardhouses, were now littered with the motionless heaps of the hungry homeless, steeling themselves for the long winter ahead.

"They are the poor souls who came to Kabul for work," Halajan explained, "when there was work to be done. Now there is nothing, and nobody, left to help them. Even if they had money, they could not afford much, with the prices from parsley to plumbers becoming so high."

"It's really that bad?" Sunny asked, remembering a time when foreign money could make an Afghan man rich overnight.

"It is," Halajan answered, pushing back her head scarf in order to check the lane beside her. "There are people who are buying just enough rice for each day, instead of the usual fifty-kilogram bags, because they are hoping for the prices to come down. Rashif has told me that it is all because people are worried that Karzai will not agree to any deal about security with the West. Nobody knows what is going to happen, so everyone is trying to make or save the money to run away if they have to."

Sunny's eyes darted around in a frenzy as she attempted to take in every single detail in her sight. She felt like pinching herself, it seemed so unreal to be back. But there was no mistaking where she was, not with the mountains of vibrant fruit piled atop the roadside carts, the clusters of blue-burqa'd women gossiping on every street corner, the wiry boys on bicycles weaving in and out of traffic. Through the glass of a car window was the absolute best way to experience life in Kabul, she always said. The only way to fully capture the depth and color of the city, in her opinion. It was like watching a movie made up of fleeting, intricate frames assembled exclusively for you.

"Look!" Halajan pointed with her chin as they approached a shiny new storefront. "Cherry Berry yogurt shop. My favorite." She lowered the window to wave at a man in a red jacket sweeping the sidewalk. "Delicious. I will have to take you there."

As they turned into the streets of the Sherpur district, Sunny pointed out to Kat a row of Kabul's infamous poppy palaces, showy mansions built from laundered money and foreign aid that had landed in private pockets. Now a surprising number of them wore battered "For rent" signs. Any Afghan with that kind of money these days, Sunny knew, would have sent it and probably themselves as well off to Dubai or some other country for safekeeping. And with so few foreigners left to pay the exorbitant rents those places commanded, many were standing empty, their garish paint fading and peeling under the Kabul sun.

"Take me by Chicken Street, Hala, please? I want to see if Sunil, that man I used to buy my furniture from, is still there with his son." But when they got there, Sunny almost didn't recognize the place. The shops she remembered so well had all been torn down, replaced by new construction, and a brand-new shopping mall rose like a phoenix at the far end of the street.

"You should see the size of the stores in there," Halajan crowed. "And they have places to park the car under the ground." Sunny marveled at the number of new high-rise apartment buildings that had sprung up since she left, although the one topped with two giant concrete pomegranates towering over the street did make her cringe. And the streets themselves! The sight of men in overalls actually picking up trash was a shock to Sunny's jet-lagged eyes.

Kabul had changed. Not really for the better or the worse, Sunny thought now as she looked out over the city from the coffeehouse roof. It was just different, and she was thrilled to be back. She reached down to scratch Poppy's neck right at the spot behind her ears that Jack had shown her so very long ago, it seemed. When she arrived at the coffeehouse with Halajan and the girls, Poppy had greeted Sunny the same way she always had, as if she had never left. Or at least she had tried to. Now the poor thing no longer had the strength to reach her paws to Sunny's chest, so Sunny had to bend down for the usual lick of the chin. It was probably her imagination, but Sunny could have sworn that Poppy had been looking behind her for Jack to show up. "I miss him too," she now said to the dog curled up at her feet. Poppy groaned and stretched and rolled over onto her back for a belly rub. Sunny could almost hear Jack's laugh booming across the rooftops and, to her own surprise, that made her smile.

She picked up her cup and took it downstairs, placed it in the sink, and headed past Ahmet and Rashif and their soon-to-be wall to the spot where Layla and Kat were at work. The toys were lined up neatly on a low shelf, and Layla was wiping down the screen of the TV Sunny had purchased for the coffeehouse years ago. "To keep the children of the women busy," Layla explained.

"Now let's get *you* busy," Kat said to a giggling Najama as she tickled the wriggling little girl in her lap. Sunny was in awe of how quickly Kat had adjusted to being here. At first she had seemed so awkward, taken aback by the overwhelming warmth of the family, and at the same time walking on eggshells, so careful not to say or do anything that might be considered wrong. But then not even twenty-four hours had passed before Sunny spied her out in the back courtyard with Halajan, the two of them laughing and sharing a smoke. What she would have given to be a fly on the wall for *that* conversation.

Back on the other side of the nearly finished partition, Halajan and Yazmina were sorting the boxes of toothpaste and bars of soap and little bottles of shampoo that Candace had sweet-talked her way into getting as a donation for the shelter, along with three dozen pairs of plastic shoes and an enormous supply of hairbrushes that had appeared at their door. Sunny pried the top off a carton and dived in to help, depositing one of each item into a small handmade tin box that would be given to an empty-handed woman to call her own. Like a little treasure chest, Sunny thought. The three of them chatted away as they worked, Sunny describing her life on the island, sharing the story of Rick and his deceit, telling them about Joe and his acts of kindness.

"And this young man, this Sky, what is his story?" Yazmina asked in a worried whisper, her eyes darting to Ahmet, who was still concentrating on the wall.

"No worries, Yaz." Sunny had to laugh at herself, answering the way Sky would have answered himself. "He's a nice kid, who helps with the grapes. A friend of Kat's," she added for good measure, to truly put Yazmina's mind at ease.

"A friend of Kat's," Yaz repeated, struggling to wrap her brain around the concept.

Sunny had been relieved when she finally forced a conversation about Sky with Layla, something she knew she had to do before they headed back to Kabul. Layla had been so obviously struggling with her emotions, but Sunny carefully explained how normal those feelings were, that they were nothing to be ashamed of. But none of this was anything Yazmina or Ahmet needed to know, and Layla and Sunny had agreed to keep the conversation between themselves, forever. Layla also claimed to have accepted things between Kat and Sky. But just as Yaz was now wrestling with the thought of a boy being an

Afghan girl's friend, Sunny knew Layla was not quite used to the whole idea of Kat and Sky being so casual with their relationship. No matter how much some things had changed in this country, Sunny knew, there were other things, things so deeply rooted in culture and tradition, that perhaps never would.

But matters like these didn't seem to be what was really worrying anyone around the coffeehouse these days. When Yazmina excused herself to go upstairs to tend to the hungry baby slung across her body, Halajan seized the opportunity to pour out her fears to Sunny. "How can you call it progress, when it goes backward?" she asked, shaking her head. "Of course," she added, "things are better than when women could not work or wear white shoes or use fingernail polish or laugh out loud, when the Taliban kept us locked in our homes like prisoners. And yes, it is true that—for now—there are more girls in school than ever before, and that there are even women who have been elected to parliament. But already we can feel the darkness returning, with brave women who dare to have jobs like men, as police or lawyers, being threatened or sometimes even killed."

"What are you bothering Sunny with now, *maadar*? Let her be. She is our guest." Ahmet shook his head at his mother and stood back to admire his wall.

"It is only the truth, Ahmet. Even you yourself have spoken of your fears of a return to the past. After all, why did we all agree that what we are doing here is so important? Somebody has to step into the shoes of those who we are trying to help, those who no longer have the money or the courage to stay and help the women of this country. As you have said, Ahmet, it is our duty as Afghans to keep up the battle."

"But I worry about you," Sunny said. "Where is your money, and your courage, going to come from?"

Ahmet dropped down onto a chair and wiped his brow. "The courage, that is easy. How can we not have the courage to do something to keep our country from losing what small gains we have made, to show those who are offended by the thought that a woman can make her own decisions and should have protection from her own family, who hear a threat in the idea that men might not control all things, that many of us want another way?"

"Why, Ahmet. You sound like a feminist if I ever heard one." Sunny's eyes went from mother to son and back again, catching Halajan chuckling to herself behind her sleeve.

"Some are blaming the West, saying this kind of thinking is an attack on our Afghan culture," Ahmet continued. "And we have been warned that those who continue to help women will become even more of a target than they are today, but we cannot just sit here and wait for others to tell us all how to live our lives, as has happened too many times before in our history. It's time for Afghans to be the ones to influence Afghanistan." He stood and picked up his hammer. "So, courage? That is no problem. Now money, that is another question."

"I still have my shop," Rashif chimed in, "and as long as there are men who will pay to have clothes that fit, I will be able to bring some money home, *inshallah*. Although there do seem to be fewer of those kind of people these days."

"I have hope that my efforts to raise money will someday bear fruit. And in the meantime, our friend Candace has promised to keep pulling the leg of the people she knows," Ahmet added.

Sunny laughed. "Putting the arm on people, you mean."

"Putting the arm on people," Ahmet repeated slowly, looking down at his own arm in an effort to understand the phrase.

"Well, let's just hope Candace uses more than one arm to get that money. You're going to have a lot of mouths to feed around here, and I'm not so sure how you're going to do that."

"We will be fine," Halajan said loudly and with such certainty that they all turned their eyes to her. She placed both hands on her hips and stood tall. "Me, I'm not worried. As my old friend Rumi says: *As you start to walk out on the way, the way appears.*"

The mist, the fog, the sky, the earth
  Inside is where I find my mirth."

"Bravo!" Whistles and applause rang through the rafters as the beaming woman with a single long, white braid took a slight bow and returned to her table. The barn was packed with locals, as it had been every Wednesday night for the past month or so. Weekends at the Screaming Peacock were always crowded, but Sunny had to get creative to bring in money throughout the rest of the week, as there were now so many counting on her for help. The word was out, thanks to Joe, that a huge chunk of the tasting room's profits were going to Kabul to support the shelter. But Wednesday nights were special, where not only a portion of the profit but also the full amount of what landed in the collection jar that was passed around during the evening went straight to Yazmina to feed and clothe everyone in what was becoming a very crowded household. And, much to Sunny's surprise and delight, the people of Twimbly were turning out to be more than generous.

Tonight's poetry slam had been Joe's idea, and already Sunny had decided to make it a monthly event. At first she'd thought that bringing in speakers for discussions about current events, just as she had done at her coffeehouse in Kabul, was the way to go. But she quickly learned that the island was strictly divided along left/right–blue/red lines, and that politics was a subject best left alone. There would be no screaming matches at the Screaming Peacock, not if she could help it.

"More wine for the back table," Joe whispered to Sunny after he invited the next wannabe poet to approach the mic. Playing waitress was definitely not Sunny's idea of a good time. She'd much prefer kicking back with the rest of them, sampling the Merlots, Cabernets and Syrahs, the Rieslings and Chardonnays that Sky had procured from vintners all around the state— winemakers who had jumped at the chance of another outlet for sales. She found herself drooling over the plates of Joe's cheese and fresh baked bread, too busy to eat until the end of the night, when they would wash glasses and count up the day's receipts. She thanked her lucky stars that Sky had agreed to ferry over from school on Wednesday nights to help, in addition to the weekends, when he was beginning to draw crowds with the passion that flowed from him into each pour, and that charming smile the kid just couldn't hold back.

However, with her swollen feet and aching back, what Sunny truly longed for was Kat's youthful energy around the place. But she had made a vow to herself not to pressure the girl. She still couldn't believe that Kat had chosen to remain behind at the coffeehouse in Kabul, although in retrospect she should have seen it coming.

At first Sunny had worried she'd made a mistake bringing Kat along. "What is the matter with that girl?" she had heard Ahmet comment to Yazmina a few days after they'd arrived, upon catching Kat smoking with his mother. "It is one thing that my mother cannot seem to control her habit, but this girl is young, and should know better than to be seen smoking."

"But, Ahmet—" Sunny tried, leaping to Kat's defense.

"Do you see how rude she is, pushing her way into conversation without even stopping to say *Hello, how are you, how is your family . . .*"

"Come on, Ahmet. That's just the way it's done back home. We get straight to the point. To not inquire every single day about every single member of every single person's family is not considered rude in America."

"But she is Afghan, Sunny."

"Well technically, Ahmet, that's not the case."

"And that hair," he continued, ignoring Sunny's remark. "What is the meaning of turning it black and white?"

Sunny was tempted to point out how *he* would have been the one considered rude, had they been in the States, the way he had gaped at Kat at first, with that hard stare an Afghan could hold forever without turning away.

It wasn't as though Kat was totally unaware of being the misfit. She'd lived practically her whole life that way, neither this nor that, neither here nor there.

"This is the one who was teaching your sister English?" Ahmet had asked Yazmina after Kat used the Dari word *sher*, meaning lion, instead of *sheer*, for milk, when she was making a meal for Najama. She was teased for her accent. "You speak as though you have a dust storm in your mouth." But because it was Halajan who said it, Kat responded with a laugh.

Sunny understood how Ahmet saw things. Yes, he was comfortable around foreigners and used to their ways. He had no problem with Sunny. But seeing an Afghan who didn't act like an Afghan—in his house with his family—was a whole other matter. Both of them had witnessed plenty of Afghan customers in the coffeehouse, those who had lived in the US or Europe, who returned acting as though they weren't Afghan at all, as though they didn't even know the language. Sunny saw firsthand how offensive it was to the others, those who were so proud of who they were. She got it. So she did whatever she could to try to ease the tension that drifted through the house like the scents from Bashir Hadi's kitchen. It wasn't until Sunny shared Kat's story with him that Ahmet finally softened toward the girl.

But it was Halajan who really took to Kat, and vice versa. They seemed to be kindred spirits. Sunny had taken to calling them Thelma and Louise by the end of her stay. It was Halajan who had first noticed the way the damaged, numbed girls seeking refuge behind the coffeehouse doors gravitated instantly to Kat, sensing in her something they felt in themselves. And it was Halajan who recognized how Kat so readily stepped up to the task of putting them at ease, as if she had been born for the job. And it was at Halajan's urging that Kat decided to stay and help for a while.

So, for now, Sunny would just have to suck it up and wait on all those tables and do all those dishes herself, serenaded by the sound of clinking glasses and clunky poetry.

She paused to wipe down the end of the long bar Sky had made from reclaimed oak. The place looks great, she thought, surveying the barn with a hand on one hip. Her Afghan treasures: the carved wooden tables, the thick wool rugs, the cobalt blue dishes, the embroidered pillows—everything fit in perfectly, as though Jack had pictured all this, down to the last detail, so long ago. And yes, they were serving the wine in teacups, just as she had done in Kabul—though she had a few dozen glasses for the true oenophiles who wouldn't be caught dead tasting from the wrong stemware. And best of all was the happy peahen she'd added right alongside her huge screaming peacock on the south end of the barn, slapped up with a can of off-white paint after she'd received the news from Kabul of the bird's miraculous return. Apparently Ahmet had heard a commotion on the coffeehouse roof, and had grabbed his gun after ordering everyone to stay inside and lock the doors. Who knew, he had later said, that the thing could fly?

She thought back on the day she'd arrived on the island, and all that had happened since. Meeting Joe, and learning everything she'd learned from his wisdom and patience, inheriting a houseful of kids and surviving, the fun they'd had giving Rick a spicy taste of his own medicine, a birth in Kabul, a new life for the coffeehouse, a new life for her. She took a good look around the barn full of smiling, chattering people, many of whom she was starting to call friends, and had to laugh. Once again, it occurred to her, Jack had totally gotten his way.

And then she found herself looking forward to next year, when the very first vintage of Dashing Jack's Screaming Peacock Rosé, from the grapes that Sunny had helped pick with her own two hands, would be ready to drink. The pink juice, now matured and balanced and mellowed with time, would flow from the bottle like liquid velvet. And, Sunny hoped, the passing seasons will have worked their magic on her as well. She envisioned herself a year older, a year wiser, pouring herself a glass and then reaching for the other bottle, the one that now held Jack's ashes, on the very top shelf of the tasting room. She'd cradle it under her arm and head out to the shady maple tree overlooking the sparkling Sound, where she'd sit and breathe in the sweet misty air, and drink to the glorious life that had brought them, and many others, so very much.

Acknowledgments

"Storytelling is the most powerful way to put ideas into the world today."

Robert McKee

Books are such a special tool—a wonderful way to share ideas, transport people to different worlds, and provide glorious escape. But books require a team. So many people have worked tirelessly to make this book happen.

Ellen Kaye, I cannot imagine writing without you. I value our working partnership, and I love that despite being so different, we can finish each other's sentences (or at least you can finish mine). It was an honor to work with you on *The House on Carnaval Street* and now *Return to the Little Coffee Shop of Kabul*. You helped me unleash the stories that were simmering in my head, fighting to escape. We are a good team, and that is something I am so proud of. You are a great friend, and remarkable writer.

Beverley Cousins and her team at Penguin Random House Australia, you are such a joy to work with. Thank you for your enthusiasm and unflagging support, for embracing the characters and giving them the chance to experience the next phase of their lives, and for your willingness to leap fearlessly across time zones to make it all happen.

Maddie West at Little, Brown UK and Sphere Fiction, thank you for always being so encouraging and for always believing in this new book. It was so comforting to know that you were only an email away whenever I needed your support. Thank you a million times over.

Marly Rusoff, thank you for taking a risk with me twelve years ago. I know, can you believe it's been twelve years? Without you, the only stories told would have been the ones coming from behind my chair at the beauty salon. You caught the vision and believed in the outlandish "hairdresser" who said she wanted to tell stories to the world. Marly, you changed my life. I know if my mom could, she would hug you and tell you thanks for taking such good care of her daughter. You are more than an agent, you are a treasure.

Michael Radulescu (Mihai), I think if I had a brother I would want him to be just like you: smart, funny and able to work magic. I am so grateful to have found a big brother in you.

Karen Kinne, my best friend. I know I can call you any time of the day or night and shriek, *Help! I've hit a wall in the plot. I'm stuck!* And you will say, *Okay Deb, grab a glass of wine and let's dig in.* You never leave me until that wall falls down. I love your creativity, but more than that I love our long-lasting friendship.

Omer Azizi, you will rise to high places. I know that for a fact. I remember when you were only fourteen and you were my translator in the real little coffee shop of Kabul. I remember our friend Lou telling me, *this kid will rule the world someday.* It has been a long and hard road for you and your family, but you made it. I am so proud of you Omer, and I cannot even begin to explain how instrumental you were in the research of this book. You know that I love your family, and being able to work with you on this project was a wish come true.

I always need to thank my amazing boys Noah and Zach Lentz, who had no choice other than to get on this wild ride with their mom. However, I also really want to thank their remarkable spouses Martha Villasana-Lentz and Aretha Lentz. Not only are they spectacular mothers to all my beautiful grandchildren—Sillas, Kai, Italya, Derik and Didier—but just hanging out with these fierce, intelligent and loving women is inspirational.

Denis Asahara—my crazy and wonderful life partner— what can I say other than you have incredible resilience. Ours is my longest relationship ever, and you have now entered into unchartered territory. You make me crazy and I love you with all my heart. I would say thank you for listening, but we both know you don't. Your family was such a huge inspiration for this book, and I thank you for sharing them with me.

A huge thanks to the Asahara and Miwa clan for sharing stories of the past and helping the characters become as authentic as possible. And a very special thanks to John Asahara, who was the compass in creating my favorite character of the book, Joe.

Thanks to Andy Besch, aka The Wine Guy, for sharing his expertise, and especially for going out into the fields to answer the question *What's it like, working a harvest?* Cheers.

Rick Rodriguez and Judy D'Ambrosio, your hospitality on "The Island" was incredible. I had so much fun, and loved learning the "island game" of "hide the fruit bowl".

Humaira Ghilzai, you tantalize the taste buds with your extraordinary recipes. Thank you for sharing the flavors of Afghanistan with the world.

Eliza Ilyas, you bring graceful awareness in every step you take. You are a beautiful and cosmopolitan example of what faith and tolerance looks like.

I am always thankful for my staff at Tippy Toes. They can rival the drama of a telenovela any day of the week!

I would also like to thank all my customers at Tippy Toes, who had to listen to me drone on and on about plots and character while I did their hair. A special thanks to Ingrid Ostick and Ann Murphy.

Many thanks to Linda Bine for being a friend to a friend, and for lending her keen editorial eye to this project.

Tashakor, thank you, Enayat Sharif for coming to my rescue with your Dari language skills.

A huge hug to Linda Crossley and Johnny Horsley, who always speak positive words into my life and show me how to reach for the stars.

And to Polly, my dear cat, who is always by my side and only a meow away.

Finally, I want to thank my readers, who responded so strongly to *The Little Coffee Shop of Kabul* and fell in love with the characters inside. And who, most importantly, asked the question *What happened next?*

About the author

Deborah Rodriguez is the author of the international bestseller *The Little Coffee Shop of Kabul*. She has also written two memoirs: *The Kabul Beauty School*, about her life in Afghanistan, and *The House on Carnaval Street*, on her experiences following her return to America. She spent five years teaching and later directing the Kabul Beauty School, the first modern beauty academy and training salon in Afghanistan.

Deborah also owned the Oasis Salon and the Cabul Coffee House, and is the founder of the nonprofit organization Oasis Rescue, which aims to teach economically disadvantaged women, and women in post-conflict and disaster-stricken areas, the art of hairdressing.

She currently lives in Mazatlán, Mexico, where she owns the Tippy Toes salon and spa.

A Q&A with Deborah Rodriguez
(contains spoilers)

In 2011 you stated you didn't feel it was wise to return to Afghanistan at that time. Is this still the case? Have you been able to return?

Afghanistan is a wonderful and very complicated country. In the last four years as the foreign presence has been decreasing, the climate of the country has been changing—but not always for the better. I have made the choice not to return to Kabul for a couple reasons. The obvious one is general safety and security; the other is very personal. I married and left an Afghan man, and am not one hundred per cent sure how that story would end if I tried to return to Kabul.

Do you keep in touch with the women you met in Kabul, and if so, did they help with your research for this new novel?

I do keep in touch with some of the women I met in Kabul. The one I talk to the most happens to be one of my first students, and to date the bravest and most amazing woman I have ever met. We both fled Afghanistan at the same time, but she fled with her family to Pakistan, and struggled for seven years as a refugee in that country. But today I am happy to say that she and her family are living a wonderful life in the United States. The entire family—but especially her son Omer—was key to the research for the new novel.

In your opinion, has the role and treatment of women in Afghanistan changed for the better since you lived there?

That's a really tough question. I feel like women's rights in Afghanistan take three steps forward, and with a blink of an eye things regress and jump ten steps back. Thankfully girls' school attendance has surged in the last fourteen years, and more and more women are in the workplace, along with holding down positions in the government. Rula Ghani (the current first lady of Afghanistan) speaking out for gender equality and religious tolerance is setting a great example for young women. But you can't turn a blind eye to the news reports after things like the siege of the city of Kunduz. The Taliban went straight to terrorizing the women and girls, burning and looting women's organizations and making it clear that they will always be watching. This is a time of great uncertainty for Afghanistan, and not just for women, but for everyone.

A clear theme of the novel is clashing cultures and finding a place where you truly belong. This is a particular issue for Kat, Layla and Joe. But it is very true of Sunny too. Was it a struggle for you when you returned to America?

Yes, clashing of cultures is a very important theme in the book, along with showing tolerance for those who are different to us.

I feel it's important not to judge a book by its cover—or a girl by her head scarf.

I did struggle with reverse culture shock when I came back from Afghanistan. I would watch and listen to people complain about things and think to myself, "Wow, this is truly a first world problem." I'd wonder how they would handle a real problem. When you see so much suffering and experience life with such strong people who have survived decades of war, you find yourself short on patience with the guy screaming in Starbucks over a mistake in his latte order.

I have adjusted in the last seven years, and moving to Mexico really made the difference for me. I don't think I am cut out to have a tidy, sanitized, non-chaotic life.

What made you pick an island in the Pacific Northwest of America as Sunny's new home? Did that region have a particular significance for you?

I was introduced to the Pacific Northwest (the Seattle area) because of my partner, Denis, and his family. Denis's father is a 92-year-old Japanese American who was in the internment camps. He made sushi while telling me stories. I instantly fell in love with this sweet, funny man and knew he had to be a part of Sunny's journey. The Seattle area fascinated me with its beauty and diversity. It seemed at every turn I was meeting someone who inspired yet another storyline, but it wasn't until I met the young Afghan woman who was my inspiration for Kat, and then took the ferry ride to the island used as the basis for the fictional Twimbly, that I knew this region had to be the next location for the new novel. The island was beautiful and the people were quirky. It seemed to be the perfect place for Sunny to sort her life out, but only if she could have her new best friend Joe nearby.

Why did you decide to kill off such a strong character as Jack before the novel starts?

That was a very difficult decision. Life is always easy when it's perfect, but I felt that more people would be able to relate to or learn from Sunny if she wasn't living with the perfect man in the perfect house, living the perfect life. We all suffer losses, and I find that for myself I grow more and become a stronger person when life tosses me upside down. When life is easy, I get lazy. Sunny has lost the love of her life, but she does much more than just survive.

Oasis Rescue is a project very close to your heart. Can you tell us a bit more about it?

I have always felt that all women need choices, no matter what their social or economic situation is. I often hear or read about young women around the world who feel they have no choice but to prostitute themselves to survive. I see predators who prey on young, poor women and take advantage of their poverty to force them to sell their bodies in order to feed their children. I can't imagine what that moment must feel like to a woman, to have to make that choice. Oasis Rescue offers scholarships to young people in the art of hairdressing. I am, and will always be, a hairdresser, and I know that offering this skill to a young boy or girl might just provide them the chance to make a choice about their own future.

Are you working on a new novel?

Yes! I can't say much yet, but I promise that it will bring together more incredible women dealing with personal and cultural challenges in locations far and wide.

For your reading group party

Reading group questions

1. Layla and Kat hold differing views on practically everything in the Afghan culture, including the wearing of the *hijab*. Do you find one opinion more valid than the other, and if so, why?

2. In Chapter 21, Joe states that "a love of country can be a very complicated thing." In that regard, how do the struggles of the characters in this book compare with one another?

3. Ahmet and his fellow students choose the issue of corruption in their country as the priority for their discussion group. What is one of the ways that corruption touches the lives of some of the characters in this story?

4. Do you find anything surprising about contemporary life in Afghanistan?

5. We see Ahmet struggling with his changing attitudes toward his country and its customs. What were the defining moments that caused him to shift back and forth on his views?

6. What do you think really keeps Sunny from leaving the island?

7. Halajan learns that a peahen cost less than a peacock. In what ways were the Afghan women thought to be worth less than men? Does it seem as though that might change?

8. Did anything surprise you about Layla's reactions to the US?

9. Halajan says, "A girl with a book is the best weapon for progress." Why is that so?

Some delicious dishes to share

Summon up the tastes and smells of Kabul with these delicious recipes, kindly supplied by Humaira Ghilzai from her inspiring cookery website Afghan Culture Unveiled, www.afghancultureunveiled.com

Afghan nachos
Chickpeas, creamy Greek yogurt and crispy pita chips

This recipe was inspired by *Taste of Beirut's** *fatteh* recipe, an ancient dish still quite popular in Lebanon. This layered dish with pita chips as the base, topped with aromatic chickpeas and creamy yogurt sauce, reminded me of nachos—it can be served as a hearty snack, an appetizer, or a meal if paired with a salad. Serve this dish in a communal platter, like nachos.

Serves 6
2 tablespoons olive oil
1 cup diced green onions (spring onions)

1 × 15 ounce (425 gram) can chickpeas, drained and rinsed
1 teaspoon cumin
1 teaspoon paprika
¼ cup finely chopped cilantro (coriander) leaves
1 cup whole (full fat) Greek yogurt
1 teaspoon sea salt
3 cloves garlic, diced
8 ounce (225 gram) bag of pita chips

In a sauté pan over high heat add the olive oil; heat. Add green onions, sauté for two minutes or until translucent. Add chickpeas, cumin, and paprika to the pan. Stir frequently so the onions don't stick to the pan. Once the aroma of cumin fills the kitchen and the chickpeas are warmed through, around five minutes, take the pan off the burner. In a small bowl, mix yogurt, salt, and garlic.

Arrange the pita chips in beautiful serving platter or bowl—top with the chickpeas and the creamy yogurt sauce.

Recipe by Humaira Ghilzai from her Afghan food and culture blog www.afghancultureunveiled.com.

* *www.tasteofbeirut.com*

Creamy Afghan eggplant dip
Laghataq

This is the perfect dish to share or take to a potluck. You can make it several days in advance and I find that everyone loves it, including children.

This dish uses a good amount of olive oil; don't skimp on the oil as it adds flavor and creaminess to the dish.

1 eggplant, cut in ¼ inch (½ centimetre) disks
1 red bell pepper (capsicum), cut in thin strips
2 medium tomatoes, roughly chopped
2 cloves garlic, diced
1 × 15 ounce (425 gram) can tomato puree
½ cup olive oil
1 tablespoon tomato paste
1 tablespoon ground cumin
1 tablespoon ground coriander
1 teaspoon paprika
½ cup Greek yogurt or labneh
1 teaspoon salt
pinch of garlic powder

Preheat oven to 300 degrees Fahrenheit (150 degrees Celsius).

Pour two tablespoons of the olive oil on a cookie sheet (baking tray) and spread around with your fingers. Arrange the eggplant disks on the greased sheet. Place the chopped tomatoes and red pepper on top of the eggplant.

Add the following ingredients in a blender: garlic, tomato puree, tomato paste, remaining olive oil, cumin, coriander, and paprika.

Blend until all ingredients are mixed and the sauce is smooth. Pour the sauce over the ingredients on the cookie sheet and make sure that it covers the eggplant. Spread the sauce with a spoon to ensure it is distributed evenly.

Bake for 1 ½ to 2 hours in preheated oven. The baking time will vary with each oven. It is important to slow cook this dish in order for all the flavors of the ingredients to be absorbed by the eggplant. To test doneness, press the eggplant and the peppers with the back of a fork; if the fork sinks in easily, it is done.

Let the eggplant cool for ½ hour before throwing all the ingredients in a food processor. Pulse three or four times, don't over-blend, make sure that you can see small chunks of the eggplant. Remove contents and place in deep serving dish. The dip can be served cold or at room temperature.

In a bowl, mix the yogurt, salt, and garlic powder until creamy. Pour the yogurt sauce on top of the dip. (For a dairy-free option, the dip can be served without the yogurt, but it is more delicious with the yogurt topping.) Serve with pita slices or pita chips.

Recipe by Humaira Ghilzai from her Afghan food and culture blog www.afghancultureunveiled.com.

Cardamom pudding with pistachios
Firnee

Firnee is a sweet, cardamom-scented Afghan pudding that is usually reserved for holidays and special events. *Firnee* is paraded out at the end of the occasion with each hostess putting her own personal "stamp" on the dish—rosewater in one, nuts in another—giving each *firnee* its own unique flavor. My personal favorite is a *firnee* that is gently scented with cardamom and topped with chopped pistachios.

Serves 4 to 6
6 tablespoons cornstarch (cornflour)
3 cups whole (full cream) milk
½ cup heavy (thickened) cream
1 cup white granulated sugar
pinch of salt
¾ teaspoon ground cardamom
½ cup slivered almonds, roasted (optional)
¼ cup roasted coconut chips (optional)
3 tablespoons finely ground pistachios
1 cup pomegranate seeds, raspberries, blueberries, or sliced strawberries (optional)

In a small bowl, mix the cornstarch with ¼ cup of the milk to form a thin paste, stirring with a fork until smooth. Pour the remainder of the milk and the cream into a medium-size saucepan and cook over high heat until simmering but not yet boiling. Add the sugar and salt and stir for about a minute until the sugar dissolves. Next, add the cornstarch mixture in a steady stream, stirring all the while. Add the cardamom, almonds and coconut. Continue to cook, stirring continuously, for another 5 minutes at a low boil until the mixture thickens.

Pour the pudding into a shallow bowl. Immediately sprinkle the nuts over the top of the *firnee*. If you really love the taste of cardamom, stir an extra ¼ teaspoon of it into the nuts before you top the pudding.

Refrigerate until chilled through, at least 2 hours. You can make the *firnee* a day ahead of time. Serve with fresh fruits when they are in season for a splash of color.

Recipe by Humaira Ghilzai from her Afghan food and culture blog www.afghancultureunveiled.com.

Afghan walnut, almond and pistachio fudge
Sheer payra

Since milk and sugar are at a premium in Afghanistan, this sweet is served at Eid holidays, weddings, baby births, and of course for very special guests.

½ cup plus 1 tablespoon warm water
1 ¼ cups white granulated sugar
¼ teaspoon salt
1 ¼ cups dry powdered milk
1 teaspoon rosewater
1 teaspoon cardamom
2 tablespoons walnuts, finely chopped
2 tablespoons almonds, finely chopped
2 tablespoons pistachios, finely chopped

Lightly butter a glass or metal pan, approximately 7 × 11 inches (18 × 28 centimetres) and 1 to 2 inches (2 ½ to 5 centimetres) deep.

Time is of essence in this recipe. For best results, have all your ingredients measured and accessible in your work area before you go to the next step.

Add the water in a heavy-bottomed saucepan, cook the sugar and salt over medium heat, stirring constantly until the sugar melts, around 3 to 4 minutes. Turn the heat up to high, bring to a boil, stir constantly for 2 minutes. A white foam will form on the syrup and it will thicken.

Remove pot from heat and move to your work area. Drizzle the dry powdered milk in the pot; as you stir, a creamy smooth mixture will form. Add rosewater, cardamom, almonds and walnuts. Mix well, making sure the nuts are distributed evenly in the batter.

Pour the mixture into the pan, scraping all the mixture from the sides of the pan. It should spread out, but if it doesn't, use the back of a spatula to flatten it evenly. Sprinkle with pistachios and set to cool, approximately 1 to 2 hours.

Cut with a sharp knife in 2 × 2 inch (5 × 5 centimetre) squares. Serve with a cup of black tea or coffee. Store any leftovers in an airtight container or Ziploc bag. Do not refrigerate, keep at room temperature.

Recipe by Humaira Ghilzai from her Afghan food and culture blog www.afghancultureunveiled.com.

One little beauty salon.
A community of women
comes together.

In a little beauty school in the war zone of Kabul, a community of
women come together, all with stories to tell.

DEBBIE, the American hairdresser who founds the training salon.
As the burqas are removed in class, curls are coiffed and make-up is
applied, Debbie's students share with her their stories – and their hearts.

ROSHANNA, a tearful young bride terrified her in-laws will discover
she's not a virgin.

MINA, forcibly married to a man in repayment of a family debt and
threatened with having her child taken away.

And **NAHIDA**, the prize pupil who bears the scars of her Taliban
husband's disapproval.

In the Kabul Beauty School, these women and many others find a small
but safe haven and the seeds of their future independence. So when
neighbours complain there's 'too much laughter inside' the academy,
teacher Debbie must hatch a plan to save the school and her students.

AVAILABLE NOW.

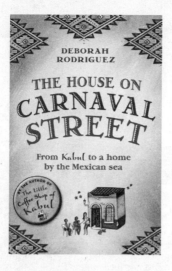

DEBORAH
RODRIGUEZ

THE HOUSE ON
CARNAVAL
STREET

From Kabul to a home
by the Mexican sea

*I hadn't been planning on making Mexico my new home, but the
little house on the sea was all that I had left...*

Intimate, honest and touching, this is the story of Deborah Rodriguez's
often hilarious journey of self-discovery. Forced to flee her life in
Afghanistan, she leaves behind her friends, her possessions and her two
beloved businesses: a hair salon and a coffee shop

But life proves no easier 'back home'. After a year living in California
where she teeters on the edge of sanity, Deborah makes a decision:
she's going to get the old Deb back. So, at the age of forty-nine, she
packs her life and her cat, Polly, into her Mini Cooper and heads south
to a pretty seaside town in Mexico. Home is now an unassuming little
house on Carnaval Street.

**If you liked *Eat, Pray, Love* you will love *The House on
Carnaval Street*. Rodriguez's story speaks to every woman,
mother, sister, wife - to anyone who has ever questioned their
relationships, their place in the world and the choices that
they've made.**

AVAILABLE NOW.